BI

THE CA.

TV

BRIAN FLYNN was born in 1885 in Leyton, Essex. He won a scholarship to the City Of London School, and from there went into the civil service. In World War I he served as Special Constable on the Home Front, also teaching "Accountancy, Languages, Maths and Elocution to men, women, boys and girls" in the evenings, and acting in his spare time.

It was a seaside family holiday that inspired Brian Flynn to turn his hand to writing in the mid-twenties. Finding most mystery novels of the time "mediocre in the extreme", he decided to compose his own. Edith, the author's wife, encouraged its completion, and after a protracted period finding a publisher, it was eventually released in 1927 by John Hamilton in the UK and Macrae Smith in the U.S. as *The Billiard-Room Mystery*.

The author died in 1958. In all, he wrote and published 57 mysteries, the vast majority featuring the super-sleuth Antony Bathurst.

BRIAN FLYNN

THE CASE OF THE BLACK TWENTY-TWO

With an introduction by
Steve Barge

DEAN STREET PRESS

INTRODUCTION

"I believe that the primary function of the mystery
story is to entertain; to stimulate the imagination and
even, at times, to supply humour. But it pleases the
connoisseur most when it presents – and reveals – genuine mystery. To reach its full height, it has to offer an
intellectual problem for the reader to consider, measure
and solve."

THUS WROTE Brian Flynn in the *Crime Book Magazine* in 1948,
setting out his ethos on writing detective fiction. At that point in
his career, Flynn had published thirty-six mystery novels, beginning with *The Billiard-Room Mystery* in 1927 – he went on,
before his death in 1958, to write twenty-one more, three under
the pseudonym Charles Wogan. So how is it that the general
reading populace – indeed, even some of the most ardent
collectors of mystery fiction – were until recently unaware of
his existence? The reputation of writers such as John Rhode
survived their work being out of print, so what made Flynn and
his books vanish so completely?

There are many factors that could have contributed to Flynn's
disappearance. For reasons unknown, he was not a member of
either The Detection Club or the Crime Writers' Association,
two of the best ways for a writer to network with others. As such,
his work never appeared in the various collaborations that those
groups published. The occasional short story in such a collection can be a way of maintaining awareness of an author's name,
but it seems that Brian Flynn wrote no short stories at all, something rare amongst crime writers.

There are a few mentions of him in various studies of the
genre over the years. Sutherland Scott, in *Blood in Their Ink*
(1953), states that Flynn, who was still writing at the time, "has
long been popular". He goes on to praise *The Mystery of the
Peacock's Eye* (1928) as containing "one of the ablest pieces
of misdirection one could wish to meet". Anyone reading that
particular review who feels like picking up the novel – out now

from Dean Street Press – should stop reading at that point, as later in the book, Scott proceeds to casually spoil the ending, although as if he assumes that everyone will have read the novel already.

It is a later review, though, that may have done much to end – temporarily, I hope – Flynn's popularity.

"Straight tripe and savorless. It is doubtful, on the evidence, if any of his others would be different."

Thus wrote Jacques Barzun and Wendell Hertig Taylor in their celebrated work, *A Catalog of Crime* (1971). The book was an ambitious attempt to collate and review every crime fiction author, past and present. They presented brief reviews of some titles, a bibliography of some authors and a short biography of others. It is by no means complete – E & M.A. Radford had written thirty-six novels at this point in time but garner no mention – but it might have helped Flynn's reputation if he too had been overlooked. Instead one of the contributors picked up *Conspiracy at Angel* (1947), the thirty-second Anthony Bathurst title. I believe that title has a number of things to enjoy about it, but as a mystery, it doesn't match the quality of the majority of Flynn's output. Dismissing a writer's entire work on the basis of a single volume is questionable, but with the amount of crime writers they were trying to catalogue, one can, just about, understand the decision. But that decision meant that they missed out on a large number of truly entertaining mysteries that fully embrace the spirit of the Golden Age of Detection, and, moreover, many readers using the book as a reference work may have missed out as well.

So who was Brian Flynn? Born in 1885 in Leyton, Essex, Flynn won a scholarship to the City Of London School, and while he went into the civil service (ranking fourth in the whole country on the entrance examination) rather than go to university, the classical education that he received there clearly stayed with him. Protracted bouts of rheumatic fever prevented him fighting in the Great War, but instead he served as a Special Constable on the Home Front – one particular job involved warning the populace about Zeppelin raids armed only with a bicycle, a whistle and a placard reading "TAKE COVER". Flynn worked for the local government while teaching "Accountancy, Languages, Maths and Elocution to men, women, boys and girls" in the evening, and acting as part of the Trevalyan Players in his spare time.

It was a seaside family holiday that inspired him to turn his hand to writing. He asked his librarian to supply him a collection of mystery novels for "deck-chair reading" only to find himself disappointed. In his own words, they were "mediocre in the extreme." There is no record of what those books were, unfortunately, but on arriving home, the following conversation, again in Brian's own words, occurred:

> "ME (unpacking the books): If I couldn't write better stuff than any of these, I'd eat my own hat.
>
> Mrs ME (after the manner of women and particularly after the manner of wives): It's a great pity you don't do a bit more and talk a bit less.
>
> The shaft struck home. I accepted the challenge, laboured like the mountain and produced *The Billiard-Room Mystery*."

"Mrs ME", or Edith as most people referred to her, deserves our gratitude. While there were some delays with that first book, including Edith finding the neglected half-finished manuscript in a drawer where it had been "resting" for six months, and a protracted period finding a publisher, it was eventually released in 1927 by John Hamilton in the UK and Macrae Smith in the U.S. According to Flynn, John Hamilton asked for five more, but in fact they only published five in total, all as part of the Sundial Mystery Library imprint. Starting with *The Five Red Fingers* (1929), Flynn was published by John Long, who would go on to publish all of his remaining novels, bar his single non-series title, *Tragedy At Trinket* (1934). About ten of his early books were reprinted in the US before the war, either by Macrae Smith, Grosset & Dunlap or Mill, and a few titles also appeared in France, Denmark, Germany and Sweden, but the majority of his output only saw print in the United Kingdom. Some titles were reprinted during his lifetime – the John Long Four-Square Thrillers paperback range featured some Flynn titles, for example – but John Long's primary focus was the library market, and some titles had relatively low print runs. Currently, the majority of Flynn's work, in particular that only published in the U.K., is extremely rare – not just expensive, but seemingly non-existent even in the second-hand book market.

In the aforementioned article, Flynn states that the tales of Sherlock Holmes were a primary inspiration for his writing, having read them at a young age. A conversation in *The Billiard-Room Mystery* hints at other influences on his writing style. A character, presumably voicing Flynn's own thoughts, states that he is a fan of "the pre-war Holmes". When pushed further, he states that:

> "Mason's M. Hanaud, Bentley's Trent, Milne's Mr Gillingham and to a lesser extent, Agatha Christie's M. Poirot are all excellent in their way, but oh! – the many dozens that aren't."

He goes on to acknowledge the strengths of Bernard Capes' "Baron" from *The Mystery of The Skeleton Key* and H.C. Bailey's Reggie Fortune, but refuses to accept Chesterton's Father Brown.

> "He's entirely too Chestertonian. He deduces that the dustman was the murderer because of the shape of the piece that had been cut from the apple-pie."

Perhaps this might be the reason that the invitation to join the Detection Club never arrived . . .

Flynn created a sleuth that shared a number of traits with Holmes, but was hardly a carbon-copy. Enter Anthony Bathurst, a polymath and gentleman sleuth, a man of contradictions whose background is never made clear to the reader. He clearly has money, as he has his own rooms in London with a pair of servants on call and went to public school (Uppingham) and university (Oxford). He is a follower of all things that fall under the banner of sport, in particular horse racing and cricket, the latter being a sport that he could, allegedly, have represented England at. He is also a bit of a show-off, littering his speech (at times) with classical quotes, the obscurer the better, provided by the copies of the *Oxford Dictionary of Quotations* and *Brewer's Dictionary of Phrase & Fable* that Flynn kept by his writing desk, although Bathurst generally restrains himself to only doing this with people who would appreciate it or to annoy the local constabulary. He is fond of amateur dramatics (as was Flynn, a well-regarded amateur thespian who appeared in at least one self-penned play, *Blue Murder*), having been a member of OUDS, the Oxford University Dramatic Society. Like Holmes, Bathurst isn't averse to the occasional disguise, and as with Watson and Holmes, sometimes even his close allies don't recognise him. General information about his background is light on the ground. His parents were Irish, but he doesn't have an accent – see *The Spiked Lion* (1933) – and his eyes are grey. We learn in *The Orange Axe* that he doesn't pursue romantic relationships due to a bad experience in his first romance. That doesn't remain the case throughout the series – he falls head over heels in love in *Fear and Trembling*, for example – but in this opening tranche of titles, we don't see Anthony distracted by the fairer sex, not even one who will only entertain gentlemen who can beat her at golf!

Unlike a number of the Holmes' stories, Flynn's Bathurst tales are all fairly clued mysteries, perhaps a nod to his admiration of Christie, but first and foremost, Flynn was out to entertain the reader. The problems posed to Bathurst have a flair about them – the simultaneous murders, miles apart, in *The Case of the Black Twenty-Two* (1928) for example, or the scheme to draw lots to commit masked murder in *The Orange Axe* – and there is a momentum to the narrative. Some mystery writers have trouble with the pace slowing between the reveal of the problem and the reveal of the murderer, but Flynn's books sidestep that, with Bathurst's investigations never seeming to sag. He writes with a wit and intellect that can make even the most prosaic of interviews with suspects enjoyable to read about, and usually provides an action-packed finale before the murderer is finally revealed. Some of those revelations, I think it is fair to say, are surprises that can rank with some of the best in crime fiction.

We are fortunate that we can finally reintroduce Brian Flynn and Anthony Lotherington Bathurst to the many fans of classic crime fiction out there.

The Case of the Black Twenty-Two (1928)

"Well, old Gerald was actually stopping at the house at the time. He always regards Bathurst as an absolute marvel. Cleared up the case when it had the Police absolutely 'stone cold'. He never tires of singing Bathurst's praises!"

THUS SPEAKS Peter Daventry, taking over the Watson role to Bathurst's Holmes in the second novel from Brian Flynn. Daventry is the brother of Gerald Daventry, who had a small role to play in Bathurst's first case, *The Billiard-Room Mystery*, and was clearly impressed by what he saw. While Daventry does not narrate the tale, most of the action is told from his perspective – Flynn would occasionally return to the first person narrative of his debut, such as in sections of *Murder En Route*, but he seems more comfortable writing in the third person.

Daventry's law partnership is involved in a double murder – Mason, a nightwatchman at an auction house and Mr Laurence Stewart, a millionaire art collector. Both were killed at the same time while miles apart, both killed by a blow to the head by a blunt instrument, their deaths linked by the theft from the auction house of items that Stewart had enlisted Daventry to bid on. Anthony Bathurst is enlisted by Daventry when Stewart's son, being unimpressed by the local constabulary, requests the aid of Scotland Yard, in the form of Inspector Goodall, and an "efficient, discreet and trustworthy private detective." Despite Bathurst having only solved one case to date, Daventry still recruits him and he finds himself enmeshed in a complex mystery involving a locked room, historic treasures and the mysterious "Black Twenty-Two".

This is the first time that Flynn put the mysterious motive for the crime in the title of the book, but it will not be the last – see, for example, the following title, *The Mystery Of The Peacock's Eye*. The mere existence of the Black Twenty-Two as an important plot point is only introduced late in the narrative, with the explanation of what it is coming extremely late in the day. The historical background to it seems to be somewhat shaky, but luckily its nature is not important to deducing the identity of the villain or villains of the piece.

This is also Flynn's first foray into the impossible murder. Later books would have some imaginative impossible crimes, such as a man dropping dead of poison in the middle of a siege (*Invisible Death*) or a man being strangled while alone on the top deck of a bus. For his first attempt, however, he stays with the trusted notion of a man being found dead in his study, locked from the inside.

A review in the *Birmingham Daily Gazette* praised the book for "some clever reconstruction before the criminals are trapped" and that "the antiquarian research required is more convincingly detailed than in most mystery stories of this type," the *Bystander* called it "a skilful piece of work", the *Daily Whig* "an exciting murder mystery", and the *Western Mail* "a fine yarn, splendidly told". The *Dundee Courier* summed it up nicely, saying "There is a realism and directness about this mystery story that ranks it among the best."

The Case Of The Black Twenty-Two was also published in the United States by Macrae Smith and, the following year, even managed to appear in Swedish, translated as *De Svarta 22*. There was also a reprint around the time of the second World War in the Cherry Tree Book range – number 174 to be precise. Collectors should beware of this version, as it is, like others in the series, only 95 pages long. The word count is about 70% of the original text, an abridgement due to the economies of war. Having read both versions, I can confidently state that the abridgement, while maintaining the crucial plot elements, does, as you might expect, feel rather rushed. Thankfully, it is the full text that we are reproducing here, so you can enjoy *The Case Of The Black Twenty-Two* as the author intended.

Steve Barge

CHAPTER I
MR. DAVENTRY RECEIVES A COMMISSION

THE FACT that it was an unusually sunny morning for an English summer day had not put Peter Daventry in the mood that it undoubtedly should have done. A riotous evening—during which he had dined not wisely but too well with a number of men who had been at Oxford with him—is not perhaps the best preparation for work on the following day, and Peter heartily cursed the relentless and inexorable fate that had made him junior partner of "Merryweather, Linnell and Daventry—Solicitors." He thrust his hands into his pockets and walked to the window of his room, gazing disconsolately at the street below.

"Cornhill!" he muttered. "And it might be anywhere else for all it means to me, or for all I care. It's a dull old world nowadays and devilish difficult to get thrills out of a business like this. After a night with the lads it gets me 'on the raw' more than ever."

He looked down at London scurrying and hurrying. Men, women, young and old, treading their way quickly, decisively and imperturbably on the various errands and ventures that Life had chosen for them. "Poor devils!" he thought. "Day in and day out the same old grind! I sometimes wonder how they stand it. I certainly don't know how I do." He walked back to the chair by his desk, carefully selected a cigarette and pressed the bell.

A middle-aged, black-coated clerk appeared in the doorway.

"You rang, Mr. Daventry? You want me?"

"Oh, no, Plunkett! Not for a moment! What on earth gave you that extraordinary idea?"

"The bell—" He indicated the table with a sort of hopeless resignation.

"Merely a matter of 'physical jerks' on my part, Plunkett. I've been standing on my head on the desk, and in the process I inadvertently butted the bell and caused you—"

Plunkett smiled feebly. He was the kind of man that always did—thirty-five years' service for the firm had made him afraid to do anything too vigorously—even to a smile. But he knew Peter Daventry and knew his little whims and ways—"he will have his little joke," he would inform his friends and acquaintances, "and till he's had it, it's best to lie low and keep quiet." It will be observed, therefore, that he had *not* encountered "Brer Rabbit."

"You wanted—?"

"This morning's post, Plunkett! Neither more nor less! Stay though—when you bring it in, you might also bring me all the papers and correspondence relating to the Langley Case." He drew at his cigarette and watched the smoke rising. Then smiled. "Breach of promise is a God-send, Plunkett! Manna from the heights of Heaven."

Plunkett stared at him, it might be said, sorrowfully—and withdrew unobtrusively. At his second appearance he placed the unopened letters and the required papers on Peter's desk.

"Thank you, Plunkett!"

"Thank you, Mr. Daventry. Mr. Linnell asked me to tell you he would like to see you in his room as soon as possible, sir. At your convenience that is to say, sir."

Peter ran the paper-knife along the back of an envelope and nodded acquiescence. "All right, Plunkett. Tell Mr. Linnell I'll blow along to him shortly."

Mr. Merryweather, the founder of the firm, had been gathered to his fathers seven years before the date of the opening of this history; but his name had been retained. As Peter remarked to his more intimate friends, "the name of 'Merryweather' had a cheerful ring about it and therefore was worth keeping!"

David Linnell was a medium-sized, clean-shaven, spare man of fifty-eight years. He had been born in Lancashire and was a firm believer in the men of the Red Rose. He fully subscribed to the theory that "what Manchester thinks to-day—the rest of the world thinks to-morrow." In conjunction with the departed Merryweather, he had built up an eminently satisfactory business in London, had attracted to it a sound and rapidly-growing "clientele," and when the question arose of Peter Daventry coming in as a partner, he had seen with all a Northerner's shrewdness and acumen that this young Oxonian would bring to the firm new business and new clients from a hitherto unexplored source.

"Good morning, Peter!" he said as Daventry entered his room.

"Good morning! Plunkett tells me you want to see me."

Mr. Linnell looked up from his seat and motioned Peter to a chair beside him.

"Sit down, Peter! And listen attentively! Ever heard of Laurence P. Stewart?" Peter had, and said so immediately.

"Naturally! The American millionaire you mean, I presume?"

"The same. Know anything about him—anything special?"

Peter thought for a moment. "Can't say that I do—beyond what all the world knows. Made his money first in Chicago and afterwards on Wall Street—I fancy he's a widower."

"Quite right. With one son—about two and twenty. I'll tell you more! About three months ago Stewart came to England. At the time Assynton Lodge was in the market. He bought it and, I believe, paid a pretty stiff figure for it. It's a very fine place—not very far from Wantage—and right in the heart of the Berkshire Downs. I understand that he intends spending the remainder of his days in this country."

"Don't think I should, if I had his money," contributed Peter. "Still—there's no accounting for taste, I suppose. What's his pet ambition—to win the Derby or become an O.B.E.?"

"Neither," replied Linnell a trifle testily. "But your question, flippant though it may have been, brings me to his association with this conversation of ours this morning." He leaned forward to pick up a letter from the desk in front of him. Then turned again towards his partner. "He has one overpowering interest in life. He is a collector—"

"Horrible word," interrupted Peter. "Makes me think of Rates and Income Tax."

"He is a collector," repeated the elder man, ignoring the interruption. "For many years now, his one hobby has been his priceless and almost unique collection of articles of what may be termed, paramount historical interest and association."

Peter began to show signs of increased attention. This sounded better! Linnell continued. "I am informed, from a source that is certainly above reproach, that Stewart is the proud possessor of over two thousand articles of great historical significance. He claims to include in his—er Museum—if I may so describe it—a Musk-Ball used by Henry VIII for instance. He has a peculiar passion it seems for objects that are supposed to have Royal associations! Which last fact brings me to the Mary, Queen of Scots business!"

Peter raised his eyebrows—then helped himself to his third cigarette. "We're apparently moving in exalted circles," he ventured.

"And a great compliment to us, as a firm—Peter. But I will proceed. If he may be said to have a passion for collecting these objects that I have mentioned of Royal association—then I can tell you that he has a perfect mania—an overwhelming obsession would be perhaps a happier phrase—for anything connected with Mary, Queen of Scots." He paused. Then looked at Peter. "Lawrence P. *Stewart*, Peter! Note the name—he has got it into his head—or had it put there possibly—that he is a legitimate descendant of that ill-fated lady. Every relic of hers at all possible of acquisition—he acquires. Now look at this letter."

He pushed the letter that he had picked up from his table, across to Peter.

"Read it!" he said authoritatively.

Peter obeyed the instruction with more than ordinary alacrity.

Assynton Lodge,
Assynton, Berkshire,
June 7th, 192—.

SIR,

I am a man of few words. Your firm has been highly recommended to me by Colonel Leach-Fletcher, for whom you have acted many times in the past in matters of extreme discretion. He speaks in the highest possible terms of your integrity and efficiency. For reasons of my own I wish you to act for me at the Sale taking place on the 10th inst. at "Day, Forshaw and Palmers'." You will purchase for me the articles scheduled in their catalogue as follows:

(No. 37) "Collar of Pearls."

(No. 38) "Antique Tapestry Fire-screen."

(No. 39) "Rosary of Amber Beads."

"all having been indisputably the property of Mary, Queen of Scots."

The purchases completed, you will bring them or cause them to be brought to the above address at your earliest convenience, when your own account will be settled by

Yours faithfully,
LAURENCE P. STEWART.

David Linnell, Esq.,

Merryweather, Linnell and Daventry.

Peter looked up at his companion. "H'm," he remarked, "seems to know what he wants. No limit I suppose, as to price?"

"None! As far as I can see! He simply says, 'You will purchase—'"

Peter glanced at the letter again.

"And we charge him what we like!"

"Money's no object to Stewart, Peter," replied Linnell. "If he's set his mind upon getting the three articles in question—nothing short of a miracle will stop him."

"Why is he employing a firm of solicitors for a job of this kind?" asked Peter.

"Can't say! But I suggest Colonel Leach-Fletcher has impressed him that we are thoroughly safe and sound—and he's out taking no risks."

"Very possibly you're right," Peter commented. "I certainly can't think of any other reason. Have you seen a catalogue of the sale?"

"I've sent for one. Immediately upon receipt of this letter! Collins has gone round to Day, Forshaw and Palmers' offices. He should be back very shortly!"

Peter walked to the window and looked out.

"Here is Collins," he said, turning to his senior, "with catalogue complete."

In a few minutes they were examining it. It was headed as follows:

At Messrs Day, Forshaw and Palmers' Rooms, The Hanover Galleries, W.1.

On Friday, June 10th, 192–, at one o'clock precisely.

Sale of Old English and French Furniture, Pictures, Porcelain Jewellery, and Objects of Art,

Formerly the property of Lord Clavering, deceased late of Clavering Court, Warwickshire.

Linnell and Peter ran their eyes down its contents. They were many and varied. Linnell read them quickly. "A William and Mary Marqueterie Walnut Cabinet, a Chippendale Wine-Cooler, a pair of Boulle Cabinets of Regency Design, Portraits by Hoppner, Paintings by De Ribera, Romney, Van Der Velde and Sir Peter Lely, Derby and Nantgarw Porcelain, Chinese Porcelain of the Sung and Ming periods, Jewellery, a Cromwellian chalice with the Hull hall-mark, a George II octofoil salver, a Georgian Epergne, an unusually large King's Pattern service, several Sèvres vases—here we are, Peter, 37, 38 and 39 . . . h'm—h'm . . . exactly as described by our client in his letter." He looked up from the catalogue.

Peter pointed to a sentence at the end of the list. "May be viewed the two days preceding the Sale from 10 to 5 o'clock."

"That's to-day and to-morrow. What do you say to me running along and having a glance at the particular stuff Stewart wants?"

"Just what I was on the point of suggesting, Peter. You've taken the very words from my mouth."

"To-day or to-morrow?"

"Please yourself—but it's a nice morning—why not take advantage of it—have an early lunch and pop up West afterwards?"

"A pleasing prospect," exclaimed Peter. "Life seems a little brighter."

Linnell smiled—then waved him away. "That's settled then."

He strolled back to his own room and looked at his watch. "Don't see any just cause or impediment why I shouldn't get along at once and see about that lunch," he said to himself. "Plunkett!" He went to his door and called down the corridor.

"Yes, Mr. Daventry." Plunkett appeared in the distance and laboriously made his way to answer to the call.

"I'm going out, Plunkett. Mr. Linnell will be here if anything should be wanted. That's all. You needn't trouble to come in."

Plunkett bowed his understanding and re-entered his daily cell.

Once outside, Peter hailed a passing taxi. "Oxford Street," he announced curtly. "The Violette." It was where he habitually lunched whenever he happened to be in its vicinity. He made for his customary table and beamed upon the waiter who came forward solicitously.

Now Peter prided himself upon the quality of his gastronomic inclinations. He scanned the menu with a fine and fitting discrimination.

"A Dry Martini, Gustave."

"Yes, sir!"

"Thick white soup, Sole au Colbert—and Roast Duck—that will do nicely to be getting on with." He smiled in anticipatory relish. Gustave did likewise before disappearing. To appear again very quickly with the Dry Martini!

Peter raised it to his lips—after all Life wasn't so very unsatisfactory when there was good food and welcome drink to be had. He sipped his cocktail appraisingly. The place was comparatively empty—it was early. At the next table sat a man and woman. They were talking eagerly and with much animation. The man was doing most of it, with the woman listening attentively and punctuating his remarks at rapid and regular intervals with a curious little vigorous inclination of her head. Peter fell to wondering about them—"a lower middle-class couple on a shopping expedition" was his verdict—arrived at simultaneously with the advent of Gustave and the soup. The fish quickly followed, and he was awaiting the coming of the "appetizing Aylesbury" as he termed it to himself when a familiar voice broke on his ears.

"Hullo, Daventry! What's brought you up this end so early in the morning?"

Peter looked up. Then he grinned cheerfully.

"Sit down, Marriott! An unexpected pleasure!"

The newcomer sank into the proffered seat, and languidly stretched out a hand for the menu. Peter had met him several times in the Law Courts and had dined with him two or three times recently.

"You haven't answered my question," said Marriott. "What brings you up here at this time of day?"

"Business, my boy, purely business. Give Gustave your order."

Marriott smiled, rattled off his desires, and turned again to Peter.

"Glad to see an improvement in you. The other day you were talking about 'chucking' it all and going out to 'God's own Country' or somewhere."

"Wish I could, Marriott, but I can't. I'm afraid the improvement about which you are babbling so delightfully will be short-lived. These peas are really excellent—you'll enjoy them!"

"Good! Any news of importance?"

"Only that the next Coal Strike is expected to last twenty-two years or thereabouts."

"Really," grinned Marriott. "Tell me something fresh. Say Queen Anne's dead!"

Peter pushed back his plate with an air of complete satisfaction and made a reply that seemed to leap to his tongue without his brain having undergone any preliminary process of thinking. It seemed to be entirely spontaneous and at the same time to him as he sat there, peculiarly appropriate. It fitted in with the morning so happily.

"So's Mary, Queen of Scots!" He blew a ring of smoke to the ceiling. As he spoke, there happened to be a lull pervading the whole room. A lull that was violently and almost instantaneously shattered! The man at the next table turned sharply as the words tingled through the air, and as he turned, with his body for the brief moment excitedly uncontrolled, his arm abruptly swept the cruet from the table to the floor.

Two waiters dashed heroically to the work of rescue and salvage. The culprit muttered a few words of apology. The lady was heard to remark something about the bad luck attendant upon spilling the salt, smiled upon the two diligent waiters, but flashed a quick look at her companion. It was a look that possessed more than one quality. It contained a suggestion of warning, a hint of rebuke and a touch of fierce annoyance. The man sat sullenly in his seat, and Peter's eyes never left his face. For exactly what reason he didn't quite know—he felt almost compelled to it. His senses seemed to be jingling a refrain to him. It rang repeatedly through his brain and its purpose was, "Well—I'm damned." At the same time he tried to persuade himself that it was just an ordinary case of carelessness and that he had drawn liberally upon his imagination to connect the incident with the words he had used.

"What's amiss, Daventry?" broke in Marriott, cutting his reverie abruptly short. "You look as though you have seen a ghost!"

Peter jerked himself back to the normal with a tremendous effort.

"It's nothing," he muttered. "That little incident surprised me—that was all."

But his eyes strayed back to the other table, and as they did so the eyes of the man there met his and held them for a brief moment truculently and challengingly. The woman appeared to be urging her companion to do something that he apparently did not favour. He shook his head doubtfully, as though he were questioning the wisdom of what she said. Peter turned to Marriott. "I'll be getting along now, if you don't mind. Gustave! Bring me my bill! What's the damage?"

"I'm nearly through myself," responded Marriott. "I'm coming along too! Which way are you going?"

"Up West. And you aren't, probably! Thank you, Gustave!"

"No! I'm bound in the other direction—you've said it! Cheerio!"

Peter waved a hand to his retreating figure and collected his change. As he did so, the couple from the other table made their way past his table on their journey out. The man was in front—the woman followed closely on his heels. As they passed, for some reason almost unknown to himself, Peter strained his ears to catch, if at all possible, any stray fragment of their conversation. He was successful. The woman was speaking in a low-toned voice, but it was not too low to carry to his ears.

"Take my advice," Peter heard her say—"let's go to-morrow—not to-day."

"Can't see it makes much difference"—her companion's reply floated back to him. They passed down the restaurant—out of sight!

Peter rose to his feet and crammed his hat on his head.

"I'm a silly ass," he said to himself. "Letting my imagination run riot—magnifying trivial incidents—giving way to distorted ideas."

He hailed his second taxi-cab that day, and settled down comfortably. "Best thing I can do," he thought, "is to go and have that look at those antiquities I'm going to buy on Friday."

Wherein he erred—for he never bought them after all.

CHAPTER II
SCHEDULE NUMBERS 37, 38 AND 39

WHEN PETER entered the Galleries there were comparatively few people present. A knot of interested art-enthusiasts had gathered in front of a superb "Reynolds" dated 1765. It was described as the "Portrait of a Lady." She held a lute in her hand and wore a satin dress cut low and edged with pearls. Although Peter was no expert in these matters, it did not take him long to realize that he was gazing at a masterpiece. But he passed on. The Galleries held other attractions that interested him more. Schedule Numbers 37, 38 and 39 were easily to be found. The three objects that had brought him to Day, Forshaw and Palmers' almost jostled each other on the left of the room as you entered. The screen stood on the floor, the Pearl Collar and Rosary lay on a small Sheraton Inlaid Mahogany side table right against it. Their only visible protection from covetous hands was a rail that barriered them from the public, about four feet high. But as Peter looked at the three things for which he had been commissioned by Mr. Laurence P. Stewart, he became acutely aware and very definitely conscious, that he in his turn was being watched. Two men of medium height were lounging near . . . their profession was obvious to him. He had come into contact with their kind too many times before in the course of his own business not to recognize them when he saw them. "Plain-clothes," he told himself. He walked across to the barrier and took a close inspection of the objects in which he was interested. As he did so he fancied the two men edged a little more closely to him. But he realized, upon looking round, that with the exception of the men to whom reference has been made, he was the only person in that particular part of the room; hence their keener interest in his movements. "Hang it all," he said to himself—"this shadowing business gets on my nerves—I'll establish my 'bona-fides.'"

He walked back to the entrance to the Galleries. A middle-aged man was superintending the transportation of what was evidently a valuable picture. He paused in his directions as Peter came up. "Anything I can do for you, sir?" Peter caught him by the arm.

"Yes. Look here! Here's my card! I'm Daventry—of 'Merryweather, Linnell and Daventry.' I want to examine items Nos. 37, 38 and 39 in the published catalogue of your sale on Friday."

The man scratched his chin—thoughtfully. Then looked again at the proffered card.

"Young Mr. Forshaw's here, sir. You're Mr. Daventry, I think you said, sir."

"That's right."

"I'll tell the young governor, sir! Can I say you've a mind to purchase?"

"Oh yes!" cut in Peter impetuously. "I'm representing my firm on behalf of a very—"

He checked himself—suddenly. It occurred to him that there was absolutely no need to mention Stewart's name at this juncture and perhaps more than one excellent reason for withholding it. He thought of Stewart's phrase concerning discretion.

"Very good, sir," said the man. "I'll bring young Mr. Forshaw along to you in half a minute."

He was as good as his word. A young man bustled up, wiping his hands upon a duster.

"Mr. Daventry?" queried Forshaw. Peter bowed!

"You wished to have a look at something included in to-morrow's sale? What is it exactly?"

"It's not an 'it,'" responded Peter jocularly. And then with scant regard for the inclination of the verb "to be"—"it's a 'them.'"

"More than *one*, sir?"

"To be precise—three—the numbers are 37, 38 and 39 in your catalogue."

"Come this way." He escorted Peter to the handrail from which he had so recently come. Then slipped underneath with ease and handed him the Collar and the Rosary. It was impossible for Peter to form any adequate idea of the value of either. His experience of jewels was very limited, and the Rosary appeared to him to possess little value apart from its historical association. However, for the sake of appearances he feigned to make a very careful study of each.

"Aren't your people afraid of having some of these things stolen?" he ventured to Forshaw.

"We take certain precautions, Mr. Daventry," was the answer. "Close watch is maintained all day and all night. Anybody attempting any 'jiggery-pokery' would get the surprise of his life."

Peter glanced at the two representatives of the Law. They lounged in a corner. Forshaw followed the direction of his eyes and smiled. "Exactly! And well armed too!" He replaced the

Pearl Collar and the Rosary as Peter handed them across to him. Then lifted up the screen and handed it over.

"I see that you advertise these three articles as having belonged to Mary, Queen of Scots," remarked Peter.

"That is so!" replied Forshaw. "They formed part of the late Lord Clavering's collection. Had been in his family, I believe, for over two hundred years. No doubt whatever on that point," he concluded decisively.

Peter looked at the screen with some interest. It stood approximately from three and a half to four feet high he estimated—on a carved-wood pedestal. Upon the tapestry, which was covered with thick glass, he could see a number of brightly colored beads. They were, to all appearances, arranged in the form of letters. Peter inspected them carefully. Then quickly grasped their meaning. The beads formed words and the words were—

"JESUS CHRIST, GOD AND SAVIOUR."

In the top left-hand corner of the tapestry was worked the Scots Queen's Royal Lion and in the right could be discerned the "fleur-de-lis." The corners at the bottom showed the Leopards and Lilies of England.

"Of more ornament than use, I'm afraid, Mr. Daventry," said Forshaw with a smile.

"I agree." He bent down to examine it more closely.

"I expect some pretty brisk bidding for that on Friday! Just the kind of thing to appeal to a collector of antiques."

"I suppose so," replied Peter. He handed it back to its temporary guardian.

"Thank you—Mr. Forshaw. I'm very much obliged to you, I'm sure, for showing me round as you have. I'll be getting along now."

Then he was suddenly impelled to ask a question. "I suppose a good many people have had a good look at these three articles already?"

"On the contrary—you're the first, Mr. Daventry. That is, of course, up to the moment. They haven't been on show very long."

Peter shook hands and laughed. "My remarks seem to miss-fire every time."

"Good afternoon, sir."

"Good afternoon." He passed by the middle-aged man at the entrance and pushed something into his hand. The man looked at it and smiled—then put his finger to his forehead in salute.

"Thank you, sir. You're a gentleman. Still—there was no necessity—"

Peter waved a sympathetic hand and departed.

Half an hour later saw him back at the office in Cornhill.

"Well?" said Linnell as he entered the room, "everything satisfactory?"

Peter sat on the corner of the table and swung his leg.

"I went up there, as we arranged, and I had a look at the stuff we've been asked to get." He paused.

"Yes?" interrogated Linnell. "What did you think of it?"

"Hard to say. The Pearl Collar is really magnificent, and the screen I should say will prove a tremendous attraction for the 'genus' collector—the species that we are deputed to represent—the Rosary, in my opinion, won't fetch anything like so much."

"H'm," said Linnell reflectively. He traced a pattern on his blotting-paper with his pen. Then he looked up at his companion.

"Has it struck you, Daventry—that we may possibly be running a big risk over this business?"

Peter looked startled. "How do you mean?"

Linnell opened a drawer and handed over a letter. "Supposing that letter hadn't come from Stewart; supposing that signature—purporting to be Stewart's—was a forgery?"

Peter's eyes opened even wider. "That's interesting. Go on!"

Linnell from Lancashire went on. And emphasized his points with quick jerks of the head. "We are instructed to *purchase*! That is to say Stewart in no way restricts us. He mentions no limit. Supposing we pay, for argument's sake, £25,000—thinking we're acting for Stewart—and then Stewart repudiates ever having commissioned us! And then, after that, we find our £25,000 worth of stuff is worth say—only £15,000. Where are we then, Daventry? I've inflated the figures purposely."

"Down the mine, Daddy," declared Peter. "But what's the Big Idea—who would ever—?"

"Who would? Seems to me Day, Forshaw and Palmers might find it a very healthy proposition," replied Linnell.

"And that's what you really think?" asked Peter incredulously.

"No—I don't!" said Linnell grimly. "But I'm damned well going to find out."

"How? Go and see Stewart?" Peter was all alertness now.

"No! I've telegraphed to him—this morning. The answer should be here at any moment! That should be sufficient."

He looked at his watch.

Peter selected a cigarette—then handed his case to Linnell.

"Thanks! I don't mind if I do."

Before Peter had had time to take his eyes from the match with which he lit his companion's cigarette—there was a tap at the door—Plunkett entered. Linnell tore open the telegram that was handed to him. Then he smiled. Peter looked over his shoulder. Then he smiled in his turn, and read aloud what he saw.

"Say! What the hell's biting you—when I say Buy—then Buy. Got that? Stewart."

That was the intelligent rendering of the message. A message which looked and sounded even cruder and terser in the unpunctuated word-arrangement of telegrams.

Linnell's smile developed into a ringing laugh. "I've been barking up the wrong tree, after all, Peter. Still—one can't be too careful. You'll go along then on Friday and—"

Plunkett reappeared in the doorway. "Another telegram, sir." Linnell looked surprised. Then read the second message.

"Say—you don't *look* before you leap—you take a magnifying glass. Same name as before."

"Mr. Stewart has a decided sense of humour," commented David Linnell. "But I'd sooner he took liberties with my *amour propre* than with my pocket."

Peter laughed.

"Some people wouldn't," continued Linnell, determined to justify himself, "but I *would*. And even if he is a millionaire—to put four words where he could have used one—should have used one in fact, is just a piece of reckless and shameless waste—and that's all there is to it."

He turned to Daventry, proudly conscious that he was safe-guarding an important principle.

"I think I'll go myself and have a glance at the stuff to-morrow, Peter—after all he's a millionaire—and business is business. Where did you lunch?"

"At the 'Violette,'" was the reply. "And, by the by, whatever you do—don't upset the cruet."

"What do you mean?" Linnell looked at him curiously.

Peter recounted the incident that had occurred earlier in the day.

"Probably quite an accident," he concluded, "and a coincidence—still it took my breath away, as it were, for just the moment."

Linnell thought for a moment or two. "Probably nothing in it, Peter. You had the thing on your mind and were over-imaginative. What are you doing to-night? Anything special?"

"I'm dining at the Club. And I may have a rubber or two afterwards."

"Good. I sha'n't be in, in the morning. I may run down to Berkshire this evening, and in any case I'll go straight on to Day, Forshaw and Palmers' first thing to-morrow. I'm really very anxious to see the actual objects of this extraordinary commission of ours!"

But just as Peter was destined never to buy them, so Linnell was fated not to see them on the morrow.

For when he arrived at Day, Forshaw and Palmers' next morning he found a condition of extreme excitement and agitation. Detective-Inspector Goodall was in charge of the case—a case that had cost Day, Forshaw and Palmers Schedule Nos. 37, 38 and 39 in their sale catalogue, and their night-watchman his life. Linnell's hand shook when he heard what had happened. The conviction came to him that he was connected with the affair. Acting upon a sudden impulse, he went in.

CHAPTER III

THE HANOVER GALLERIES MURDER

JUST INSIDE the room he was stopped. Two six-feet members of the Metropolitan Police barred his further entrance.

"Sorry, sir," said one of them, "but our orders are to admit nobody."

Linnell paused—then under the influence of a sudden idea—he produced his card.

"Give that to the Inspector who has the case in hand, will you?" he said; " it's just possible I may be able to help him." He looked straight at the officer.

"Very well, sir," rejoined the latter. "I'll see what I can do for you." He spoke to his colleague. "You stay here—I'll go and have a word with the Chief about this gentleman."

He was soon back. "Detective-Inspector Goodall will see you, sir! This way, if you please!"

He piloted Linnell down the lengthy room. A group of men were standing at the far end. Goodall was in the center of the group. Linnell saw a clean-shaven man of medium height and stoutish build—dressed in a double-breasted blue serge suit. He awaited Linnell's approach with uplifted eyebrows.

"Mr. Linnell?" he interrogated—quickly and decisively. "Of—?"

"Merryweather, Linnell and Daventry—Cornhill," replied Linnell—to the point as always. "I am the senior partner of the firm."

"You have important information for me, I understand," cut in Goodall.

"Information," corrected Linnell. "You must be the judge of its importance."

"Well, I'm listening, Mr. Linnell. Go ahead!"

"Before I tell you what I know—would you, in your turn, be good enough to tell me if the rumours that are travelling round outside—are correct? Are you investigating a case of murder and robbery?"

"I am! A robbery has taken place here since shutting-up hours last evening—and a poor devil of a watchman been bashed on the head—he's as dead as mutton. Where do you come in?"

"Maybe not at all, Inspector. But my firm had a rather peculiar commission entrusted to it yesterday in relation to the sale that was to have taken place here to-morrow. And it struck me when I heard—"

"Aren't you a bit imaginative, Mr. Linnell?" demanded Goodall. "How could anything you—still—let's hear all about it."

"I was going to," remonstrated Linnell mildly. "We were commissioned to buy three articles that were advertised as having belonged to Mary, Queen of—"

"What?" blazed Goodall. "The devil you were. They're the only three articles we can trace to have been stolen. Who commissioned you?"

Although Linnell was really surprised at this announcement—yet in one way he was not. His mind seemed prepared for it—some sixth and subtle sense had been pounding at his brain ever since his arrival at this place that Stewart's instructions and the tragedy that confronted him were in some manner connected with each other. It was the shadowy belief in this that had prompted him to try to interview the Inspector.

"Mr. Laurence P. Stewart of Assynton, Berkshire," he replied quietly.

"The millionaire?" exclaimed a tall man from the group.

"Yes," said Linnell.

"You know this man Stewart, Mr. Day?" asked Goodall, turning to the speaker.

"Only by reputation," rejoined Day. "It's the American millionaire—you must have heard of him, Inspector! Forshaw here, met him once or twice over in the States—I never have."

"That's so," intervened Forshaw with a positive movement of the head. "I met him in New York a year or two after the War."

"Go on, Mr. Linnell," said the Inspector. "You said his instructions to your firm were 'peculiar'—that was the adjective you used. I reckon you've some more to tell us."

Here young Forshaw broke in. "The gentleman who called here yesterday—a Mr. Daventry—he was a representative of your firm, I think?"

"Quite correct," affirmed Linnell. "My partner! My only partner, I should have said."

Goodall swung round on to Forshaw Junior. "Called here yesterday? What about?" he grumbled in his deep voice.

"The Mary, Queen of Scots' stuff." Goodall looked a trifle annoyed.

"You didn't tell me," he muttered. "Why didn't you?"

"I simply haven't had a chance yet," came the reply with just a hint of rebellious obstinacy, "you've been doing best part of the talking. I should have told you though before you'd finished." Forshaw shrugged his shoulders.

Goodall glared—then reverted to Linnell. "Fire away, Mr. Linnell. What exactly were your instructions?"

"Yesterday morning I received a letter from the gentleman I just mentioned—Laurence P. Stewart—authorizing me to buy the three articles that you have just informed me have been stolen—er—numbers 37, 38 and 39 in the sale catalogue."

"Well?" rapped Goodall—"I can't see anything . . ."

Linnell went on. "The whole thing was peculiar in this respect. I was entirely unacquainted with the gentleman—the commission was right out of our usual type of business—no price was mentioned—I was given *carte blanche*—I know absolutely nothing about this particular species of—er—antiques—and what is more"—here he paused and looked Goodall straight in the eyes—"I had no absolute proof that the affair was genuine."

Goodall nodded approvingly. "You took steps, of course, to—"

"I wired to Berkshire and the reply was satisfactory—at all events—"

"What reply did you get?" Goodall was showing signs of impatience.

"It came by telegram—you shall see it. It's at my office."

"You were satisfied?"

"Yes, Inspector."

"One little point, Mr. Linnell, before you proceed any farther. Why did Mr. Stewart select your firm to carry out this commission? Any idea?"

"He explained that in his letter. He said he had been told of us by a very respected and esteemed client of ours—a Colonel Leach-Fletcher."

"Was that true?" demanded Goodall.

"Colonel Leach-Fletcher is a client of ours—certainly—I can say nothing as to the alleged recommendation. You can see the letter with the telegram."

"I will. Anything else?"

"Not very much. The telegram reassured me—Mr. Daventry, my partner, came and had a look over here yesterday—and I had come with similar purpose this morning—only to find this trouble."

"How did you know, Mr. Linnell?"—Goodall's voice sounded very distinctly, almost as though he were launching an accusation—"that these three particular objects had been stolen? It seems to me—"

"I didn't," replied Linnell in an almost aggrieved manner. "I thought you understood that when I entered. I had no knowledge of it whatever. I only obeyed my instincts."

"H'm," grunted the Inspector. "Yes, Doctor?"

This last remark was addressed to a gentleman who had come authoritatively down the room.

"The poor fellow's quite dead, of course. Been dead, I should say, about eight hours when I examined him. Four particularly savage blows on the skull I think—part of the brain actually protruding—whoever did it—meant doing it."

"Struck from behind, do you think, Doctor?" queried Goodall.

"Very probably—the parietal bone is badly smashed."

Goodall turned to Day. "What time did this night-watchman come on duty, Mr. Day?"

"At midnight, Inspector! The first watchman is on duty from six o'clock—when we close—till twelve, when poor Mason relieved him. I've sent for Druce—that's the other watchman—he should be along here in a few moments."

"Well, this poor fellow in the other room can't tell us anything—so we shall have to rely on Druce. I hope he will be of some help."

"Was he found dead in this room, Inspector?" asked Linnell—"or—"

"Just over there"—pointed Goodall to a spot about a dozen yards away—"right in front of the handrail. Doctor Archer examined him first down there—then we had him taken into Mr. Day's private office."

"Where the rug is?" interrogated Linnell. He looked at the rug on the floor.

"That's it," answered Goodall. "There's a nasty mess underneath—that's why the rug's there!"

"How did they get in and out?"

"Well, Mr. Linnell—as to that—they got out with the night-watchman's keys—we can't find them anywhere—how they got in is a matter of conjecture—that's what I want to see this other watchman, Druce, about."

"But I presume you've formed some conclusions? There must be some—"

"There's very little," replied Goodall. "Very little indeed. No forced entrance at all. Not even a foot mark or finger-print. Three articles stolen—a night-watchman dead on the floor. Motive—burglary! Which makes the murder a subordinate factor in the crime. Which makes the murdered man almost impersonal! And I'm supposed to put my hands on this murderer in less than twenty-four hours—and that out of a little matter of six millions of people."

"You're supposed—"

Goodall shrugged his shoulders. "If I don't—my wife or some other damned good-natured friend will confront me with an article in the London press shrieking 'the decadence of Scotland Yard.'"

Linnell looked at him curiously. To say the least he was impressed. That this sturdy and efficient police-representative would prove no mean antagonist he felt sure.

Mr. Day came bustling forward. "Druce is here, Inspector," he announced.

"Bring him along here, Mr. Day." Goodall's eyes brightened perceptibly.

Druce came slowly forward—nervously plucking with his fingers at the cap he held in his hand. He was a wizened-faced man—of about sixty years of age. He had had no encounters with the Police before—all his life he had "kept honest"—and this new experience, therefore, had had a somewhat unsettling effect upon him.

"You are Edward Druce—one of the night-watchmen here?" commenced Goodall.

"Yes, sir."

"How long have you worked here?"

Druce hesitated and half-turned towards Mr. Day. "Is it five or—?"

"Six years, Druce, you've been with us," supplemented his employer, "six years last Easter."

Druce nodded. "That's it, sir. And I hope I've always given satisfaction."

A glint of humour shot through Goodall's eyes.

"What time were you relieved last night?" he asked.

"About five to twelve, sir, or thereabouts."

"Mason came on then? Was that about his usual time?"

"It were, sir," replied Druce. "He never varied much, sir, did Mason—steady and reliable he were—always. What's come to him, sir?"

"He's dead, Druce," came the relentless reply, "murdered in the night."

Druce went ashen pale. He licked his lips as the horror of the news struck home to him. "Murdered?" he managed to gasp.

"Now tell me, Druce," proceeded Goodall, "did anything about Mason last night strike you as peculiar or—extraordinary?"

Druce shook his head. "No, sir—nothing." This decisively! "He 'ad a joke on his lips, sir, when he came up the stairs with me—just as he usually had. Told me I could go 'ome and do some gardenin'—before I went to 'Kip.' Twelve o'clock at night, sir, that was."

"You went downstairs to open the doors to let him in?"

"Yes, sir. He always give three loud sharp knocks."

"And you noticed nothing then—or at any other time during the evening that you regarded as unusual or abnormal? Think carefully!"

Druce pondered over the question. "No—I can't say as how"— then a sudden reminiscence seemed to awake in him—"well, sir—now you mention it, there was an incident, so to speak, when Jim Mason come to the—nothing at all important, sir—" he spoke deprecatingly.

"Let's hear it," rapped Goodall. "Every word of it!"

Every vestige of blood went from the night-watch-man's face. "I'm sorry I didn't think of it before, sir," he muttered, "I hope there's no harm done—"

"Let's have it," bellowed Goodall, "every second's of import-ance!"

"Well, sir," said Druce—"it was like this. When I 'eard Jim Mason knock—he give his three knocks just as usual—I went downstairs to let 'im in. When I opened the door he was stan-din' there just in the ordinary way—when a female comes up to us. Wanted to know what time the Galleries opened the next morning—that was all she enquired, sir! I told her 'ten o'clock.' Then she pointed down the street and asked if that way was the right direction for the Marble Arch."

"And was it?" snapped Goodall eagerly.

"Yes," said Druce with some surprise. "That's so, sir!"

"What did Mason do while this conversation was taking place?"

"Mason, sir? He showed 'er the way the same as wot I did."

"Of course he did," cut in Goodall with decision. "And I expect she wanted a deal of showing, didn't she?"

"She did seem a bit mazed-like," murmured Druce.

"I'll warrant she did," said the Inspector. "Just long enough for the murderer to slip in behind your backs and up the stairs in front of Mason."

Druce went goggle-eyed. "Gosh! Who'd 'ave thought of that?"

"Not you, evidently," returned Goodall. "If you had have done, your mate might still be alive. It's no use, though, wasting time on regrets or recriminations."

He stepped into the private room used by Day as his office.

"Is this door locked of an evening when the place closes?" he asked.

"Always," responded Day. "Or, at least, it should be!"

"Who was in charge here yesterday evening?" queried the Inspector swiftly.

"I was." Young Forshaw stepped forward.

"Did you lock this door when you left?"

"To the best of my memory—yes. But it's a mechanical sort of job—you know, Inspector—the kind of thing you do so often from mere force of habit—that the doing it leaves no very clear impression on your mind."

Goodall nodded in acceptance. He knew exactly what the speaker meant.

"Still," went on Forshaw, "I'm fairly certain I did it." He thought it over carefully.

"How many keys are there?" broke in the Inspector.

Day took it upon himself to answer. "Four. Each of the partners has one—and Ronald Forshaw here also. He's more often in charge here of an evening than anybody—he has to have a key."

"Now tell me again," interjected Goodall, "who gave the alarm? The cleaner, you said, didn't you?"

"That's so," replied Day. "The watchman on duty between twelve midnight and seven A.M. is always relieved by a Mrs. Turner—she sweeps and cleans the place up generally. When she arrived she got no answer, of course. Couldn't get in! So she got into touch with the people next door, who 'phoned me. I came down post-haste. I guessed there was trouble because I knew we had some valuable things here."

Goodall pursed his lips. "The door of your office was locked when you arrived?"

Day knitted his brows. Then a sudden flush of colour welled and broke into the ordinary paleness of his face. "Inspector," he said, "write me down a dunderhead. The door of my office was closed but not locked. I remember it distinctly now. I brought the keys of the front door along—my own keys—we all came in together—my partners and I—we found poor Mason on the floor there and I rushed to the phone for you and Doctor Archer. I never gave a thought to the fact that the door of my office wasn't locked. The idea of the murder drove it completely from my mind."

He paused—a little crestfallen and apologetic. Goodall turned to the group of listeners somewhat dramatically. "That's how the murderer got in and managed the job," he declared. "Got in while the attention of the two watchmen was being distracted by the woman 'decoy'—made his way quickly up here—picked the lock of that door"—he pointed to the door of the private office— "hid in the office till the time came for action—then pounced on Mason from behind."

Linnell interposed. "Would he have sufficient time, do you think, Inspector, to pick the lock before Mason and Druce could get up here?"

"Depends on Mason and Druce and the time they spent downstairs," replied Goodall. He swung round like lightning on the man concerned. Druce reddened. "How long were you before you and Mason came upstairs?"

Druce shifted his feet uneasily. "Not more than a matter of a few minutes, sir. Say five minutes!" Goodall flashed a look of understanding at him. "I suppose you stayed at the foot of the staircase for a 'few draws,' eh?" He turned on his heel to Mr. Day. "Smoking forbidden here during the watchmen's shifts, Mr. Day?"

Day inclined his head in assent.

"Thought so. Well, Druce, am I right?"

"Well, sir, Mason certainly did have a puff or two—only for a few minutes though."

"Why did you come back with him—upstairs again—when you were going home?"

"For my things, sir. I never collected 'em together when I 'eard 'im knock. I always went straight down to 'im."

Goodall nodded. "You and Mason were certainly long enough absent from the room to give this fellow his chance and Mason paid for his mistake with his life, poor chap. Now—about this woman, Druce—what was she like? Describe her!"

Druce shook his head with evident misgiving. "I'm afraid I can't 'elp you much there, sir. I ain't much of a 'and at descriptions—my daughter Poppy now—if she were 'ere she'd be able to—"

"Describe a woman she'd never seen, I suppose," snapped Goodall. "Come now."

Druce pulled up with a jerk. "Well, she 'ad on dark clothes and some sort of an 'at—and was about middle height." He concluded hopefully.

Goodall turned away with a gesture of dismay. "And yet we're informed that all undiscovered crimes are the fault of the Police," he said bitterly. "When we get civilian help like this."

"What age would you say the woman was, Druce?" asked Mr. Day.

Druce hesitated. He seemed to find this another poser. Then he committed himself.

"Well, I ain't certain, sir, not by no manner of means, but I should say somewhere between thirty and forty."

"Dark or fair?"

"I couldn't see, sir. Honest, I couldn't—so it's no use askin' me, sir."

Day turned in Goodall's direction. "I'm afraid that's about all we shall get, Inspector," he declared semi-humorously. "Do you want to ask him any more?"

"I'm thirsting to," drawled Goodall. "He's such a mine of information. Let him go," he muttered with a tinge of disgust.

Druce turned with relief written on every line of his face. "Thank you, sir. Thank you, gentlemen. I'm glad to 'ave been of assistance to you." He made his way to the door. Then he turned to the group again.

"I'll tell you what I *did* notice about that woman, now I come to think of it," he announced with an air of extreme wisdom.

"You don't say!" declared Goodall. "Don't tell me she walked with one shoulder lower than the other—all suspected persons do."

"No!" replied Druce with disappointment in his tone. "Nothink so important as that, sir. But when she walked away up the street, sir, she sneezed several times. That's what I've just thought of, sir."

Goodall threw his head up hopelessly. "Can you beat that?" he said plaintively. "The stiff!" He heard Druce slowly descending the stairs, proudly aware no doubt of a very perfect piece of Pelmanism.

"There you are," asserted Goodall, "there you have—"

His remarks were interrupted by a ring of the telephone from the private office. Mr. Day went into his room and picked up the receiver.

The others outside heard him say, "Yes! He's here now. I'll bring him to the 'phone."

He came out. "Mr. Linnell," he announced, "Mr. Daventry, your partner, would like to speak to you on the telephone."

"Thank you," said Linnell. He entered and took the message.

"What?" he said. "Good God, Peter—you can't mean it. It's impossible."

He stayed a minute or two longer—then replaced the receiver with trembling finger. For the moment he had a hard task to control himself. Then he pulled himself together and re-entered the Gallery.

"Gentlemen," he said very gravely, "Mr. Laurence P. Stewart was murdered last night in his library at Assynton. He was found with his skull battered in!"

CHAPTER IV

PETER DAVENTRY IS MINDFUL OF MR. BATHURST

To SAY that Goodall and his companions were dumbfounded is no exaggeration. Events were crowding upon them this morning with a vengeance. The announcement of this second murder took their breath away. It startled them and threw them off their balance much more effectively than the first calamity had done. Mason was a night-watchman! Stewart was a millionaire! The former could be very easily replaced—the latter's death was a tragedy in more senses than one. Goodall knew perfectly well that any failure on his part to find the murderer of Mason would occasion no questions in Parliament and would cause the Home Secretary no loss of sleep. But now that Laurence P. Stewart was caught in the wheels of the murder-machinery he was painfully conscious that he must be "up and doing." The case might be his, too!

"How did that news reach you, Mr. Linnell?" was his first question.

"From my partner, Mr. Daventry. He has just had a 'phone-call from Stewart's home in Berkshire—from Stewart's son, I understood him to say."

"What made Stewart's son telephone so quickly to your office?"

Linnell rubbed his cheek with his fingers. "He didn't explain the reason to me just now—Daventry didn't, I mean. I can only surmise that young Stewart knew that we had received instructions from his father concerning the sale of those antiques and wished possibly to countermand them—considering the fresh and tragic circumstances."

"H'm," muttered the Inspector. "I suppose that's possible. When was Stewart murdered, did you say?"

"They believe—some time last night. Naturally, I wasn't able to glean extensive details—even if my partner had been in a position to give them to me. But from what he did tell me, I imagine that the body was discovered early this morning."

Goodall looked thoughtful. "Hardly looks like the same people! Assynton must be a matter of seventy miles from London—getting on for a couple of hours' journey at least—that means they would have to leave there somewhere about nine-thirty, assuming Stewart to have been killed first, and accepting Druce's evidence as reliable—h'm—possible but not probable—have to find out when Stewart was last seen alive."

He turned to Linnell. "Extremely useful your turning up here, Mr. Linnell. There does seem to be a connection between the two affairs—difficult though it may be to discover it. I'll come and see your Mr. Daventry later on."

"I shall be delighted. There's our address." He handed his card to the Inspector.

Goodall fingered it, thinking carefully. "Mr. Forshaw!" he called. "Mr. Forshaw, Junior!"

"Yes, Inspector!"

"You stated just now that you interviewed Mr. Linnell's partner yesterday."

"That's so, Inspector. Yesterday afternoon, to be precise."

"What happened exactly—tell me?"

"Well, it was like this! This gentleman, Mr. Daventry, asked to be allowed to have a look at the Stuart stuff—the three articles that have been stolen. I showed them to him. He examined them rather carefully. . . . that's all I think . . . oh . . . he commented on the possibility of them being stolen . . . I remember that fact, because I took the trouble to explain the precautions that were always taken to safeguard our property."

"You had a watch on the stuff then?" queried Goodall.

Day intervened and took up the thread from Forshaw. "Two of your people were here, Inspector. During the hours the Galleries were open to the public! In 'plain-clothes' of course, and armed! It's our usual plan when we have sales of anything at all valuable. It's been our practice for many years now."

Goodall signified that he understood. Then he turned to young Forshaw again. "What else did this Daventry do?"

Forshaw passed his hands across his brow in an attempt at recollection.

"Nothing, I think! That is to say—oh, I remember—he asked how many other people had been to examine the three articles he was handling."

"What was your answer? That question interests me too."

"My answer was 'nobody' . . . It was true," Forshaw replied simply.

Goodall looked across at Linnell.

"Now I wonder what made your partner—"

"Look here, Inspector," broke in Linnell with a gesture of annoyance, "for goodness sake don't start imagining things. Daventry was interested in Stuart articles purely from the standpoint of a competitive purchaser, about to act on behalf of a client—surely you don't—"

Goodall patted him on the arm. "Don't get a 'peeve,' Mr. Linnell. It's my job to ask questions and very often a random sort of question hits a target quite unexpectedly. Don't forget that the presence of both you and your partner in this affair is downright queer. Right from the beginning—to the point we've reached now—you admitted as much yourself when you came in."

But Mr. Linnell's professional dignity had been touched—he remained quite silent under the Inspector's attempt at justification. He walked across to the others. "I think I'll go, gentlemen. My partner will, no doubt, desire to discuss matters with me as soon as possible. You know where to find me if you should want me."

He bowed to the company and made his exit.

Upon arrival at his offices in Cornhill he found Peter awaiting him with anxious impatience.

"I'm jolly glad to see you," was his greeting. "There's been a second message from Assynton—young Stewart was particularly anxious to talk to you—he seemed quite annoyed when I told him you were still away from the office."

"Peter," said Linnell, "we've been caught in a most curious set of circumstances. When you 'phoned me just now, at Day, Forshaw and Palmers', what do you imagine I was doing?"

Peter looked at him blankly. "Doing? Why—having a look round of course:—the same as I had. What are you driving at?"

"I'm not driving at anything, Peter. I'm just giving you some information. When I arrived at the show-rooms this morning I had rather a 'jolt.' The police were there—the Galleries had been robbed during the night—and what is even more dreadful than that, a night-watchman employed there had been brutally murdered."

Peter gasped. "Good Lord! My telephone message to you must have been a shock."

"It was! I could hardly believe my ears! I decided not to say anything to you over the 'phone but to come back here."

Peter thrust his hands into his trousers-pockets. "Funny thing—we seem in it both ends—don't we? The whole thing is very queer. Both here and in Berkshire."

Linnell shook his head. "Not really. We just happened to be in at the Galleries end because Stewart sent us there—but I haven't finished yet."

Peter uttered a cry of amazement. "Don't say there are any more—"

Linnell cut into his remarks. "I told you the Galleries had been robbed during the night. I didn't tell you what had actually been stolen. As far as the police could tell when I left them, the only three things that had been taken were *the very three that Stewart commissioned us to buy!*"

He paused and walked to the window. Then turned and confronted Peter.

"What do you make of that? Extraordinary, isn't it? To say the least!"

Peter whistled softly. "I said we seemed to be well in it. I feel sure now. And what's more, Linnell, I've got a feeling we haven't heard or seen the last of it either, by a long way. You mark my words."

Linnell smiled. "I agree with you! As a matter of fact, I shouldn't be at all surprised if Detective-Inspector Goodall hasn't already got a certain Peter Daventry on his list of 'suspects.' I hope your alibi's good."

"What on earth are you gibbering about?" demanded Peter. "And who the hell's Detective-Inspector Goodall?"

"I'm not gibbering, my dear fellow. Detective-Inspector Goodall is the gentleman from Scotland Yard that is investigating the Galleries murder, and he has, of course, been informed of your interest in the Stuart relics and of your call there yesterday. Young Forshaw told him. Then there was my call to-day—I got in 'at the death' as you might say—I could see he thought it was damned suspicious conduct—all of it—I explained our connection with the affair—"

"You told him of Stewart's commission? Was that wise? Yet awhile?"

"I think so, Peter! My professional experience has taught me the value of frankness and truth—even as a solicitor—that is why I never entered Parliament."

"But why suspect *me*?" reiterated Peter. "Is every intending purchaser on the—?"

"The police *must* suspect *somebody*. Why not flatter yourself at their attention? But tell me all you've heard about the Berkshire end of the tangle."

Peter swung his legs as he sat . . . somewhat petulantly. "The message came through about half-past ten—the first message, I mean—Stewart's secretary put it through—I think he said his name was Morgan or Llewellyn—I'm not sure. He asked if you were in—I told him 'no'—then he asked for me. I said it was all right and he told me that young Mr. Stewart wanted me. The poor chap seemed very agitated—his father had been found dead in the library that morning. Murdered—his head beaten in! Would we cancel our instructions about the sale to-morrow? As far as he was able he was getting into touch with all his father's immediate business activities . . . in the case of a millionaire, he explained, it was of the utmost importance . . . affected the money market so. That was about all, I fancy. Then I 'phoned the news on to you—I knew I should find you there. By the way, did you run down to Assynton last night?"

"Didn't have time. When was the second telephone message?"

"About twenty minutes before you returned," said Peter.

"What did he want?"

"He asked for you, again. It seems he isn't too satisfied with the quality of the local Police Force—he's asking for Scotland Yard to send a man down—says he's prepared to pay anything to get at the truth and arrest the murderer. Also he wanted your advice. Could you recommend an efficient, discreet, and trustworthy private detective? They were the three adjectives he used."

"Why does he appeal to me, I wonder?"

"I asked him that. He says he hasn't been in England more than a few months and it occurred to him that we might help him. He also wants one of us to go down—his father's solicitors, I understand, are in New York."

"H'm," muttered Linnell. "I can appreciate his position. But I'm afraid I'm no use to him in the matter of the private detective. I don't know anybody I should care to send down there—it isn't as though it were a case of keeping a person under observation." He shook his head doubtfully.

"Nor I, either," supplemented Peter. "What about his idea of one of us going down there—shall I go? What do you think yourself?"

"I think you might go," replied Linnell. "It should be more in your line than mine—you're younger to begin with. Can't you do a bit of 'sleuthing' on your own account? Sherlock Holmes has had many imitators!"

"I might. It will make quite an interesting and 'piquant' situation—a 'suspect' one moment—a 'sleuth' the next. I remember my brother Gerald—by Jove, Linnell, I've got it—Anthony Bathurst! Why on earth didn't I think of him before?"

"Who's that? What do you mean?"

"Why, if you want a man to act for young Stewart, you couldn't possibly find a better!"

"What is he—a private inquiry agent?"

"Not on your life—he's a sort of free lance—tinkers about at a good many things. He was up at Oxford about the same time as Gerald. That is to say, about three years after me. Can you remember the Considine Manor affair?"

"Considine Manor? Wasn't it a murder down in Sussex somewhere?"

"You've got it. Well, old Gerald was actually stopping in the house at the time. He always regards Bathurst as an absolute marvel. Cleared up the case when it had got the Police absolutely 'stone cold.' He never tires of singing Bathurst's praises!"

" Where is he now? Do you know?"

Peter stroked his chin. Hadn't Gerald told him Bathurst was living in London somewhere?

"No, I don't. There you've got me! Still—old Gerald may know. I'll give him a ring." He unhooked the receiver. "Give me 'Wedderburn and Rathbone,' will you—the Accountants—Devonshire Place will you *please*—I've forgotten the number. Oh! Thank you!"

He waited for a moment or two. "Yes. Mr. Gerald Daventry, that's it! Oh—hallo, Gerald—Peter speaking. Could you possibly put me into touch with Anthony Bathurst? Eh? . . . Yes, something after his own heart, where . . . Leyton . . . thanks very much."

He turned to Linnell. "Gerald says we shall probably find him at Leyton this afternoon, on the members pavilion. Middlesex are playing Essex, and he rarely misses any of the Middlesex games. He'll come down himself—Gerald, I mean—and if Bathurst is there—he'll introduce us."

"All right, then, Peter. You get along—and if it can be arranged satisfactorily, we'll 'phone Stewart when you return."

"Why don't you come along too? Come and see your adopted shire!"

"No. I'll stay here. I've had enough excitement for one day."

Peter grinned. "You're a superlative optimist," he exclaimed, "I must introduce you to a friend of mine who's a baseball 'fan.' He'd be tickled to death to hear you connect cricket with excitement."

A step sounded in the corridor outside. Linnell and Peter glanced quickly in the direction of the door. Then Linnell heard a voice that he recognized only too well.

"Come in, Inspector," he announced. "I was half expecting you."

"Thank you, Mr. Linnell. I thought no harm would be done if I came along and dropped in on you as I suggested. This gentleman, I presume, is Mr. Daventry?" His keen eyes ran Peter up and down.

Peter bowed. "Quite right, Inspector. The man in whom you are interested, I believe."

Goodall shot a quick glance at him—then laughed quietly. "Mr. Linnell's been talking, I suppose! I certainly got a bit curious—but there—curiosity's part of my job—and I can't afford to take anything for granted."

"Any more news, Inspector?" intervened Linnell affably.

"Up to the moment—no! I came straight on here. I want to have a look at one or two things! That letter from Stewart—may I see it?"

Linnell opened a drawer and handed the letter to him.

"H'm," muttered Goodall. "Assynton postmark—June 7th." He read it. "I fancy you gave me to understand that you knew nothing about Stewart, till you got this letter. Am I right?"

"That is so, Inspector. My only knowledge of him was just ordinary public knowledge."

"I see. What did you do after you got the letter?"

"I thought it over and wired back. To get confirmation, as it were!"

"And you got a reply?"

"This!"

Linnell gave him the extravagant telegram—then waited for the smile to ripple over Goodall's face.

"Seems to be a man who knew his own mind. Doesn't seem possible the man's dead." His eyes narrowed as he stood thinking.

"Tell Inspector Goodall what you've just told me, Peter! About young Stewart 'phoning here."

Goodall became all attention.

"That interesting! Fire away, Mr. Daventry!"

Peter repeated the information he had previously given Linnell, taking care, however, to suppress any reference to the Berkshire police or the desire for a private detective.

Goodall listened carefully. "It doesn't help me much," he commented when Peter had finished. Then looked him straight between the eyes.

"Oh! Mr. Daventry!" Goodall spoke as though an afterthought had struck him. "After you visited the Galleries yesterday—where did you go?" Peter's cheeks went a dull red—it seemed to him he was being humiliated.

"Came back here! Mr. Linnell can confirm that—if you doubt my word."

"Thank you! And after that?" He fingered his note-book.

"I dined at my club—then went to a show."

"Thank—you—your club is—and the show was—?"

"The Isthmian—Piccadilly—and 'On Approval'! Anything more, Mr. Inspector?"

"That will do for the present." Goodall closed his note-book with a snap.

Peter's eyes blazed at him angrily. "And if you're interested in any more of my comings and goings—I may as well tell you that I'm just off down to Leyton to put in an hour or two at the Middlesex and Essex match."

But Goodall remained imperturbable under the shaft of sarcasm. "Wish I could come with you! I like watching cricket—particularly Lancashire and Glamorganshire—they always seem to me to lack supporters so—it means such a terrible lot of travelling, you see, for their relations to go to watch them." The Inspector grinned.

Peter's ill-temper vanished instantaneously at Goodall's sally. He held out his hand and shook the Inspector's. Goodall took it—crossed to Linnell—and departed.

"I'll bring Bathurst along, then, as arranged—if I'm lucky enough to find him."

Linnell made a gesture of assent. "If he'll come! Then we'll get on to Assynton and tell them." Daventry soon motored down to the ground and quickly found his brother. Together they made their way onto the pavilion, Gerald being a member of the M.C.C. and of the three Metropolitan counties. But all attempts to unearth the man for whom they were searching proved unavailing.

Then Gerald met a kindred spirit. "Bathurst?" he said. "Yes—I can help you—he won't be here to-day at all—he told me—now, why the devil was it?—I've a cursed rotten memory"— he assumed an air of painful mental effort—then suddenly his face cleared. "Oh, I know—he's playing 'Squash' at 'Princes' this afternoon—you'll see him if you pop along up there. Is it anything important?"

"It is rather," replied Gerald. "And I'm awfully obliged to you."

"Pleasure, old son. Shall we drift along and have one off the ice?"

They drifted and after the one had multiplied considerably the two Daventrys motored back up to Knightsbridge.

"The uninitiated would never dream of a club like 'Princes' hiding here, would they, Peter?" queried his brother as they entered. "I remember being very interested the first time I came."

Bathurst was soon run to earth.

"Haven't seen you for nearly a year, Daventry! Your brother? Delighted! Fit?"

"Very fit—thanks—and you?"

"Never better!" His words did not belie him. Anthony Bathurst, in whatever company of men he found himself, was usually the fittest of the lot. He excelled at nearly all ball games and took extraordinary pains to keep thoroughly "trained." And his mental powers were equally outstanding. Peter Daventry speedily realized something of the admiration that he knew his brother felt for the man to whom he had just been introduced. He was aware of that atmosphere of "personality" that distinguishes a select company.

"What brings you along here?" queried Anthony. "Playing— are you?"

"No," responded Gerald. "I've brought Peter here to see you! It's his funeral."

Anthony waved them into a couple of deck-chairs. "What about?"

"He's got a story for you that you may possibly find interesting. Have a cigarette, lie back in your chair, and listen. Now, Peter—say your mouthful." Peter complied with his brother's request. Bathurst lay listening—apparently lazily—but Peter quickly discovered that his faculties were acutely alert. When he reached the murder of Mason—the night-watchman, Anthony's eyes betrayed understanding.

"I read a short account in the early editions today. Seemed just an interrupted robbery case to me then . . . of course . . . you say the identical *three* things . . . go on."

At the point when Peter told of the death of Stewart, Bathurst listened most attentively. "Extraordinary," he commented at the finish of Peter's narrative. "Quite a fascinating little problem. And you say Stewart's son would like me to have a look at it for him—eh?"

"He wants me to bring somebody down with me and I suddenly thought of you—I had heard so much of you from Gerald."

Anthony took a cigarette and lit up carefully. "I've nothing pressing at the moment. I'm your man if you're sure you want me."

"That's great. When can you come along?" Anthony looked at his watch. "I should have liked to commence my little investigations at this end. But I suppose I can't—I must get down to Assynton to see Stewart—that's evident—there's a train at Paddington at five minutes to seven. That will get us down before nine. I'll meet you on the platform, Daventry."

"Right!" declared Peter, "6:55 then."

"Yes—and Daventry—I think you'd better bring a revolver."

CHAPTER V
THE ASSYNTON LODGE MURDER

SERGEANT CLEGG assumed an air of profound sagacity, which did not altogether become him too well. At the moment he was a prey to conflicting emotions. A police-officer's career in an obscure Berkshire village doesn't get too many chances for personal "spot-light." And although he felt that his big chance had come, he had a nasty feeling somewhere at the back of his mind that the case was going to prove *too* big. However, he turned to the son of the murdered man and to the Doctor who had accompanied him into the library and made his preliminary announcement—importantly!

"Nothing in here must be touched. Nothing—*whatever*."

"Nothing has been disturbed, Sergeant Clegg. Doctor Gunner arrived only a few minutes in front of you."

"That's all right, then, Mr. Stewart! You might make your examination, Doctor, with as little disturbance of the corpse as possible—will you? I haven't got a photographer handy—that business will have to come later."

The murdered man was seated in a chair at his desk—the cause of death being painfully visible to all. He had received a heavy blow or blows from behind—the back of his skull was smashed like an egg-shell. He had apparently been in the act of writing when killed—for his pen had almost entirely fallen from his grasp—the butt being just retained between thumb and forefinger. He was dressed in a dark-blue dressing-gown and on his feet were bedroom slippers. The dressing-gown had been put on over his pajama sleeping suit and he gave every appearance of having come downstairs from his bedroom. The doctor busied himself for a few moments over his gruesome task. Meanwhile the Sergeant turned to the young man who found himself so suddenly bereaved. He cleared his throat—twice.

"Tell me the details, Mr. Stewart, as far as you are able." Stewart shook his head.

"I know very little. The maid who does the library every morning was amazed this morning to find the door locked. She couldn't understand it, so she informed Butterworth, the butler. He went along and found that what she had reported was correct. He sought me out and we found Mr. Llewellyn, my father's secretary. We went to my father's bedroom. It was empty—the bed had not been slept in. So we decided to burst open the library door.

You can see for yourselves how we found my father. I immediately telephoned for you and for Doctor Gunner."

"The door was locked, you say. Where was the key?"

"In the lock—on the inside."

Clegg strolled across to the French doors that opened on to the garden. "These are fastened all right. All the bolts are shot." He stooped down and examined them.

"By gum—that's funny. How did the murderer escape? Bit of a puzzle—eh?"

Stewart saw the drift of his remarks. "Extraordinary, isn't it?" he ventured.

Clegg walked over to the desk and looked at it carefully. Beside the dead man's hand there rested a sheet of notepaper. The Sergeant took it up. "Looks as though this is what he was writing when the blow fell," he suggested.

Scrawled on the paper were the words, "Urgent in the morning! M. L." "This your father's handwriting, Mr. Stewart?" he asked.

The young man looked over his shoulder. "Yes," he said. "Without a doubt—although it looks to me as though it had been written very hurriedly or in a moment of extreme agitation—it isn't as firm as usual."

Clegg leaned over the dead man and felt in the pockets of his dressing-gown.

The right-hand pocket was empty. He gave a sharp exclamation when he took from the left—a revolver. He looked at it carefully. "Loaded in five chambers," he declared—"the sixth has been discharged." His eyes traveled slowly round the room. Then they came back to Stewart. "Did you hear anything like a shot any time last evening or during the night?"

Stewart shook his head in dissent. "Nothing at all!"

"Is this your father's revolver?"

"It looks like it—though it's a common pattern."

Clegg turned to the Doctor. "Finished your little investigation, Doctor?"

"Yes," was the reply. "Been dead about twelve hours, I should say, and received three blows I think! I'll leave him as nearly as possible as he was when I came in. I'll make arrangements for moving him later."

"Thank you, Doctor!" Clegg returned to young Stewart. "I suppose your father had had no recent quarrel with anybody?"

"N—no. Not that I'm aware of! Of course a man with his vast financial interests didn't go through life without making some enemies—and pretty vindictive ones at that—but I can think of nothing special—certainly not recently."

He spoke with deep feeling in his voice, and Clegg wasn't absolutely sure that there hadn't been just a trace of hesitation in the first part of his answer.

"How old was your father, Mr. Stewart?" he continued.

"Fifty-three in July—on the twenty-second of next month. We have been in England only a matter of a few months."

"From America, wasn't it? I remember your coming here."

"New York—previously we had lived at Washington and Chicago."

"You the only member of the family living here?"

"My father's ward, Miss Lennox, lives here also. She is like a member of the family."

"Who else is in the house?"

"My father's private secretary—a Mr. Morgan Llewellyn—Butterworth, the butler, and his wife, who acts as housekeeper, and the servants."

"Any idea, Mr. Stewart, who was the last person to see your father alive?"

"I don't know that I can answer that question with certainty. I had been out during the evening—playing tennis. I returned about a quarter to ten. My father was in here with Colonel Leach-Fletcher—that's a neighbour of ours—I simply put my head round the door and said 'Good-night.'"

"Didn't you go in and speak to the Colonel?"

"Oh no! He's a constant visitor here, has been on very friendly terms with my father ever since we came here. I never feel on 'company manners' with him."

"Any idea what time the Colonel left?"

"No—Butterworth could probably tell you."

"Butterworth's the butler, isn't he? And the secretary's name is Llewellyn? How long have they been with you?"

"Butterworth came into my father's service when we were living at Washington. He was butler to Sir Julian Kennedy, the British Ambassador at Washington at that time. When Sir Julian died—about fifteen years ago I should say—speaking from memory—my father offered him employment. My father"—his voice broke a trifle—the realization that his father was dead was becoming more poignant to him as time passed—"regarded him as invaluable."

"And Mr. Llewellyn? How long has he been with your father?"

"About two years. He came to us when we were in New York."

"The butler's wife—you said just now, I think—acts as house-keeper?"

"Yes. There are four maids here, also."

"Any comments to make on them?" The Sergeant puffed out his cheeks and endeavoured to look impressive.

"I have nothing against any of them."

"You'll forgive me, I hope, putting the question, Mr. Stewart—especially at a time like this—had your father any entanglements as you might say with the opposite sex?" The indelicacy of his query affected the Sergeant so profoundly as to produce a superfluous aspirate.

But once again he was destined to draw a blank.

"You can make your mind easy on that point, Sergeant. My mother died ten years ago when I was twelve. It was a great blow to my father—they idolized each other—I don't think the thought of another woman since has ever entered my father's mind." He kept his gaze resolutely averted from the still figure at the desk. Doctor Gunner, before he had slipped out, had reverently laid a white towel over the head and face. But the boy's nerves were rapidly getting on edge, and he felt he would be unable to endure this phlegmatic policeman very much longer. Clegg, however, was nothing if not "thorough." His favorite philosophy was to contemplate the epic struggle of the hare and the tortoise and whenever he was tempted to hitch his personal wagon to a star he always took excessive care to see it was well secured. "I don't believe in taking a lot of risks," he was wont to say to his staff at Assynton. "Care may have killed the cat, but it's never been known to have killed a policeman."

This case that Fate had tossed so unexpectedly into his lap was beginning to worry him a trifle. It was so much bigger than anything he had previously handled. Once again the conviction was borne upon him that in all likelihood it would prove eventually to be too much for him. However, "sufficient unto the day is the evil thereof" might have been his uppermost thought as he squared his ponderous shoulders and walked across the room. As you entered, the desk stood on the left with its back to the left-hand wall. The leathern arm-chair in which the dead man sat was drawn up to the desk in the usual way. A person seated in this arm-chair would therefore show the left-hand side of his face to anybody entering by the door. Facing the door stood a bookcase—sectional. It was of many more sections than is usual. Stewart was evidently a lover of books—the "standard" authors jostled each other and Coventry Patmore rubbed shoulders with Renan, Baudelaire and Verlaine. On the right were French windows commanding the garden. No part of it, however, brought Sergeant Clegg his badly needed inspiration. Nothing in the room seemed to him to tell any story other than its natural one. He walked back to the door. That door worried him. "Key in the lock on the inside," he muttered—"bolts on the French doors shot—top and bottom—and a dead man inside the room."

He made his disconsolate way to the fireplace—on the bookcase's right. Bending down, he stepped into the hearth and attempted to look up the chimney. The attempt proved completely unsuccessful as a source of inspiration. It was speedily made plain to the Sergeant that the murderer of Laurence P. Stewart had not escaped in that direction. Then an idea struck him.

"Have you communicated with your father's solicitors, Mr. Stewart?"

Stewart shook his head. "No, my father's solicitors are Crake and Ferguson—New York. I'm going to get Mr. Llewellyn to cable them as soon as possible."

"New York's a long way away. It's a pity you haven't somebody nearer."

"I may be able to get into touch with somebody who may assist me—till Crake and Ferguson move in the matter. I had considered that possibility myself."

Clegg concurred with a heavy shake of the head.

"Good. Now I must get a move on, too. I had better have an interview with some of these others." He consulted his notebook with judicial gravity.

"Ring for this Mr. Llewellyn—will you, Mr. Stewart—please?"

Within a few minutes the summons was answered. The secretary was a man somewhere in the early thirties. Of good height and slim, with the hair thinning considerably on the front of his head, his general appearance, aided by the pince-nez that he wore, suggested what may be termed not unkindly an academic superciliousness. His eyes were a rather unusual shade of reddish-brown and gave an acute observer an impression of brooding watchfulness. He entered the room quietly, yet perhaps warily.

"You wished to see me, I believe?"

Sergeant Clegg grunted a somewhat reluctant affirmative.

"I am conducting a preliminary investigation, Mr. Llewellyn, into the death of your employer, Mr. Laurence Stewart. If it lies in your power at all to help me, I want you to do so."

"I am perfectly willing to tell you all I know—which I'm afraid isn't very much."

"Thank you. When were you first informed of the tragedy?"

"This morning—about eight o'clock—just about an hour and a half ago. I was in my bedroom dressing when Mr. Charles Stewart came to my door and told me he feared something was amiss with his father. I finished my toilet hastily and joined him and the butler, Butterworth. The maid, it appeared, had been unable to get into the library—the door was locked. The three of us burst down the door and were horrified to find Mr. Stewart as he is." He inclined his head in the direction of the motionless body.

"What did you do then?"

"Well, we rushed up to him—but it didn't take us very long to realize that he was dead."

"And then?"

"Mr. Charles Stewart gave me certain orders to convey to the servants while he telephoned for you and for the doctor."

"I am told, Mr. Llewellyn, that after you three gentlemen burst the door open—you found the key in the lock on the inside."

"That is true. Mr. Charles Stewart called my attention to it specially."

"And the French doors were also fastened—all the bolts firm in the slots?"

"Yes."

"When did you last see your employer alive?"

"At dinner, last night."

"Was it your custom to dine with him?"

"Usually I did. Our dinner party generally consisted of Mr. Stewart, his son, Miss Lennox, and me."

"Was that the case last evening?"

Charles Stewart intervened. "I did not dine here last evening. I was out. I think I told you. I was playing tennis."

Clegg nodded his head. "That's all right, sir! I understand!"

Llewellyn proceeded. "Colonel Leach-Fletcher completed our party last evening—but really, I don't see—"

"Had this Colonel any particular reason for dining here last evening?"

Stewart allowed a faint smile to illumine his features. "What on earth do you mean, Sergeant? Colonel Leach-Fletcher dined here at my poor father's invitation—he didn't suddenly announce that he intended to stop for dinner."

Llewellyn's brooding eyes seemed to smoulder for a brief instant—then they flickered back to their habitual watchfulness. He allowed himself the vestige of a smile. His smile broadened as the Sergeant made a clumsy attempt at extrication.

"Naturally, naturally, gentlemen. Exactly what I meant." He followed the secretary's eyes and observed them rest on the desk-table in front of the dead man. "It seems that Mr. Stewart was writing a message of some kind when he was struck down?"

"Yes," came Llewellyn's quick response, almost automatically. "Mr. Charles Stewart and I noticed that when we first found the body."

"What do you think its meaning is?" Llewellyn raised his eyebrows in interrogation. The poise of his head and the somewhat peremptory significance contained in his gesture, accentuated his suggestion of superciliousness.

He held out his hand. "May I see it again? I hardly—"

Clegg took the paper from beneath the dead man's hand. "Not much to go on, I admit! But Mr. Stewart had evidently received important news of some kind that he regarded as very urgent. To sit down to write it there and then—" he stopped abruptly. "M. L." he quoted. "They might be a person's initials even," he declared.

Stewart felt a flood of sudden excitement run through his veins. He watched Llewellyn's face keenly and could not avoid seeing the sudden glint flash through the striking eyes. But once again the flame was but momentary and died down as quickly as it had been born.

When the secretary answered he was coolness personified. "They might. It's very probable. They might even be mine. I am called Morgan Llewellyn."

He paused and watched the effect of his declaration upon his questioner. Then continued, even cooler than he had appeared before, "But I can suggest no good reason to make me think that they are."

Both Clegg and Charles Stewart watched him very closely. And to each of them there came the feeling—in the first case, slowly and of deliberation, and in the second case, quickly and instinctively—that his coolness was assumed and his seemingly frank indifference something of a calculated pose.

Clegg harked back. "Going back a little way, Mr. Llewellyn, you stated that you last saw Mr. Stewart at dinner. What happened after dinner?"

Again Llewellyn's answer came quickly. "After dinner, Mr. Stewart intimated to me that he was going into the library with Colonel Leach-Fletcher and that he wouldn't require anything further from me. I think that he had something to discuss with the Colonel, who is a keen collector like Mr. Stewart—was. I was free to do as I pleased."

"What did you do?"

"I spent the rest of the evening with Miss Lennox in the music-room."

"What time would that be?"

"From about half-past eight till ten o'clock, I should say!"

Clegg made a note of the times. "One more question, Mr. Llewellyn! Did you go straight to bed after that?"

"I did. I was in bed, I should think, by half-past ten."

"Now think very carefully, Mr. Llewellyn. Did you at any time during the evening or during the night hear anything like a revolver shot?"

Llewellyn started up in his chair, stung by surprise. "Certainly not!"

Clegg glanced at Stewart. "Confirms your statement, Mr. Stewart. I can't think myself that the shot was fired in here. The fact of the revolver being in your father's pocket—not in his hand the fact that there is a complete absence of any signs of a struggle—both those facts seem to me to point to the shot having been fired elsewhere—at some other time."

Stewart appeared to agree. "I heard nothing. I told you I didn't."

The Sergeant thought for a moment. "How far away are your bedrooms?" he demanded.

"Mine is on the floor above this," answered Charles Stewart. "Llewellyn's is above that."

"Where is your father's?"

"Next to mine! The only other bedroom on that floor is used by Miss Lennox."

"And the servants?"

"On the same floor as Llewellyn's. On the other wing."

"Thank you, Mr. Stewart. I don't think I shall need Mr. Llewellyn any more for the present. Thank you, Mr. Llewellyn."

The secretary bowed and thanked the Sergeant, not without a touch of irony.

Charles Stewart turned to him as he walked to the door.

"You might get that cable off to New York, that I mentioned to you previously, and also 'phone to that firm in Cornhill who were acting for my father to-morrow, will you? Explain the circumstances and tell them to consider their instructions cancelled. I can t see any reason why I should go ahead with those purchases now. Stay, though, a minute—get them for me and I'll speak to them—I'll tell them all about the whole affair. Probably that will avoid any misunderstanding."

Llewellyn took his instructions quietly and went out. Charles Stewart gestured to the Sergeant.

"My father intended to purchase two or three more very special antiques—he was always anxious to add to his collection. Now that this dreadful thing has happened—I don't care to go on with it."

"I understand exactly how you feel, sir. It does you credit."

"Whom will you see next, Sergeant? Or have you finished for the time being?"

Clegg looked at his note-book—then wetted the point of his pencil, thoughtfully.

"I should like a few words with the lady that's been mentioned, Mr. Stewart. This ward of your father's—Miss Lennox."

Stewart turned quickly. "I don't think she'll be able to—"

The door moved and Llewellyn entered. Charles Stewart frowned.

"I've got through to Cornhill, Mr. Stewart. If you would come along—they're holding the line. Mr. Linnell is out—Mr. Daventry, the junior partner, is speaking."

"Right." He turned again towards Clegg. "Pardon me for a minute or two, Sergeant. I'll just transact this little piece of business and on my way back I'll tell Miss Lennox you would like to speak to her. You will see her in another room, of course." He looked across at the desk significantly. Clegg showed his agreement. The glorious June sunshine flooded through the French doors and bathed the room with its shimmering shafts. It seemed completely incongruous in that room where so recently tragedy had dwelt. Shadows would have become it more fittingly than sunshine. The presence of the dead man stirred an emotional chord in Clegg's being and he shivered. He walked away from the desk beside which he had been standing towards the French doors and looked out into the garden. For a moment or two he stood there thinking—his shivery feeling vanishing under the warming and comforting influence of the summer sun. He glanced down at the curtains that hung, one at the side of each door—then started. Bending down quickly, he picked out something that had been lying hidden there—something that nestled a pure white against the creamy-white of the curtains. It was a lady's handkerchief, fragrant, fragile and delicate. Holding it somewhat gingerly, he opened it! In the corner were embroidered initials—"M. L."

"By Gum!" said Sergeant Clegg.

CHAPTER VI
MARJORIE LENNOX DOESN'T MINCE MATTERS

THE SERGEANT felt hope surging in his breast. Up to this moment his investigations had yielded little, but this sudden discovery, he felt, had at last set him moving. This "M. L.," whoever it might be, had undoubtedly an important bearing on the case. Twice this morning previously these initials had confronted him. He subjected the handkerchief to a most careful scrutiny. It was a lace square of about six inches and exhaled a dainty fragrance that in other circumstances even the Sergeant might have found distinctly alluring. For he was something of a Romantic! And in consequence had an inclination towards a leniency to what he himself always described as "the fair sex." He heard Stewart's voice outside and hastily pocketed the delicate trifle that the curtains had concealed. When Stewart entered he found the Sergeant engaged in a careful examination of the bookcase.

"I have arranged that you see Miss Lennox in the music-room. Will that suit you, Sergeant?"

Clegg thanked him, but stayed where he was. "That will do very nicely, Mr. Stewart," he replied. "But would you mind telling the constable on duty at the front entrance to report to me for just a moment—or sending somebody with a message to that effect? Thank you."

"I want you for a little while, Potter," he said to the man when he came in. "You're to keep at this door here and to see that nobody enters! You understand—*nobody!* If you have any trouble over it—send for me. I shall only be the other side of the hall."

P.C. Potter saluted smartly. "Right—Sergeant. Is the body in here?"

"You've said it! Now you understand." The constable assumed a bearing of importance. Clegg walked across the hall and entered the music-room. He felt somehow that the approaching interview might prove disturbing. All the same he was anxious to meet the lady in question, for he felt sure that the handkerchief was hers. The possession of this gave him an advantage, he considered. He started with something in his favour—otherwise he might have viewed the position with less complacency. For he had yet to make the acquaintance of the lady in question.

"This is Sergeant Clegg, Marjorie," announced Charles Stewart as he entered. "He wants to ask you one or two things about my father to see if you can help him in any way to discover the truth of what happened last night—he won't worry you for long I am sure."

Marjorie Lennox rose quietly from the low chair upon which she had been seated.

"I am ready to tell the Sergeant anything."

And at that moment the truth came home to Sergeant Clegg—unerringly—that unless he "watched his step" very carefully he would be as wax in the hands of the highly-capable Miss Lennox. He found himself fervently wishing that he belonged to the ranks of the "strong, silent men"—certainly not to the Romantics. For Marjorie Lennox had a delicate beauty and a dainty charm that were instantly arresting. She was "petite", it is true, but she had that semi-disdainful, semi-challenging roguishness that many men find so hard to resist. It was easy to find fault with her features, for her nose was appreciably "retroussé"—but this very tip-tiltedness only served, if anything, to enhance her attractiveness. She had glorious blue eyes—twin pools of pure cornflower, and a complexion that made one immediately think of roses and cream. Added to this she possessed a demure gracefulness that almost perfected her, giving her a Dresden china sort of setting—from the depths of which she was destined to play havoc with the hearts of men. And of course she fulfilled that destiny to the limit of her dainty power! Sergeant Clegg threw an inexorable rein over his romanticism and did his duty. A little throat clearing once again prefaced his first remark.

"Thank you, Miss—" he hesitated momentarily.

"Lennox," she broke in quickly. "Marjorie Lennox. I am—or rather, I was—Mr. Stewart's ward." She sank back in her chair again.

"Yes, miss. I understand that much. How long have you lived with Mr. Stewart?"

"Ever since I was a little girl of three. My father was a very old friend of Uncle Laurence's—I always called Mr. Stewart 'uncle'"—she explained with engaging candour—"and when my father died I came to Uncle Laurence to live. My mother died when I was born," she added simply.

"Was your father in good circumstances when he died—can you remember?"

Marjorie Lennox flushed. "I believe not. Certainly his circumstances were quite different from those of Uncle Laurence. What has that to do—?"

Clegg wagged his head half apologetically. "I see! I see! Now, coming to the events of last night—I've no wish to distress you, Miss Lennox, but there's just this. You dined, I believe, with Mr. Stewart, Colonel Leach-Fletcher and Mr. Morgan. Is that so?" He ticked the three names off on his fingers.

"Yes. There were just the four of us. Charles did not return for dinner."

"And after dinner?"

Marjorie flashed him a searching—penetrating glance. "Do you mean what did I do after dinner or—"

"If you please, miss." The Sergeant became acutely aware of his constitutional chivalry, but sternly suppressed it.

"I came in here. It is my usual practice after dinner. Uncle Laurence used to like me to play to him—he was passionately fond of music. But last night he went into the library."

"Did you stay in here for the rest of the evening?"

"Yes—no—no, I'm wrong! It was about nine o'clock when I left here."

She amended her statement with the utmost composure and Clegg couldn't be sure if she had made a genuine mistake or was desirous of concealing something. But he remembered Llewellyn's story and the two didn't tally! Llewellyn had made no mention of Miss Lennox having left the music-room at nine o'clock! He had stated that he spent the *remainder* of the evening with her. Now—according to Marjorie Lennox—he had been alone for an hour. That is to say there was at least one hour of his time for which he had not accounted. Now Clegg was slow-moving and inspiration visited him but seldom, but he took care, and he quickly came to the conclusion that hereabouts in his inquiry extreme care would be necessary if he were to achieve any success. He decided to hasten slowly.

"Where did you go then, Miss Lennox?" he followed up.

"To my room. My uncle was still engaged with Colonel Leach-Fletcher in the library, and I didn't wish to disturb them."

"Did you see Mr. Stewart again before you retired for the night?"

"No—I was tired. It had been a rather hot day, down here, as you probably know yourself. And I seem to mind the heat. I thought I would go to bed early."

"You are quite certain you didn't go into the library?"

"Positive." Miss Lennox flicked an imaginary speck of dust from her sleeve.

"When did you last go in there?"

"To the library? I didn't go in at any time yesterday. Why do you ask?"

She was lying! Clegg knew it! But he wasn't certain why he knew it. His knowledge didn't emanate altogether from the fact of the lace handkerchief lying in his pocket. It came rather from the lady herself. Nonchalant, despite her grief, utterly self-controlled, she nevertheless failed to impress him with the quality of simple sincerity. He was fairly certain that she was acting a part. His present and immediate task was to discover "why"! He had half intended to tax her here and now with the handkerchief, but in the later light of what she had just told him—he decided to keep quiet—for a time at least.

"I fancied I was told by Mr. Stewart here that he saw you in there."

"No, Sergeant. Your memory has failed you! I said nothing of the kind." Charles Stewart appeared anxious to clear up this misunderstanding. It seemed to him that Marjorie needed protection.

"Sorry, sir." Sergeant Clegg made his apology.

But it didn't deceive Miss Lennox. Just as Clegg had realized her insincerity, so she in her turn knew that this rather lame explanation of his question to her had not been the truth. She immediately put herself on the defensive. Inclined as she had been in the first place to under-rate this policeman, she effected a mental readjustment.

She awaited his next question—outwardly unchanged, but inwardly more vigilant. When it came it surprised her.

"Did you hear anything unusual in the night, Miss Lennox?" Somewhat relieved, she breathed more freely, but her defensive tension remained unrelaxed.

"Nothing! I slept like a top." The blue eyes regarded him ingenuously.

"Thank you. One last question, Miss Lennox. You have lived a long time with Mr. Laurence Stewart, almost as long I suppose as Mr. Charles Stewart here—and ladies, if you'll excuse me saying such a thing, are very often more in a man's confidence than gentlemen! For instance, you were as a daughter to the poor gentleman"—he broke off suddenly—and Marjorie Lennox began to sob quietly—her handkerchief pressed to her eyes. There was genuine sorrow here—Sergeant Clegg had sufficient sense to recognize it when it came his way and it was reflected in young Stewart as well. His white face grew whiter—the ordeal of this dreadful day was oppressing him more and more and Marjorie's convulsive sobbing tore his heart-strings. He knew he must have help. He would get it as soon as he could. This was too much. Sergeant Clegg felt his courage sink into his boots. This sobbing was more than a Romantic could stand—the more so because he himself had provoked it. He must do something to stop it. He placed his hand on her shoulder—an act that he was always to remember.

"Come, come. What I mean is this. If Mr. Stewart regarded you in the light of a daughter—did he ever *confide* in you? Any secret? Any trouble? Had he any enemies that might have wanted to do him harm?"

She looked up. "He had no secrets at all. He wasn't the kind. But since you've asked me—I'll tell you—something."

She sprang to her feet. Her eyes shone like stars and her hands were clenched together. Her whole manner altered.

"There *is* a man who wanted to do him harm. A man none of you would ever suspect. He's in the house now—why should I shield him?"

Charles Stewart threw out his hand and attempted to restrain her. But she flung the proffered hand away imperiously, while Stewart looked at her reproachfully.

"Sergeant Clegg asked me," she asserted vehemently. "Sergeant Clegg shall know. The man is Morgan Llewellyn!!!"

Clegg received the announcement stolidly—he was progressing! Charles Stewart gave a gasp of astonishment and turned to her with an air of remonstrance.

"You're mad, Marjorie! You've no right to bring an accusation of that kind. Why should Llewellyn have harmed my father?"

Clegg waited eagerly for the answer. He even got his note-book ready.

Marjorie Lennox faced her so-called cousin defiantly—her blue eyes challenging his grey ones. For a moment there was a silent battle for the mastery. Then before either of the men could stop her, she swept majestically from the room!

CHAPTER VII

BUTTERWORTH IS APPREHENSIVE OF THE FUTURE

FOR THE second time on that eventful morning Sergeant Clegg felt at loggerheads with circumstances. For the second time he felt that the Law had received a set-back—that he, its accredited representative, had been flouted!

Charles Stewart looked at him somewhat anxiously. How was he going to take this feminine outburst? Stewart attempted to smooth things over. "A trifle hysterical, I fancy, Sergeant, and it's scarcely to be wondered at. She's had a trying time—I know what it's been like to me—it must be a thousand times worse for her."

Clegg nodded. "H'm. Now that's most extraordinary. There's an 'M. L.' on the paper under your father's hand—then there turns up a 'Morgan Llewellyn'—then I find a 'Marjorie Lennox' and a—" he pulled himself up. He would keep the handkerchief incident absolutely to himself. "And to crown all—one of the 'M. L.'s' finishes up by accusing the other 'M. L.'" He sighed and then gave expression to the point that had been his constant worry since his arrival. "What was the weapon the murderer used?"

Stewart broke in upon him. "With all deference, Sergeant, I shouldn't place any reliance at all on what Miss Lennox said. She's distraught."

"She's not, Mr. Stewart. She's not the kind. She meant some-thing—I'll take my Bible oath on that."

Stewart shook his head as though unconvinced. "Women are whimsical, Sergeant."

"I know. None better. I've been married seventeen years and I'm still learning things—but there you are! I'd like to see this butler of yours now—what's his name, Butterworth?"

"Right! In here?"

"No—in the library. I'll get along in there again. Bring Butterworth, will you, Mr. Stewart?"

"Well, Potter," said the Sergeant as he regained the library door, "everything O. K.?"

Potter touched his helmet—satisfaction oozing from his finger-tips. "Yes, Sergeant—nobody's crossed the threshold since you left, Sergeant. A young lady came across the corridor just now and wanted me to let her pull down the blinds or something—she said the sun ruined the carpet at this time of the day—but I explained as genteelly as I could about orders being orders." He beamed at this account of his devotion to duty. Clegg scratched his chin. The plot was getting thicker!

"What sort of a young lady, Potter?"

"On the small side, Sergeant. A regular dainty piece she was and no mistake!"

"How long ago was this?"

"Only a few minutes, Sergeant. You only just missed her."

"Now what does she want in here," thought Clegg as he entered. Her handkerchief? Something else? Or both? His musings were cut abruptly short by the entrance of Stewart with the butler. Butterworth was a man with a presence. Tall and well set-up, he carried his sixty odd years with impressive dignity. When he had left the service of Sir Julian Kennedy for that of the man whom they were now mourning, it had not been without a certain amount of misgiving. After all, as he was fond of relating to a carefully chosen circle, the British aristocracy was a thing apart. Sir Julian had been a diplomat of the old school, and in the words of Butterworth, "we were 'looked up to' by the 'elite' of Washington." He had accepted Stewart's offer of employment with a certain suggestion of condescension—and after he had turned down two less remunerative offers, it was a tribute to his strength of character that this apparent condescension still remained obvious in the manner of his acceptance. Certainly it was sufficiently manifest to impress Laurence Stewart. But the Butterworth of this morning was not the Butterworth that had lamented Sir Julian Kennedy. Fifteen years had made a considerable difference in him, and a man who has turned sixty, fears the "menace of the years" more than the man turned forty. He had hoped to finish his days with this rich American. Last night's tragedy had definitely closured that idea. Butterworth loved England—the English countryside; he loved "breathing English air" and "suns of home," and it was extremely improbable that Charles Stewart would continue the establishment on his father's lines. The boy had spent most of his life in America and in all probability he would return there. Therefore Butterworth was not free from anxiety this morning. He was face to face with upheaval—and he disliked change exceedingly.

"Good morning, Sergeant," he said, on his entrance. "I understand you wish to speak to me."

Clegg was visibly impressed. He realized that he was in close touch with a "personage." Butterworth had intended that he should.

"Yes—Mr.—Butterworth. It would help me considerably in my investigations"—Clegg was at pains to do at least some share of the "impressing" business—"if you could tell me for certain when you last saw Mr. Stewart alive."

"I can do that without any difficulty. I showed Colonel Leach-Fletcher out a few minutes after ten. My master told me that it was not his intention to sit up late—would I lock up at half-past ten. At ten-thirty precisely I came in here, as was my usual practice, Sergeant Clegg, to lock up for the night. My master had retired, as he had previously said that he should. I bolted the French doors—replaced the tantalus—and locked the library door. I then attended to the other living rooms down here, and shortly afterwards retired to rest myself. It was Mr. Stewart's special orders that I should always personally perform the locking up duty every night. He was extremely particular with regard to it."

Clegg nodded gravely to express his complete understanding.

"How long did it take you?" he asked, knitting his brows.

"I was in bed by ten-forty and asleep almost immediately. I am a sound sleeper, Sergeant."

"And nothing awakened you?"

"Nothing whatever! The first intimation that I had that anything unusual had occurred was early this morning. Barton—one of the maids—was unable to gain admission to the library. She referred the matter to me—I came and tried the door—it was locked and the key gone. I went to Mr. Charles at once. We got Mr. Llewellyn and came down here together. We eventually burst the door open."

"One moment, Butterworth! Are you perfectly certain that the key was in the lock on the *inside* and that the French doors were bolted when you entered?"

Butterworth paused for a brief moment to assimilate thoroughly the full significance of the question. Then he nodded in agreement.

"Yes, I am. Mr. Charles called our attention to the key, and I can swear to the bolts on the French doors having been shot tight. I saw them—you can rely on both those facts."

Charles Stewart interposed. "I can vouch for that too, Clegg! Also Llewellyn. Rest easy on that point." Clegg stroked his chin between thumb and forefinger, seemingly disinclined to accept this piece of soothing advice. There was no denying, however, the vital importance of what the butler had stated.

"Anything else, Butterworth?"

"We found my master dead, Mr. Clegg. Exactly as I can see him sitting now." His voice broke. "It was a great blow to me. For all of us, no doubt; but one describes one's own feelings best. No servant ever worked for a better master. I loved Mr. Stewart and I'm pleased and proud to think that he had a little affection for me. I don't quite know what will happen to me now—I'm not a young man—"

Charles Stewart put a hand on his shoulder. "There is no need to worry, Butterworth. I should be sorry to fail *one* of my father's servants."

Butterworth's eyes clouded with sorrow. "Thank you, Mr. Charles—thank you."

He rose from the chair he had been occupying. Then turned with unmistakable dignity to Clegg. "Is there anything further you want of me?" he said.

"You haven't any idea, Butterworth, I suppose, of anybody likely to have done this?"

"What do you mean, Sergeant?"

"I mean this." Clegg breathed heavily in his desire to do justice to the dignity and importance of the Law. "Did Mr. Stewart have any enemies?"

"If he had, I didn't know them. He never confided such an idea to me."

"How was Mr. Stewart when you last saw him? Bright and cheery like?"

"Just as usual. Nothing different from the ordinary."

"Didn't appear to have anything on his mind?" asked Clegg.

"Not to worry him. I think he was a bit eager about the sale that was taking place."

"Sale?" Clegg seemed momentarily at a loss.

"I told you, Sergeant," Charles interposed. "My father intended to purchase some—"

"Quite right, sir," apologized the Sergeant. "It was the use of the word 'sale' that sent me astray for the moment. He seemed 'eager'—you say?"

"That is the word. It describes my master's feelings exactly— that is, if I am any judge. Anything fresh towards a gratification of his hobby always made him like a schoolboy on a half-holiday."

The Sergeant understood perfectly. But Charles Stewart, as though in doubt about this, stepped forward with an offer of assistance. "You can have access to all the correspondence relative to the intended purchases, Sergeant—with the greatest pleasure. Mr. Llewellyn will let you see it—I will instruct him to do so."

"Thank you, Mr. Charles! I should certainly like to glance over it."

"You shall. Do you want Butterworth any more?"

Clegg considered the matter. It was evidently a weighty one, for it occasioned much frowning and facial contortion. At last a reply was forthcoming.

"The servants, Butterworth; the other servants here—anything suspicious about any of them?" he said slowly.

"Nothing, Sergeant Clegg! There's my wife, who acts as housekeeper—I can speak for her—I've been married thirty-seven years and I'm perfectly satisfied. There are four maids, Barton, Regan, Evans and Winter—the cook, Mrs. Briggs—and Maidment the gardener. Then there's O'Connor—he assists the gardener—does odd jobs. We call him the boot-boy. Of course the last two—O'Connor and Maidment—don't sleep here—they live in the village."

Clegg noted the personnel and the additional information thereto with becoming solemnity. Then he deliberately closed his note-book. The gesture seemed to convey to his two companions that the preliminary investigation was finished. A nod from the Sergeant confirmed this conviction and Butterworth withdrew—gravely and silently—the perfect butler to the last.

"I'm going to get another 'phone message through to London, Sergeant," exclaimed Charles Stewart. Clegg detected a note of anxiety in his tone. He scanned the young man's face interrogatively. Stewart flushed, but quickly came to the point. "Look here, Sergeant Clegg—frankly I think we're up against it. There seems to me to be some dark mystery here that will need the best brains of your profession to solve. I'm not slighting you—*in any way*, when I say that, either."

Clegg sucked his pencil. "I wouldn't say that you weren't right. Still—we'll be doing our best."

He walked to the door—then turned. "I'll make arrangements about your father"—he nodded towards the body—"and then get down to make my report. Good morning, sir! I'm very sorry, sir." He stepped into the corridor—then started. Butterworth was waiting there and caught him by the arm. He seemed to be labouring under some tremendous excitement. "Something I didn't tell you, Sergeant, I *last saw* Mr. Stewart at *ten o'clock*, but I *heard* his *voice* about *ten minutes after that*—

in that room!" He stabbed with his finger at the library. "And I heard another voice, too! I heard the voice of Miss Lennox, I'm *certain!*"

CHAPTER VIII

THE 6:55 CARRIES A TRIO OF DISTINCTION

PETER DAVENTRY glanced at the clock on Paddington platform. He saw with undisguised relief that he was a good quarter of an hour to the good. "Curse this beastly wrist-watch," he muttered to himself—"it gets worse every day—fairly put the wind up me that time." He walked to the platform indicator—digested the information thereon applicable to the 6:55—"Didcot, Wantage Rd., Assynton"—and drifted over to the appropriate platform. Arrived there, he scanned the horizon for Anthony Bathurst. The platform was pretty crowded and he could not see the man he wanted. It was unlike Bathurst to arrive at 6:45 for 6:55. He argued that it was a sheer waste of very valuable minutes. Daventry commenced his second tour up the platform when a voice at his shoulder jolted his equilibrium and suddenly brought him to a standstill.

"Good evening, Mr. Daventry." Detective-Inspector Goodall smiled genially and extended what looked like an amicable hand. "Going to try the Berkshire air?"

Peter gasped feebly but retained sufficient presence of mind to grasp the extended hand—mechanically it must be admitted. Goodall clasped it warmly, but Peter could almost feel the handcuffs on his wrists. "Y—es. I'm going down to Assynton." Then his indignation mastered his surprise and his resentment. "But why the devil are you trailing *me*, Inspector—for it's pretty evident you *are* trailing me," he concluded with asperity.

"Not on your life, Mr. Daventry," replied Goodall—the picture of unruffled imperturbability. "You mustn't get jumpy like that—or I shall begin to suspect you after all." He smiled again.

"Well then, it's a wonderful coincidence to meet you here," remarked Peter ruefully.

"Not so wonderful—if you think for a moment." Peter's face cleared magically.

"Ass that I am," he declared. "You're bound for the same destination, of course."

"Now we're talking," said Goodall. "The local people down at Assynton have asked 'the Yard' to take a look at things down there—just at the very moment, too, when we at 'the Yard' were trying to piece the two murders together, somehow! I'm going down. But what about you, Mr. Daventry?"

"I'm representing my firm—Mr. Stewart's son has asked me to run down."

"How about a nice compartment, then, with a couple of corner seats? This train isn't a 'corridor,' worse luck."

"Well—as a matter of fact"—temporized Peter—"I'm waiting for somebody!"

Goodall instantly became all interest. "Really? I had no idea—you wish to be alone?"

Peter denied the idea strenuously—feeling all the time that he was heading straight for the Valley of Suspicion again. "Not at all. Only too pleased to travel with you, Inspector. I'm sure my friend will be—"

"Delighted," said Anthony Bathurst. "Introduce me, Daventry, will you?"

Peter accepted the invitation gladly. He was downright pleased that Bathurst had turned up when he did. This fellow Goodall seemed to know a jolly sight more about a chap than was thoroughly comfortable. He was curious to see how Anthony Bathurst would be affected by Detective-Inspector Goodall. He made the introduction.

"I am honoured," remarked Bathurst. "Scotland Yard must consider the Assynton Lodge murder as extremely 'difficult' for it to engage the attention of Inspector Goodall."

He bowed to the Inspector, who, however, seemed impervious to the compliment.

"You flatter me, Mr. Bathurst," was his rejoinder. He turned to Daventry. "We'd better get in—if we don't want to be left behind."

"On the contrary," smiled Bathurst—entering the compartment last of the three—"I paid you a compliment. Flattery is merely a counterfeit business. A flatterer usually seeks to gain favour—a compliment is a tribute made to ability by reason of recognition."

Goodall melted a trifle. "Thank you," he yielded. The train glided out of the station and they settled down more comfortably. The flamboyant beauty of the June day was dying hard in a glorious evening.

As they approached the first fringes of the countryside and caught the wonderful streaks of the westering sun flung over copse, wood and water—flooding the tranquillity of green and white with red-gold radiance—the tragic nature of their journey seemed to grow more remote in the minds of the three of them. Anthony waved his hand at the country decorated so beautifully.

"Look at it, gentlemen," he exclaimed. "We shall be too busy during the next two or three days to think of beauty—murder's a soul-destroying business—let us enjoy it while we may!"

Goodall looked across the carriage with raised eyebrows. "We?"—he questioned.

Peter dashed in courageously. "Mr. Bathurst is also coming down at young Stewart's request," he volunteered. "He's in a bit of a fix, I think, new to England and all that, you know—he feels he wants a sort of steadying hand." He beamed at Goodall—guilelessly.

But it was unnecessary. "The usual term, I believe, Mr. Daventry, is to watch a person's interests." Goodall appeared to be on the frigid side.

"I would have preferred to have had a look at the case from the Galleries murder end, Inspector, but Fate has decreed otherwise—however, it may be all for the best."

Goodall's face again registered surprise. "You seem remarkably well informed, Mr. Bathurst—"

Anthony raised an explanatory hand. "Mr. Daventry has posted me pretty soundly, thank you. He interviewed me this afternoon. I understand the main facts of the case are these." He gave a brief but explicit résumé of the affair as it had been presented to him. "That's about all, I fancy, Inspector?" He looked at Goodall for corroboration.

Now Goodall could have supplemented Bathurst's information with one or two additional facts, which was precisely what Mr. Bathurst intended should happen. But the Inspector was not yet quite certain of his bearings and Mr. Bathurst's exposition of the facts had been sufficiently masterly to prompt him to refrain. He gave Bathurst a confirmatory nod and said nothing.

"At any rate," proceeded Anthony—"we are fortunate in one respect—that is to say from the stand-point of investigation. With regard to the first murder we do know the motive."

"The first murder?" queried Goodall. "Which of the two was that—I should be pleased to know?"

Anthony smiled. "I was not referring to the order in which the two men were murdered—although I appreciate your point. At the moment I don't know when Stewart was killed. All I know is that he was found dead this morning. By the term 'the first murder' I meant the murder of Mason, the night-watchman. It was the first of which I heard. It was the first of which you heard. It happened in London, where we live. Cigarette, Inspector? You, Daventry?" They accepted his invitation—Goodall a little nettled. He had provoked an encounter and chosen his weapons, but had not been brilliantly successful. But he had the sense to accept what Anthony had said.

"Quite right, Mr. Bathurst. I just wanted to make sure. I rather believe in making sure, you know—I tested *your* alibi, by the way, Mr. Daventry, this afternoon."

Peter grinned. "Well—and how *was* it? I'll guarantee you couldn't shake it."

"I'm not going to arrest you—sit still!" He leaned over to Bathurst with his elbows on his knees.

"You reckon then we know the motive for the Hanover Galleries job?"

"Well, it's pretty plain, I should say. Possession of the Stuart antiques—robbery! Which makes it a clean-cut case! This end we aren't so well off." He looked at Goodall with that humorous twist to his mouth that his friends knew so well. When they saw it they knew that things were running pretty smoothly. "To know the motive of any crime gives you a flying start, Inspector." He tossed his cigarette end through the window.

Goodall scratched his chin, reflectively. "That's all very well, as far as it goes. Robbery—you say, for possession of the Stuart antiques. Worth what? I'm not an expert—but for the sake of argument we'll put it at a matter of hundreds. And we sha'n't be so very far out, at that! Now, Mr. Bathurst, what was there so peculiarly attractive about these antiques—or about one of them—to spell Mason's murder?" He leaned forward still further in his seat and his voice cut across the compartment quietly insistent and definitely certain. "To kill Laurence Stewart? To send you—and you—and me, to Assynton, on a summer evening—*wondering*! Eh, Mr. Bathurst—tell me that!" His eyes blazed with a mingled excitement and determination, as he watched his *vis-à-vis*. Bathurst rubbed his hands, appreciatively!

"Excellent, Inspector, excellent. That's a question that I should very much like to be able to answer."

"Which of the antiques, Mr. Bathurst? Which one? And not a clue that you can call a clue as to where they've gone—except a sneezing woman," he remarked semi-humorously.

"Tell me," said Anthony, "I'm interested." He listened carefully while Goodall—despite his opposite intention when the journey started—related the trenchant evidence of Edward Druce—night-watch-man.

"So they were at the Hanover Galleries at midnight, were they? That's important! That gives us a definite time-anchor." He spoke to Goodall with decision. "I think with you, Inspector Goodall, that the two cases are connected without a doubt. But it's a mistake to theorize without data—let's wait till we pick up the threads a bit this end. As you say—which one of the three antiques were they after? It's as bad as 'finding the lady'—with Mary, Queen of Scots, as the lady."

He grinned at Daventry, who had been following the interchange of ideas with the keenest possible attention. Suddenly Peter slapped his thigh with excitement.

"By Jove!" he cried, "Mary, Queen of Scots—that reminds me—what an idiot I've been not to tell you before."

Then he paused with a hint of apology. "So much has happened since, that it has been driven completely out of my mind."

"You become more interesting hourly, Daventry," remarked Anthony. "Out with it, whatever it is—before you forget it again." Peter waved the sarcasm aside.

"It's a pretty trivial matter," he commenced, "but I know you 'sleuth' people always like to hear full particulars about everything—the usual phraseology is 'no matter how unimportant it may seem'"—he grinned—then went on again. "You observe, of course, that I have read several detective stories!" Goodall wrinkled his nose somewhat contemptuously. But Peter was perfectly hardened against that kind of discouragement. "When Linnell and I first heard from Stewart about the purchase of these antiques it was arranged between the two of us that I should pop along to Day, Forshaw and Palmers' to have a squint at the stuff. Well, I did so—on my way I blew in to the 'Violette' for a mouthful of grub. While I was there I ran into a pal of mine—Marriott, by name—we got gassing to each other about the usual thousand and one things. Well—I'm afraid I'm telling this pretty badly"— Goodall's face was a study—"but sitting at the next table were a man and a woman. I noticed them particularly for two reasons. Firstly the 'Violette' was comparatively deserted—it was early, you see—and secondly they seemed to be having a 'pow-wow' of some importance to them. They were just an ordinary looking couple—scarcely anything distinctive about them—no help for you there, Inspector. Well, I made an inane sort of remark to old Marriott and he replied—as idiots will—'Queen Anne's dead.' Then I did a mad sort of thing—I'd been thinking of Mary, Queen of Scots, all the morning—at any rate since getting Stewart's jolly old letter—and some inexplicable imp of mischief made me say, 'So's Mary, Queen of Scots.'" He stopped again to see the effect he was producing upon his companions. Each was listening in his own way. Goodall's slightly cavalier attitude had relaxed somewhat, and Anthony was giving him that nonchalant attention that he employed to mask unusual mental activity. Peter let his words sink in. "Directly I said it, the chap at the next table seemed—mind you, I only say 'seemed'—to give a sudden sort of start. He swept round in his chair and sent the cruet and all its contents flying on to the floor—three bags full." He shrugged his shoulders. "Of course I can't swear that it was what I said that had poked the gust up him, but it did seem like it to me, gentlemen."

"What happened then?" cut in Goodall.

"Nothing much," answered Peter—"the waiters rushed to repair the damage—that was all."

"H'm," commented the Inspector. "I know Lironi, the proprietor of the 'Violette,' pretty well. If I think it important enough I could see him—he might know something about them—they might be fairly regular customers of his. It depends on what I strike down here in Berkshire." He looked across at Bathurst, who was sitting with his head sunk on one shoulder. Suddenly the latter sat up.

"What did the woman do, Daventry—anything noticeable?"

"Well, there again—it's hard to say, definitely. But in my opinion she was pretty savage about the incident. She certainly tried to joke it off to the waiters, but I'm fairly confident she chewed the merchant's ear off a bit—looked to me like it," he affirmed.

Bathurst nodded. "I thought perhaps the truest indication of the value of the incident might be supplied by the conduct of the woman." He spoke to Inspector Goodall. "Sherlock Holmes has laid it down, Inspector, that in moments of sudden alarm and anxiety, a single woman rushes for her jewel case—a married woman for her baby. This incident throws a further light on the question. It may be added now that the married woman on occasion gives her husband wordy castigation—as the present-day 'argot' would put it—she 'ticks him off'!" He smiled. "Don't you think so?"

"I don't know that this particular pair represented husband and wife, Mr. Bathurst," protested Goodall.

"I wouldn't bank on the marriage certificate, myself, Inspector," returned Anthony. "But there is just this to be said for what Daventry has told us. A woman crops up in two of our little scenes. There's a woman in this incident and there's the woman whose thirst for information took her to Day, Forshaw and Palmers' at the identical moment when Mason and Druce, the two night-watchmen, were changing shifts." He thought for a moment or two. "It's certainly a point to be considered," he concluded.

"There aren't many 'crooks' that haven't a woman in tow, nowadays," declared Goodall. "The equality of the sexes has become very far-reaching. Still it's deuced smart work for the same gang to have pulled off both these jobs—I can't quite take that in myself—not yet."

"Who's in charge of the case down here?" queried Anthony. "Anybody you've run against before?"

Goodall shook his head. "A Sergeant Clegg was called to Assynton Lodge this morning—he's the local man—he's at Assynton. They 'phoned to 'the Yard' this afternoon—felt the case was a nasty one—likely to prove too big for friend Clegg. When the news reached me I told our people of Mr. Linnell's information which seemed to link up the two cases, and it was decided then and there that I should come down." He rubbed his cheek with his forefinger. "About twenty-four hours late," he murmured as a kind of afterthought. "The scent cold—another man—possibly with an assistant or two—done his best to destroy most of the things that might help one—talk about 'locking the door behind the stolen steed'—can you beat it?"

"Not too helpful, I admit, Inspector," argued Anthony. "Still, even now there may be something to pick up—you never know—there's always the 'human element' to be considered in every case."

"All murderers don't make glaring mistakes, Mr. Bathurst, don't you run away with that idea—if they did—Scotland Yard would have precious few failures to record. Take my advice—don't you go relying on the human element for mistakes—*always*." He took his hat from the rack and put it on his head. "I fancy we're running into Assynton." He looked at his watch. "A little matter of four minutes late!" Anthony uncoiled his length from the seat. "I didn't mean that, Inspector! By the 'human element' I meant the people in the case—the circle round the dead man— the people we shall encounter—there's always the factor of their personal psychologies. Do you follow me?"

Goodall grunted as the train drew up. Darkness was beginning to suggest itself. A heavy figure emerged from the recesses of the booking office and presented itself to them—semi-important, yet at the same time—semi-apologetic.

"Detective-Inspector Goodall?" he inquired.

"That's me," replied Goodall. "And you?" He peered forward at the man that had met him.

"Sergeant Clegg, Inspector." He saluted. "And downright glad to see you."

"Thank you," said Inspector Goodall.

CHAPTER IX

MR. BATHURST OPENS HIS BEDROOM DOOR

INSPECTOR GOODALL motioned towards Anthony and Peter. "These two gentlemen have travelled down with me, Sergeant Clegg. They have been sent for by Mr. Charles Stewart."

He introduced them. Sergeant Clegg was visibly impressed. "Pleased to meet you, gentlemen," he announced—"though it's a sad business, to be sure, that has thrown us together." He turned to the Inspector. "I've taken the trouble to book a room for you, Inspector, at the 'Red Dolphin'—quite an excellent place. What will you do—go straight there for now, and start work in the morning, or would you prefer to get into your stride at once?" He looked somewhat anxiously at Goodall as though he attached very great importance to his decision.

"Tell me, first of all, what you've done, Clegg," said the Inspector.

"I was called to the case this morning, Inspector, and I interviewed everybody that might be termed 'principals'—you shall have their facts almost verbatim—I've been polishing 'em up from my notebook. I've had 'photos' taken this afternoon of the body and of the library generally, so that poor Mr. Stewart could be taken away—and I've had the room fixed and fastened so that nobody can get into it." He breathed heavily—weighed down with an acute sense of his responsibility. Goodall's reply transported him.

"Excellent, Clegg," he declared, "excellent. I'm for the 'Red Dolphin' and supper, bed and breakfast."

"Very good, Inspector! What time shall I see you in the morning, then?"

"I'll be along directly after breakfast—say about half-past nine. I shall probably do much better if I approach the case in the first place with a mind refreshed from a good night's rest than if I were to commence right now—make it half-past nine, then, Clegg."

He turned to Anthony and Peter Daventry. "You two gentlemen are going to the Lodge now, of course. Good-night. I shall see you in the morning, too."

The three shook hands, and Goodall and Clegg swung off to the delights afforded by the hospitality of the "Red Dolphin." Bathurst pointed to a smart car that was drawn up in the station-yard.

"Ours—I think, Daventry," he said. An equally smart chauffeur swung from the driver's seat and touched his cap.

"Assynton Lodge, sir?" he inquired of Bathurst.

They entered and the car purred its way to its destination. It was not long before they found themselves sweeping up the drive that took them to the main entrance.

"Nine minutes' run," announced Bathurst. Charles Stewart met them in the hall.

"I got your telegram, Mr. Daventry," he said, "and I've arranged for dinner to be served for you directly you are ready."

"Thanks—that's extremely good of you," responded Peter, "and I'm sure you'll be pleased to hear that I've been able to bring somebody with me—as you suggested—this gentleman is Mr. Anthony Bathurst. He will be pleased to help you in any way whatever."

"It's a great relief to know that," replied Stewart. "Butterworth"—he turned to the butler—"show these gentlemen to their rooms—you're on the second floor," he explained. Butterworth carried out his instructions quietly and efficiently. "Dinner will be served in half an hour, gentlemen," he announced.

"I have arranged that we three dine alone," said Stewart upon their return. "Miss Lennox—my late father's ward—has a bad headache and begs to be excused, and Mr. Llewellyn, my father's secretary, dined earlier as he is very busy. My father's sudden and tragic death has entailed, as you may guess, a tremendous amount of important correspondence." His fingers drummed on the table-cloth. "My father's solicitors are Messrs. Crake and Ferguson, of New York. I have had a cable sent to them today—till I hear from them I don't exactly know how matters altogether stand financially."

Peter Daventry expressed his sympathy.

"Mr. Stewart," said Bathurst, "I am delighted to take this case for you—though, of course, very sincerely deploring the sad circumstances and your own personal loss. If it isn't asking too much of you—would you be good enough to tell me all you know of the facts of the case—take your own time and tell me entirely in your own way?"

"Before you start, Mr. Stewart," intervened Peter, impetuously, "have you heard of the other—" but a well-directed kick on the shin from Bathurst under the table dried up the torrent of his information quite abruptly but most effectively.

"Don't worry Mr. Stewart, Daventry," said Anthony gravely. "Let him tell us as I suggested." Stewart proceeded to tell the story of his father's death. Soon came Bathurst's first interruption.

"You say that when you burst open the door the key was in the lock on the inside and also that the French doors were shut and bolted?" Anthony leaned forward across the dinner table and pointed his query with keen interest.

"Yes, Mr. Bathurst. Extraordinary though it may sound—the facts were so."

Anthony rubbed his hands together. "Most interesting," he muttered, "most interesting. Go on."

"My poor father," continued Stewart with evident distress, "was seated in his chair at his desk-table—his head on his hands— his skull badly smashed—he had been dead some hours—struck down in some foul, dastardly way from behind." He stopped and tried to control his feelings, which were obviously beginning to master him. After a short interval of silence—sympathetically observed by the two others—he continued again. "Apparently he had been writing when he was attacked, for a pen had almost fallen from his hand and on the desk in front of him lay a sheet of note-paper. On it had been written the words, 'Urgent in the morning, M. L.'"

Anthony shot his second question across to the speaker. "In your father's handwriting, Mr. Stewart?"

"Beyond doubt, Mr. Bathurst." Anthony waved to him to proceed.

"In the left-hand pocket of my father's dressing-gown was his revolver—loaded in five chambers only. None of us can remember hearing a shot during the night, so that we don't know when the one shot was fired—in the night or on some previous occasion."

Anthony stopped him with his hand uplifted.

"One minute, Mr. Stewart. Was it your father's habit to carry firearms in the pocket of his dressing-gown? Have you ever known him to do it? Think carefully—this is most important."

"Well, of course, naturally, I don't sleep with my father—I rarely see him after he has retired for the night—but I certainly wasn't aware that he made a habit of carrying a revolver. It doesn't surprise me, though, to know that he had a revolver pretty handy, because we house a number of very valuable things here—still—I'll say this—I've never seen him with a revolver in his hand."

Anthony accepted the statement—then followed it up with another question. "Your father was a right-handed man, of course, Mr. Stewart?"

"Yes. Always. Doctor Gunner gave it as his opinion that he had been dead about twelve hours. That wasn't quite possible, as he was alive at ten o'clock last night."

"Who saw him?"

Stewart hesitated for a moment. "Two of us here can prove that my father was alive round about ten o'clock last night. I spoke to him about a quarter to ten, and Butterworth, the butler, spoke to him a few minutes after ten. My father gave Butterworth instructions to lock up about that time." Bathurst nodded.

"I see. So Butterworth was the last person to see your father alive—as far as is known?"

"Yes. A Colonel Leach-Fletcher dined here with my father last night. Butterworth saw him out about ten. When I spoke to my father at nine-forty-five the Colonel was with him then, in the library."

"An old friend of your father's, I presume—I understand from Mr. Daventry here that it was on Colonel Leach-Fletcher's recommendation that your father got into touch with his firm?"

"I believe that is so, Mr. Bathurst—but I should hesitate before I described the Colonel as an old friend of my father's—his friendship only dates back to the time when we first came here."

Anthony pulled at his lower lip with his thumb and forefinger. Had Daventry known him better he would have understood from this gesture that certain features of the problem were worrying him. Then suddenly his face betrayed eagerness.

"Three more questions, Mr. Stewart, if you'll pardon me. This sheet of note-paper found under your father's hand—the writing on it—if my memory serves me correctly—was 'Urgent in the morning—M. L.'—I am right, am I not?" He looked at Stewart. The latter nodded. Anthony went straight on. "This 'M. L.'—the initials probably of somebody or something—I've been wondering about them. You mentioned just now, Mr. Stewart, two other members of your father's household—a Miss Lennox, his ward, and a Mr. Llewellyn, his secretary. I feel bound to ask you if the Christian name of either of these two people begins with 'M'—yes." He fingered the stem of his champagne glass with undisguised approval—then carefully watched the face of his young host while he awaited his answer.

"Very curiously, Mr. Bathurst, both Mr. Llewellyn and Miss Lennox have those initials—Miss Lennox is 'Marjorie' and Llewellyn is 'Morgan.'" He spoke with apparent composure, but Peter Daventry—most interested of spectators—was not quite sure that some, at least, of the unconcern was not deliberately assumed. He began to wonder why. Who was who in this house upon which such a tragic shadow had been cast? What dark passions had been loosed but a few hours since that had meant death, sudden and terrible, for an unsuspecting victim? What was Bathurst's opinion? What was he thinking? Had he noticed Stewart's counterfeit composure? Bathurst, however, appeared to be tremendously interested. He lifted his eyebrows at the piquancy of the situation as revealed to him.

"Really?" he said. "We are confronted with two 'M. L.'s' then. Now that's distinctly fascinating." He paused. "Was it a message, Mr. Stewart, do you think, to either of them—or even—" he stopped and pondered—eyes narrowed.

"A message or an instruction, Mr. Bathurst, would almost certainly affect Llewellyn, Mr. Bathurst—I think we may safely discard any idea of Miss Lennox being implicated." He spoke quite quietly, but yet Peter Daventry fell to introspection once again. He felt certain that he was able to detect a tinge of anxiety in the voice—almost, in fact, that in what Stewart had said the wish had been father to the thought. But Bathurst, to all appearances, accepted the situation as Stewart had presented it. He went to another question.

"You stated a little while since that your father had a number of valuable things in the house. Quite a natural thing for a man of his wealth, of course. Has anything been stolen? Anything missed?" Stewart shook his head in denial of the idea. "As far as we know, Mr. Bathurst—*nothing* has been taken. Certainly no money has been stolen. My father's personal jewellery is in his bedroom—untouched—just where he left it."

Anthony thought for a moment. "Papers! Documents! Was there any evidence that anything of that nature had been taken from the library? Did any drawers appear to have been ransacked?"

"There were no signs of disorder in the library at all. Everything there seemed quite normal."

But Bathurst persisted. "Your father's collection, Mr. Stewart—that was very valuable, I believe. Have steps been taken to see that this is intact? Where is the collection kept?"

"In what we call the Museum Room—next to the library. I don't know that it occurred to me—or even to any of us—to go in there—there was no connection you see." He looked across at Anthony.

"Is the Museum Room kept locked?" demanded the latter.

"Not necessarily during the day," came the answer. "My father might be in and out several times during an ordinary day—he might even have been in there last night with Colonel Leach-Fletcher for all we know. Butterworth will be able to tell us," he concluded, rather lamely, Daventry thought, "we can ask Butterworth if he locked the Museum Room when he locked up last night."

"You don't mind if I smoke?" put in Bathurst. "The key of this Museum Room now—where would it be kept—in the door?" He lit his cigarette, and tossed the match into an ash-tray.

"No—I don't think so. In fact, I'm sure not. The key of a room like that would be hung up each night in Butterworth's service-room. He would unlock the room some time during the following morning."

"So that we may say—anybody had access to it—knowing that the key was kept there?"

"I suppose so," replied Stewart. "But I'm quite certain the Museum Room door was shut all right when the alarm was given this morning." He sat back in his chair firmly as though to give point to his words.

"That's pretty conclusive then," admitted Anthony. "Still—I think we'll have a look at this Museum Room—nevertheless!

You see it might supply that motive I'm looking for." He rubbed his chin with his finger. "Otherwise—"

Stewart rose from his chair at the head of the table. "Would you care to come and look now, Mr. Bathurst?"

Anthony motioned him back again. "In the morning, Mr. Stewart, in the morning. That will be time enough. Tell me—I'm rather curious to know—the point is of extreme importance— have you any list or catalogue of your father's collection?"

Stewart looked somewhat surprised. "It would be some task for you to go through all the things in the Museum Room, Mr. Bathurst—but I believe I am right in saying that Llewellyn has compiled something in the way of a catalogue. You shall see a copy in the morning, if you would care to."

"I should—very much," responded Anthony. "I have just the glimmering of an idea—that's all—and I think it's just possible the catalogue may help me." He looked at Daventry, who had been trying hard to follow him—unsuccessfully.

"What started you off?" inquired Peter—"that key of the Museum Room business? Personally, I can't see anything much—"

Bathurst interrupted. "No—not that, Daventry. I happened to be thinking about 'M. L.'—that was all." He rubbed his hands as the idea took shape. "And I'll lay a guinea to a gooseberry," he proceeded, "that I'm 'warm' as the youngsters say. If I'm not— well, then, we shall have to start all over again."

He smiled at his two companions. "But we sha'n't have to. You see."

Stewart did not appear to share this piece of optimism—he shook his head rather hopelessly, but Peter Daventry remembered the judgment of his brother Gerald and was able to catch something of the Bathurst tradition.

"One last question," said Anthony. "What was the opinion of the Sergeant who came along this morning about the weapon with which the crime was committed? Did he have any ideas about that, do you know? Did he seem confident of making any arrest?"

Stewart dismissed the suggestion immediately it was made. "I was quite unimpressed by him. In fact that was the chief reason why I asked Mr. Daventry's people to help me and why I suggested Scotland Yard could do worse than have a look at things. I don't think he formed any ideas about the crime at all! The question you have just raised about the weapon that was used puzzled the Sergeant, I should say, from my observation of him, pretty considerably. There wasn't a trace of anything!" He seemed to have almost reached his limit of physical endurance, and Anthony was quick to detect it.

"Daventry," he said, "I'm afraid I haven't shown Mr. Stewart too much consideration—he's worn out, and I must leave any further questions till to-morrow morning." He glanced at his wrist-watch. "It's well past ten and we're all tired. A good night's rest will do us all good." He rose and walked across to his young host with outstretched hand. "Good-night, Mr. Stewart, and my most sincere sympathy! I know it's easy to say that, but I'll say something else as well." He paused for a second and his jaw set with the lines of indomitable purpose. "I have every hope, even at this early stage of the case, of getting the handcuffs on the right wrists—which should comfort you a little!"

Stewart was very pale when he answered, and his answer was brief. "Thank you, Mr. Bathurst. Good-night!"

Peter added his salutations and they made their way upstairs.

"No need to trouble Butterworth," exclaimed Anthony, "we know our rooms. Here's mine—there's yours, Daventry. Good-night!"

Anthony walked to the window and opened it. He was fond of darkness and it was just beginning to get dark. Darkness and its attendant tranquillity he always found invaluable conditions for the process of concentration—he had often discovered the solution to a mystifying problem out of this communion. He smoked a cigarette through and lit another. "What was it," he said to himself as he stood there by the open window, "that caused Stewart to come downstairs and enter the library? What happened in the library to make him scrawl the message that he described as 'urgent'?" He commenced a third cigarette. "And who trod softly behind as he sat there writing—and killed him?" He undressed and got into bed. "A pretty little problem—espe-

cially when we think of the Hanover Galleries affair on top."
That was his last conscious thought before he slept. He had
the knack of getting to sleep almost instantaneously and also
the complementary faculty of awaking at the slightest sound.
He was destined to awake suddenly that night. And he knew
instantly and instinctively what had awakened him—a stealthy
step, had gone past his bedroom door—he was certain of it! He
looked at the luminous face of his wrist-watch. "Twenty-two
minutes past one," he muttered. "Not an ordinary time for legitimate night-wanderings." He tiptoed to his bedroom door and
drew it very slightly ajar; then listened intently for what seemed
like ages. It was very quiet beneath him. Had the step been on
its way back? Suddenly he heard a sound that sent his heart
racing perilously—somebody was ascending the stairs! He shut
the door silently and held the handle tight. The step passed—
almost noiselessly. Anthony waited a second, then pulled his
door gently open, and looked out on to the corridor. He was just
able to distinguish the figure of a man, entering the room next
but one. A man—slim and of good height. Judged by his walk—
comparatively young. Anthony whistled very softly, as he sat on
the side of his bed to think things over. "Now, who the devil was
that?" he muttered, "and why does he wander o' nights?" In the
morning at breakfast his first query was answered.

"Let me introduce you," said Charles Stewart. "Mr. Bathurst—Mr. Morgan Llewellyn—my late father's secretary."

CHAPTER X
THE INCIDENT OF THE BOOT-BOY'S BICYCLE

MR. BATHURST bowed his acknowledgment. And at the same
time felt that matters were progressing. Progressing, perhaps,
a trifle *too* quickly, and at a rate that, to a less alert intelligence
than Mr. Bathurst's, might prove extremely disconcerting.
Under cover of a few casual and perfunctory remarks he studied

Llewellyn carefully and at the same time reviewed the events of the morning. For Mr. Bathurst had been up betimes. The music of the Berkshire birds had been his first consciousness of this glorious morning. He had risen to the "Te Deum" of the bird-choir and had joined with them in a thanksgiving for "the immaculate hours"; and when he found himself downstairs his watch showed the time to be a few minutes past seven. He made his way into the garden and marvelled at the magic of the morning. What was the geography of the library in relation to the garden? Passing through a charming rockery with a fountain plashing deliciously in the centre of a clear-watered pool, he came on to a stretch of perfectly kept grass that stretched almost to the French doors of the library itself. Under the morning sun this patch of exquisite emerald seemed fit for the flying feet of angels. Anthony retraced his steps—he would leave the library question till he could get inside to have a look properly. He strolled through the rockery, then turned and came out on to the road. He would have a walk before breakfast, for a thought was beginning to take shape within his brain. He cut along briskly and soon discovered that he was descending the hill to Assynton village. At the foot of the hill on the fringe of Assynton itself, he stopped. It was an iron foundry that claimed his attention, for Mr. Bathurst had always been intrigued by the industry of the early morning. The clang of the hammers was as music to his ear. To him it represented one of the real essences of England— there were others—a barge moving steadily on a canal—the scraping of a bricklayer's trowel—a fishing fleet standing in to the harbour heavy with the fruit of its toil—all of them tingling as it were—with the impetus of the newness of the morning. These things to Anthony Bathurst meant much. He listened as the clanging quivered incessantly on the almost virgin stillness of the June air. Suddenly he noticed a man signalling to him from the open door. Bathurst turned into the yard and approached him. A magnificent man, with a sweeping breadth of shoulder, came out of the foundry and stood waiting. His black eyes sparkled genially and he pulled at a bushy black beard as Anthony came up. He must have stood at least six feet two, and his leathern apron became him handsomely. He touched his forehead.

"Beggin' your pardon, sir, for takin' what may appear a liberty. But I should like a word with you, sir." He looked behind him somewhat anxiously, then drew Bathurst a few yards farther away from the foundry door. "If I'm not mistaken, sir, aren't you one of the gentlemen what's lookin' into matters up at the Lodge?" He jerked with his thumb in the direction of "up the hill."

Anthony regarded the black-bearded giant with curious interest. "I haven't the least idea how you know that," he replied, "but you're quite right—I am! News seems to travel quickly in these parts."

Blackbeard's teeth flashed in a smile. "No great mystery about that, sir," he explained. "I saw you in the company of Sergeant Clegg last night with another gentleman that looked uncommonly like a police-detective. And I ain't too bad at puttin' two and two together." He grinned again.

"I see," said Anthony. "And what was it you wanted to tell me? I take it that there *is* something—you haven't called me in here merely to wish me good morning?" He eyed the foundry-man quizzically.

"No, sir, I haven't, and that's a fact! And what I've got to say, I'd sooner say to you than to the police, for I've no love for that fraternity—you can take it from me." He spat with some vigour as a garnish to his remark; then proceeded to embellish what he had said. "Especially for Sergeant Amos Clegg. But I like the look of you, sir, and when my boy told me what he told me yesterday midday I advised him to keep a still tongue in his head till I told him to loosen it. When I spotted you last night, sir—I made up my mind that *I'd* do the tellin' and to *you*!"

"Thank you for the compliment," returned Anthony smiling. "I appreciate it, I assure you. I shall be very pleased to hear what you wish to tell me. Fire away!" The giant glanced round, then lowered his voice appreciably. "My name's Michael O'Connor and I'm the father of Patrick O'Connor—him as they call boot-boy up at the Lodge—Mr. Stewart's place. Patrick was eighteen on the 17th of March and has worked for poor Mr. Stewart for three or four months now. He does lots of odd jobs about the place and gives the gardener a hand—I'm tellin' you this just to give you a rough idea of who he is—so to speak. Now Patrick's a good lad—though he's mine and say it I shouldn't—honest and willin'. He gets sent out a good deal, so Mr. Stewart provided him with a bicycle to run his errands on. He don't sleep up at the Lodge and he's supposed to leave the bicycle there when he gets away of an evening—which is usually about seven. The machine goes into old Maidment's potting-shed. Maidment's the gardener. That's where Patrick put it the night before last." He stroked his beard and pushed his face nearer to Bathurst. "When he went to the Lodge yesterday mornin' and heard all about the murder there wasn't much work for him, as you may well guess—so he thought he'd give his bicycle a bit of a clean-up. What does he find when he looks at it?" He paused dramatically and drew himself to his full height. "That it had been used by somebody since my Patrick left it in the shed." He spat again. "And how do you think he knew?" he chuckled—then without giving Bathurst time to venture an opinion, continued, "Look down there, sir," he said, pointing down the road that wound into Assynton village. "See the steam-roller?" Bathurst both saw and heard it—puffing and grinding after the manner of steam-rollers and flaunting the White Horse of Kent. "The road into Assynton is bein' done up," continued O'Connor—"with tarred macadam. The sun for two or three days now has been melting the new stuff that's been put down—it sticks to your boots if you walk in it. And my Patrick tells me that *the tyres of his bicycle were all* marked with it." He concluded on a note of triumph. Then looked at Bathurst with an invitation for approval.

"Good lad," contributed Anthony. "He's told nobody besides you?" O'Connor shook his leonine head.

"He was a bit frightened-like, I think, sir, so he brought his troubles to his father—I teach my young'uns to do that! But it proves this, sir, *somebody used the bicycle the night of the murder.*"

Anthony nodded in corroboration. "I suppose he's sure he didn't pick the stuff up himself on some errand?"

"Absolutely, sir. He says he came into the village twice the day before yesterday, and took great care to miss the part of the road that's been tarred. But a person riding in the dark, sir, wouldn't notice it—'specially if he had somethin' on his mind." He sniffed—and the sniff carried a wealth of meaning.

"Perfectly true," agreed Anthony, "and I'm much obliged to you for the information—this road into the village leads straight to the station, doesn't it—it was getting dark when I drove up last night?"

"That's right, sir," replied O'Connor—"straight up through Assynton."

Bathurst pushed a Treasury note into his hand, which, after some demur, he accepted.

"I'll be getting back now, O'Connor, and I'll have a quiet chat with Patrick at the first opportunity. I'll tell him you've seen me—that will establish my credentials."

He swung back in the direction of the Lodge—musing over the encounter, and over the incident of the footsteps during the night. When Stewart introduced Morgan Llewellyn and he was able to identify the gentleman as the wanderer who had disturbed his sleep, he concluded that he had quite enough to think over for his first morning. Peter greeted him at the breakfast-table.

"Been out, Bathurst? So early?"

"Just a short stroll, Daventry. I was anxious to have a look round and I hadn't the heart to rout you out, old man! I went across the downs a bit and worked down towards the village." He turned to Stewart. "The birds were simply wonderful. I even enjoyed those melancholy 'pee-wits'!"

"We'll get breakfast over as soon as we possibly can, gentlemen," exclaimed Stewart. "I expect the Scotland Yard representative will be up here pretty early. I should like you to be present, Mr. Bathurst, when he enters the library—Sergeant Clegg closed the room up, you know, when he left yesterday."

Llewellyn sniffed contemptuously. "A brilliant piece of work—that! One of us might have wanted to use the room—for a legitimate purpose, I mean." He wiped the glasses of his pince-nez with his silk handkerchief. As he did so, Bathurst observed the peculiar quality of his eyes and at the same time formed the opinion that Mr. Morgan Llewellyn might very well prove to be a dangerous customer if things didn't please him over-well.

"Mr. Stewart," said Anthony, addressing his host, "what sort of a lad is Patrick O'Connor—the boot-boy?"

Stewart stared at him with a certain strain of amazement on his face.

"Really," he said, "I didn't know that you were sufficiently acquainted with our staff here to be able to ask that question! I suppose it's a case of the early bird, eh?"

Anthony's grey eyes twinkled delightfully! "We all have our little secrets, Mr. Stewart," he responded. "You mustn't probe me too thoroughly—tell me rather of Master O'Connor." He looked round at Peter Daventry—"He's got a fine name, you know, Daventry—'Patrick O'Connor'—hark to the music of the 'r' and the 'n'!"

"Quite a reliable lad," came Stewart's answer. "As far as I know. Certainly I know nothing unfavourable."

"What time does he get here in the morning?" asked Anthony.

"About half-past six, I believe," replied Stewart. "You should know—you've seen him, I take it, this morning?"

"On the contrary—I've never set eyes on him." Bathurst smiled gravely.

He felt the glances of the three men fixed intently on him.

"Well, you've certainly wasted no time," declared Llewellyn, "though how exactly you've been to work, I can't guess."

"I sha'n't ask you to," laughed Anthony. "It might be trying you too highly, and I mustn't do that."

Peter Daventry began to wish that he hadn't slept so soundly—Mr. Bathurst's methods were beginning to fascinate him. Breakfast over, he came across and joined Anthony. The latter went up and spoke quietly to Charles Stewart.

"By all means," was Stewart's reply, "I'll let you know directly I want you."

"Come and have a breath of air, Daventry," said Anthony. "It's a perfectly wonderful morning."

They strolled out into the garden; Anthony took a cigarette and handed his case to his companion. "I want a few minutes' conversation with this boot-boy, Patrick O'Connor—I have a fancy that it may prove to be somewhat enlightening—and don't forget, Daventry, anything we may hear, either now or later on, we'll keep to ourselves, unless we decide otherwise."

Peter saluted with mock gravity. "I'll be the soul of tacit discretion," he exclaimed. "Have you really stumbled across a clue already?"

Bathurst's face relaxed into a smile. "Clues are tumbling over each other—I've really had the luck of the old gentleman himself up to the moment. The ball's running altogether too kindly— doubtless I shall get a rude awakening soon. Come over on the grass there and I'll tell you something!"

Peter accepted his bidding with alacrity. Anthony carefully chose another cigarette. "I'll tell you this," he said, speaking in low tones, "before we go across to find O'Connor. But first—a question! How did you sleep last night? Anything disturb you?"

Peter knitted his brows. "No! Nothing! But I was dog-tired and slept like a top—whichever way that may actually be."

Anthony pointed across to the wall of the garden against which could be seen nestling a burden of magnificent nectarines. "Be interested—apparently—in something that I'm showing you—I don't want anybody in the house to think I'm discussing the case with you—for all I know we are being watched."

Peter grimaced, but began to play his part as per instructions. "The situation is becoming decidedly interesting," he muttered. "Why do you ask me about how I slept?"

Anthony made a gesture with his arm towards another part of the garden before he answered. "At twenty-two minutes past one this morning I awoke very suddenly. I'm a very light sleeper and the slightest sound is sufficient to wake me. What I had heard was a step passing my bedroom door. Of course

I couldn't be sure which direction the steps had taken. But I slipped out of bed and opened my door. I stood listening for some time and then I heard the steps coming back. Whoever it was, was coming upstairs again. Naturally I had to bolt back into my bedroom, but I held the door handle so that I could open it quickly and noiselessly immediately the prowler had passed. I just had time to see the gentleman disappear into the room next to yours. You may guess that I went back to bed and did a little bit of quiet thinking."

"By Jove!" exclaimed Peter. "The plot thickens! Who the blazes was it—any idea?"

"I know who it was," replied Anthony. "It was the gentleman who had 'brekker' with us this morning—Mr. Morgan Llewellyn! You may remember what he thought about the library being shut up."

Peter whistled softly. "You mean that he was trying to get in there, in the night?"

"I think it extremely probable," declared Anthony. "And the question is what is it that's attracting him there? That's what we've got to find out—that's why I've told you."

"Did he get in do you think?" queried Peter, "because if he did, the mischief's done."

"Not he," grinned Anthony. "Sergeant Clegg saw to that, quite thoroughly. Now come along over to the other side. We'll see if we can run across Patrick O'Connor."

Maidment, the gardener, was earthing up potatoes in the kitchen garden as they approached. He straightened himself as he wished them "Good morning."

"O'Connor," he said, in answer to Anthony's question. "You'll find him up there in the potting-shed." He pointed past the cucumber frames that lay on his right to a shed at the end of the path. "Perhaps you'd like me to be accompanying you?" he continued. "Maybe I'll be able to help you?" Anthony waved his offer on one side. "Thanks—but we'll see him alone—you stay here."

As they reached the shed, a tall lad stepped out, and Bathurst immediately recognized that here was a case of inherited physique. He seemed surprised to see his visitors and made as though to turn back into the potting-shed.

Anthony touched him on the arm—then bent down and whispered something into his ear. The lad's face cleared and he beckoned them inside.

"You gentlemen gave me a bit of a start," he declared. "I'm a bit jumpy I suppose since yesterday. This sort of thing gets on your nerves, you know, sir—you can't help it."

Peter Daventry wondered what the message was that Bathurst had passed on. What possible connection could there be between the two of them?

But his wonderings were summarily cut short. Anthony's next remark showed that he was speedily getting to business.

"Where is the bicycle, O'Connor?"

O'Connor walked across to the farther corner and wheeled the machine down to them. He pointed to both front and back tyres. "There you are, sir! You can see for yourself!"

Anthony went down on his haunches and smelt the tyres. "Quite certain you didn't pick it up yourself, O'Connor—on another part of the road, for instance?"

"I'll take my dyin' oath I never did, sir. The day before the murder was discovered I went down into Assynton twice—once just before lunch time and the second time about a quarter-past four. I was extry careful about riding over the new road because I hates my bike all messed and mucked up, so I jumped off when I came to it and wheeled it along the path. As for pickin' it up anywhere else, sir—there ain't no other part of the road round here, sir, what's bein' done up." His eyes flashed, and Anthony realized again that here stood the son of his father.

"Do you always keep the machine in this shed?" he asked.

Patrick O'Connor nodded an affirmative. "Always, sir!"

Anthony threw a critical glance round the potting-shed. "When you came in yesterday morning and found your bicycle like that—was there anything else here that caught your attention—was the shed just as usual—everything in its place— nothing touched or disturbed?"

O'Connor thought for a moment—then shook his head. "Not that I noticed, sir."

Anthony walked to the door and looked out; then he retraced his steps. "Re bicycles, O'Connor! Are there any other bicycles kept at Assynton Lodge—or is this the only one on the premises?"

O'Connor flung his head back with decision. "This is the only cycle here, sir, so that whoever used it on the night of the murder either struck lucky or *knew that it was in here*." He lowered his voice on the last few words. Peter saw Anthony's face as O'Connor spoke—then he turned sharply. Maidment, arriving apparently from the clouds, was framed against the doorway of the potting-shed. His approach had been noiseless and unexpected, for even Bathurst seemed slightly taken off his guard!

"Mr. Charles's compliments," announced the gardener, "and he will be glad to see you two gentlemen in the library."

CHAPTER XI

WITH A GIVEN CENTRE, MR. BATHURST DESCRIBES A CIRCLE

STEWART MET them at the French doors. "Inspector Goodall and Sergeant Clegg are here already. We shall have to postpone our visit to the Museum Room till later. Come in, will you?" Clegg and Goodall had already got to work.

"Nothing has been touched, sir," said the former, "since I was first called in. Except for the removal of the dead man, the room is exactly as it was yesterday morning."

"Good," replied Goodall. "I've read all your notes on the case—the key was in the lock on the inside when the door was burst open, and the bolts of the French doors were securely shot. Darned peculiar!"

Stewart made as if to offer an explanation of something, but the Inspector checked him. "I'm fully acquainted with all the circumstances of the case, sir! I've read Sergeant Clegg's notes thoroughly—not only those concerning the crime itself but also those dealing with the interviews he had with the various people when he was here—so you can write me down thoroughly *au fait* with the whole business." Stewart bowed. Goodall took a tape measure from his pocket and walked to the chair where Laurence Stewart had been murdered. "Is this chair exactly in position?" he queried of the Sergeant. Clegg came and surveyed the situation gravely. Then announced his opinion.

"As near as makes no odds, Inspector."

Goodall first of all measured from the chair to the library door and then from the chair to the French doors. He then examined the lock of the door and the bolts of the other two doors.

"H'm," he said—then scratched his chin thoughtfully. "The Doctor's report"—he drew a document from his breast-pocket and perused it for a moment or two—"states that your father was struck three times, Mr. Stewart. The first blow rendered him unconscious, in all probability, Doctor Gunner thinks, and the second and third finished him completely. Mr. Bathurst—you might help me in a little experiment. I'm going to try to reconstruct the crime." He looked at Anthony and did not wait for his reply. "Sit here, will you, as Mr. Stewart sat. Now you're Mr. Stewart and I'm the murderer." He walked back to the French doors, which he opened, and then went outside, pulling them together. He then opened them noiselessly and tiptoed across the heavy pile carpet. He reached Bathurst and raised his hand as though to strike. "Did you hear me?" he asked.

"Not your steps—I heard you breathing—that was all—but of course I was aware that you were advancing on me. I can quite believe the murdered man was taken by surprise in that way and heard nothing." He rose from the chair. "Congratulations, Inspector."

Goodall came up to the desk. "Is this the piece of note-paper, Clegg? Just where you found it?"

"Yes, Inspector!" Bathurst joined the Inspector. The message was there just as it had been written by the dead man. Bathurst let the Inspector read it—then extended his hand for it. "May I see it?"

Goodall passed it over. Anthony produced his magnifying glass and then covered all the writing with another sheet of paper—that is to say, from urgent to "M. L." Then he carefully examined with his glass the part of the paper immediately following the letter "L." Peter Daventry watched him curiously. After a moment or two he put down the sheet of paper and replaced his magnifying glass. Clegg's eyelid flickered as he caught a glance from Goodall, but the latter gave no other sign of interest. He clasped his hands behind his back and walked to the bookcase—then suddenly turned on his heel.

"Where's that revolver you mentioned, Clegg—let's have a look at it." The Sergeant took it from the right-hand drawer of the desk.

"This was in Mr. Stewart's left-hand pocket," he declared—"and one shot has been fired." He passed it across to the Inspector.

"That's not to say it was fired at the time of the murder," rejoined his superior. "All the evidence you've collected is absolutely contrary."

"You mean that nobody admits having heard it?" intervened Anthony.

"I do," said Goodall.

"With your permission, Inspector—not quite the same thing," came the reply.

Goodall fingered his cheek. "No sign of the bullet, Mr. Bathurst, if you're suggesting that a shot was fired in here."

Clegg smiled broadly. There was no gainsaying the Inspector's last remark. Anthony shrugged his shoulders good-humouredly and went back to the desk again. Peter noticed that his eyes were sweeping backwards and forwards over that particular part of it directly in front of where Stewart's head had rested. Suddenly he picked up the ink-bowl and held it up carefully to the light. He swirled the ink round and round in the bowl three or four times and watched its black eddy with the greatest keenness. Apparently what he saw gave him entire satisfaction—which his face showed when he replaced the ink-bowl on the desk. He rubbed the palms of his hands together. "You were quite right,

Inspector, regarding your theory of the crime. I hope to put my hand on the—"

"Criminal, Mr. Bathurst?" broke in Charles Stewart. "What makes you so optimistic?"

"No! I was about to say 'on the weapon,' Mr. Stewart. But the other will naturally follow."

"I'm rather curious to follow you, Mr. Bathurst," said Goodall. He walked to the desk and picked up the ink-bowl. "Ah!" he muttered, after a moment—"I think I see your drift." He nodded his head two or three times—then came back to Charles Stewart again. "I'm going into the garden for a few moments—when I return I should like to see Miss Lennox and Mr. Llewellyn, your father's secretary. Perhaps you would be good enough to tell them." He passed through the French doors—the indefatigable Clegg at his heels. Anthony and Peter watched them go through the rockery and disappear out of sight. "Where's he gone now?" questioned Peter.

"He's bound to have a look outside," was Anthony's reply. "He may pick up the O'Connor information—he should do—he's a pretty shrewd fellow."

Out of sight of the library, Clegg touched the Inspector on the coat-sleeve. "What I wanted to tell you was this. I wanted you to come into it fresh—with no suspicions so to speak—so I didn't tell you everything till you'd had a bit of a look round." He gazed round warily to make sure that they were not overlooked or overheard. Then he thrust his hand into the breast-pocket of his tunic and handed Goodall a dainty lace handkerchief. "I found that caught in the curtains hanging by those French doors yesterday morning," he explained breathlessly. "Do you see the initials? That belongs to the dead man's ward—Miss Lennox."

Goodall handled it with great interest. "Now that's very curious, Clegg," he observed. "Miss Lennox eh? And I understand that Butterworth, the butler, accuses her of having been with the dead man at ten minutes past ten on the night of the murder—h'm. She, in her turn, puts the rough edge of her tongue round Mr. Morgan Llewellyn—h'm! Clegg—where the hell are we getting to?"

Clegg coughed discreetly. "There was the other point I mentioned, Inspector, on top of all that," he pointed out steadfastly. Goodall considered for a second. Then he remembered what Clegg meant.

"She attempted to get into the library you mean, don't you, when you left your man on duty there?"

"Not a doubt about it," replied the Sergeant.

"Before I see her or this secretary fellow—I'm going to have a few words with some of the servants—come along with me—we may perhaps pick something up that may be valuable."

Clegg fell into step. Goodall went on to outline his difficulties. "There's one feature of the case that's rather strange, Clegg. Nothing appears to have been stolen from here at all—no search seems to have been made for anything—there's not a drawer ransacked or disturbed. Now in this other affair that I told you about—this Hanover Galleries murder—three objects that the dead man here was desperately keen on getting hold of were stolen—they were apparently the motive for the murder. Yet nothing's gone from here." He turned to Clegg somewhat impatiently. The Sergeant wagged his big head solemnly.

"Aye," he conceded—"that's the very identical point that struck me. But"—he thrust his face very close to Goodall's—"is it certain that the two murders *are* connected—have you never heard tell of the long arm of coincidence?" He pronounced the last word to rhyme with "guidance," much to Goodall's professional disgust.

"No," affirmed the latter, "there's no doubt in my own mind that there is a connection somewhere, and it's up to me to find it—I can't agree with your coincidence theory, Clegg."

The latter pushed his chest out and accepted Goodall's statement as final, registering at the same time a mental resolution that for the future he would emit no theories. He would listen!

Anthony, meanwhile, was still at work in the library, finding Peter Daventry a highly appreciative audience. "The important features of the case as I see them are these, Daventry. (a) The one shot fired from Stewart's revolver and the taking of that revolver by Clegg from the *left-hand* pocket of Stewart's dressing-gown,

(b) The use of Patrick O'Connor's bicycle some time during the evening or some time during the night, (c) The message left by the dead man with its reference to 'M. L.' (d) The dirty condition of the ink in the ink-bowl, (e) The apparently impossible conditions under which the murder was committed—the room is locked on the inside at both exits." He blew a cloud of smoke from his cigarette. "Add to that the somewhat unusual and rather absorbing detail—the fascination for Stuart antiques, themselves associated with a particularly brutal murder in London almost contemporaneously—and we have all the ingredients for as pretty a problem as ever was." Then suddenly a thought seemed to strike him. "By Jove," he said, "that coal cabinet, Daventry. I wonder if it's worthwhile looking in there—it's just possible the murderer may have—" He dashed across to the coal cabinet. It was of the type that swung outwards on a hinge. He pulled it towards him. Then he knelt down in front of it. Taking a sheet of note-paper from his pocket, he very carefully picked out some objects from the contents of the scuttle. Daventry wasn't able to see what they were as Anthony placed them on the piece of paper. He couldn't restrain his curiosity any longer. "What is it, Bathurst? What have you found in there?"

"A long shot," chuckled Anthony, "but it's happened to have come off." He held the paper out to his companion. "It struck me when I looked at that coal-scuttle just now, that a person clearing little pieces of dirt and mud from the surface of that table"—he pointed to the desk where Stewart had been found dead—"might very easily dispose of them in the scuttle—it might well be the handiest and most convenient place—look here then!" Daventry looked at the paper held out on the palm of Anthony's hand. There were seven or eight dried pellets of mud and four small light brown stones such as may be found in any garden. Anthony went on with his explanation. "There isn't very much coal there—as you may see if you look—fires have been discontinued for some time now, I expect—so it didn't give me very much trouble to find these chaps." He smiled with infinite satisfaction, but Peter Daventry wasn't too clear at all. "I can understand that part of the business," he conceded—"where I'm floundering is over the part of the affair before we come to that. I haven't the foggiest notion how you ever deduced their existence!"

"When I get the chance," replied Anthony, "I think I shall be able to show you at least one other stone just like these four little fellows that I've taken from the coal-scuttle—I can't now—the Inspector and Clegg may be back at any minute." He walked to the French doors and looked out—then turned back to Daventry. "There they come," he exclaimed.

"That stone, Bathurst," cut in Peter hastily.

"Is *in this room*," replied Anthony, "but not a word for the time being."

Clegg stepped into the room, immediately followed by Goodall. To Daventry's amazement, Anthony went straight over to them. "Well, Inspector, what did you make of the matter of O'Connor's bicycle?"

"You rather take my breath away, Mr. Bathurst," said Goodall very quietly. "Permit me to return your question—what did you?"

"I had no doubt you would pick it up," he said, "and I'll answer your question quite frankly." He walked across to the bookcase, and standing with his back to it had his three hearers in front of him, Peter on his right, and the two officers on his left. "O'Connor's bicycle, gentlemen, was used last night to carry somebody from this house into Assynton. In my opinion it carried the murderer of Stewart—if not the murderer, certainly his or her accomplice—but I fancy the murderer." He watched the three faces to see the effect of his opinion. Goodall became critical at once.

"Who placed the bicycle in the shed then?" he asked cautiously.

Bathurst's reply came just as quickly. "The murderer, of course."

Goodall screwed up his face as though unconvinced. "You mean, then, that the murderer returned—that the murderer lives—"

Anthony interrupted him. "I mean that if my theory holds good—that the *murderer* used the machine and not an accomplice—he is either in this house now or very near it. He or *she*."

But Goodall stuck to his guns. "But why go away to come back again?—that's what beats me."

"More than one reason might supply a reasonable answer to that question, Inspector. The murderer may have wished to hide something, for instance. He may have gone to meet somebody even. Thirdly, he may have gone to deliver an important message." He paused to consider the three possibilities he had named. Then looked straight across to Goodall. "I am inclined to the third suggestion myself, Inspector. Rather strongly as a matter of fact." He came away from the bookcase, giving Peter Daventry an impression—vague perhaps—that the final word had been spoken.

Goodall shook his head rather doubtfully. "Theories are all very well in their way, Mr. Bathurst—but if I were to go chasing after all the theories I have put in front of me—I should be well set to work—can't you give me something more definite on which your theories have been based—something more tangible?"

Anthony thrust his hands into his pockets with a gesture of impatience. "Of course I can, Inspector. Surely you don't think I make statements of this kind irresponsibly? 'Pon my soul, I feel rather like picking up your challenge and being much more explicit than I had intended to be." He paced to the bookcase and then came back again. "That bicycle was almost certainly ridden into Assynton after the murder had been committed. For the reason, in my opinion, that immediate communication had to be established between this end of the tangle and the other—or if you prefer it—between Assynton Lodge and the *people that murdered Mason at the Hanover Galleries the same night*." He paused, and Peter Daventry noticed that Inspector Goodall was listening keenly and critically—punctuating Anthony's remarks with sharp, quick movements of the head. "I deduce an urgent telephone message," continued Anthony, "something had happened here that made instantaneous action *imperative*—the 'phone was the only way. Obviously the 'phone in the house itself must not be used—the nearest is in Assynton village—the nearest that would also be safest. If you like, I will embroider my theory somewhat." He smiled as he sensed the improvement in his "atmosphere." He was beginning to "get over!"—"I deduce also, Inspector, that this urgent telephone message was very probably to an hotel. I think that we are dealing with a dangerous set of criminals who mean to stick at nothing to gain their ends and who in all likelihood had prepared their plans very thoroughly to meet all emergencies. If quick telephone communication formed a link in their connection system those of them who are conducting the operations from the other end were probably stopping at a quiet hotel. They don't appeal to me as likely to be permanent residents in the West End of London, so I incline to the probability of an hotel." He turned to Inspector Goodall decisively. "Let me make a suggestion, Inspector! Try to trace a telephone message from Assynton about 11:20 on the night before last." Goodall broke in with an exclamation of incredulity. But Bathurst held up his hand and went straight on. "A message to an hotel—I'll give you a list that I fancy will contain the identical one."

Goodall raised his hands. "You travel a darned sight too fast, Mr. Bathurst. Hold hard a minute—there's a pretty wide gulf of difference between outlining your suggestions and putting them into solid practice. For instance, you assert quite confidently that the time was 11:20. How—"

"Tut-tut, man," broke in Anthony—"that shouldn't surprise you. Your mysterious woman arrived at the Hanover Galleries at twelve o'clock or thereabouts—I've endeavoured to fill in the time with what happened here between ten o'clock and then—I put the murder at eleven o'clock approximately, and I've allowed twenty minutes for the cycle ride." Goodall nodded slowly as Anthony made his points. "Granted all that—Mr. Bathurst—I don't say I accept it all—how about that list of hotels you talk about drawing up and handing to me—there isn't exactly a famine in hotels in London—it seems to me it will be 'some list'." He smiled at Anthony with just a tinge of sarcasm.

"Just a little matter of geometry, Inspector," came the somewhat baffling answer.

"Geometry?" queried Goodall.

"Yes," said Anthony, "with a given centre and a radius say of one mile—describe a circle—the hotel will be found within that circle—the lady was at work on the real business by midnight—remember." The Inspector's face cleared.

"Of course! I see now what you mean. Your centre will be the Hanover Galleries?"

"Exactly," replied Mr. Bathurst.

CHAPTER XII

THE SECOND SCREEN OF MARY STUART

GOODALL TURNED to Clegg and fired off a rapid fusillade of instructions to which that worthy gave the most respectful attention. "At once, Inspector?" he questioned.

"Quicker than that," snapped Goodall, "and stand no nonsense from anybody."

Anthony gave him a glance of approval. Then watched Clegg depart with heavy and important tread. "Tell Mr. Charles Stewart we should like to speak to him for a moment," he called to the Sergeant as he made his way towards the hall—"you'll find him close handy." Goodall then came forward.

"I want Mr. Stewart," he said. "He promised that I should interview Miss Lennox and the late Mr. Stewart's secretary—also I'm afraid I've been keeping him waiting."

"Would you mind postponing the interviews for a little while, Inspector?" asked Anthony. "I've another suggestion to make."

"Let's hear it then."

"Please yourself, of course," proceeded Anthony, "have them in now by all means if you consider it very important. But what I was going to suggest was this. I should very much like to have a look at this Museum Room of Mr. Stewart's. I've got a shrewd idea that it won't prove to be entirely unprofitable."

Goodall thought for a moment and then signified his agreement. "Very well, Mr. Bathurst—that will suit me very well—I can see the others later."

As he spoke Charles Stewart returned.

"That trifling matter of the Museum Room, Mr. Stewart," exclaimed Anthony. "Did you remember to get that little catalogue from Mr. Llewellyn that you promised me? If you did I should like to go in there and have that tour of inspection I discussed with you last evening."

Stewart made an exclamation of regret. "My apologies, Mr. Bathurst, it slipped my memory—but I'll soon rectify that." He touched the bell. "Mr. Llewellyn," he said as the secretary appeared, "didn't you compile for my father some time ago a catalogue of the contents of the Museum Room?"

Anthony watched the secretary's face with the utmost intentness as he replied. "Yes, Mr. Charles. That is so! Your father was very keen on having it done."

Charles Stewart nodded eagerly. "Bring me a copy, will you, please? In here—at once!"

Llewellyn left quite imperturbably and Stewart offered a hint of explanation to the others. "My father thought a tremendous lot of Llewellyn, gentlemen—and one of the reasons of his great confidence in him was because of Llewellyn's keen interest in *all* of my father's concerns. He wasn't a chap who just did his bare duty and no more—he seemed able to identify himself intimately with each one of my father's many interests—and not least with his mania for collecting."

Anthony stopped him. "Is Llewellyn a 'devotee' of the 'antique artistic'?" he asked.

"My father found him a most zealous assistant in it, Mr. Bathurst," replied Charles Stewart, "that's all I can tell you. I'm afraid I was much less interested myself."

A tap on the library door heralded the secretary's reappearance. "There is a copy of what you wanted, Mr. Charles," he declared. Stewart took it and rapidly glanced over it. "That is a list," continued Llewellyn, "of every single article in your father's collection."

Charles Stewart handed the list to Anthony. "Here you are, Mr. Bathurst! Would you like a copy, too, Inspector?"

Goodall declined with a shake of the head. "All I want I can get from Mr. Bathurst," he answered. "Remember—this is more his 'stunt' than mine. I haven't yet been informed that anything has been stolen from the room in question"—he looked hard at his questioner. Stewart's reply came with just the slightest touch of asperity.

"Mr. Bathurst doesn't get any inspired information from me, Inspector, if that's what you're hinting at. He knows that I rather disagree with his idea. The room was closed when the alarm was given, and I've never suggested to anybody that anything has been stolen."

Goodall partly shifted his ground. "Why then is our friend here so insistent on the point?"

Anthony made an attempt at explanation. "I'm not exactly insistent, Inspector," he explained, "don't misunderstand me! I haven't perhaps very much reason at the back of my idea, but I'm just curious to get a look at these treasures that the late Mr. Stewart valued so highly. I have a strong feeling that the visit may help us considerably."

Here Goodall's gesture stopped him.

"Your theory, of course, Mr. Bathurst, if I may call it such, being based on the Hanover Galleries murder—eh?"

"Yes," replied Anthony quickly, "it seems to me that the whole case revolves round the Stuart heirlooms—if you can so describe them."

"Well," intervened Stewart, "the matter can very soon be settled—we'll go to the room. Get the key, Mr. Llewellyn, will you—you'll probably find it hanging up in the service-room. Come along, gentlemen." It was the work of a moment for Llewellyn to get the key and for Stewart to unlock the door of the room. The five men entered. As far as could be seen the room presented an appearance of complete order. A more heterogeneous collection it would have been impossible to imagine. Tables of old and exquisite workmanship supported the smaller articles—the larger finding their place on the floor and against the four walls. Four glass cases protected other treasures. Manuscripts, missals, musical instruments of all ages, weapons, rings, snuff-boxes, furniture of all kinds were to be found, with suits of ancient armour and specimens of fragile glass.

"There are over two thousand articles in this room, gentlemen," announced Morgan Llewellyn, "and the catalogue that I was privileged to compile lists and partly describes every one of the two thousand odd. If you look at the end of the catalogue, Mr. Bathurst, you'll see the exact number there are." Bathurst turned to the end. "Two thousand and forty-four," he declared. Goodall smiled at Llewellyn and Stewart.

"Well, it's pretty evident that no burglarious entry was made here, gentlemen. Nothing here appears to have been disturbed." He turned to the others for corroboration of his opinion.

Stewart shook his head doubtfully. "It would be most difficult, gentlemen, to trace anything that *had* been stolen. My father doubtless would have been able to tell at once, but I fear that now—"

He stopped and shook his head again.

"I appreciate what Mr. Stewart says entirely," supported Llewellyn. "I was intimately connected with this particular side of Mr. Stewart, senior, but I should hesitate to assert that I could say that anything was missing. Of course, I could tell if some of the things had been taken—some of the more special objects for instance. For example"—he walked to a table that stood to the left of the door. On it lay what looked like a circlet of dull and twisted metal. Llewellyn picked it up. "The ancient Crown of the Kings of England—believed to have last graced the head of Charles the First. Mr. Stewart paid a tremendous price for this—and the sale was secret. It was purchased by him from one of the most famous names in England. I should have known at once, for example, if this had been missing." He replaced it on the table, and his eyes smouldered with the covetous zeal of the collector. Laurence Stewart's enthusiasm had apparently been infectious. Bathurst found himself pondering over it. Llewellyn crossed to the wall and unhooked a piece of armour that had been hanging there. "Look at this! This is a gorget. Who do you think is supposed to have worn it?" Goodall took it and examined it curiously.

"No idea," he said. It was a species of breastplate shaped like a half-moon.

"That," continued Llewellyn, well launched now on a subject close to his heart, "is supposed to have been worn by the Black Prince at the Battle of Crécy. That is a second thing that I should have missed instantly."

Inspector Goodall cut in. "Let's put it like this, Mr. Llewellyn, or you, Mr. Stewart! Do either of you miss anything at all—that's the quickest way to get to grips with the question?"

Llewellyn made a tour of the room. "I miss nothing, Inspector."

Charles Stewart shook his head rather despondently. "I can't help you and that's a fact, Inspector. You must leave it at that." He looked at Anthony Bathurst, who was, however, busy at the moment turning over the leaves of Llewellyn's catalogue.

"Well then, if that's the case," rejoined Goodall, "no particularly good purpose will be served by us stopping in here any longer. I'm afraid Mr. Bathurst has given us a 'stumer' this time."

"Half a minute," interposed Anthony quietly. "You've all had an innings, now it's my turn. Listen to me for two minutes. Mr. Llewellyn"—he turned to the secretary—"consider for a moment item number eight hundred and sixty-six in the catalogue, will you?"

Apparently the number conveyed nothing to Llewellyn, for his face was unchanged.

"Eight—six—six?" he inquired.

"I'll read you the description I find here," proceeded Anthony. "Antique fire-screen, of beaten metal-work—about four feet high. Originally the property of Mary, Queen of Scots." He tucked the catalogue under his arm. "I'd like to have a look at that," he said, "I'm interested."

Llewellyn raised his forefinger. "You shall, Mr. Bathurst, I do know it now you mention it—it's in this corner—behind this collection of Waterford glass." He crossed to the right-hand corner of the room. Anthony scratched the back of his neck—watching Llewellyn pick his way between the tables. Suddenly the secretary stopped, and although his back was towards them, more than one of the four detected an anxiety in the manner of his stopping. Then he turned—his face white and working with excitement. "It's gone, gentlemen," he cried. "It's not here—come and look yourself, Mr. Stewart." Charles Stewart walked quickly to the corner.

"There's no screen here," he declared.

"Mightn't it be somewhere else?" asked the Inspector. "Are these things always kept in precisely the same spot?"

"Always, Inspector," replied Morgan Llewellyn promptly. "Mr. Stewart was most particular about that."

"Isn't it possible that Mr. Stewart himself may have removed it—on the eve of his intended purchases—for comparison or something?" suggested Daventry.

"No," said Llewellyn. "I think not. I'm certain Mr. Stewart would have told me if he had done so."

"Goodall," said Anthony, with a suspicion of the didactic in his manner, "I can now assure you of at least one thing! Mason, the night-watchman, was murdered for possession of the other Stuart screen!"

"And my father—" broke in Charles Stewart with emotion.

"I am not sure," replied Anthony with his hand on Stewart's shoulder, "yet! Time is precious," he continued, "we're moving at last. Who can give me a more detailed description of this screen that was kept here—I am anxious to know more about it? Can you, Mr. Llewellyn?"

Llewellyn hesitated. But Peter was unable to decide what it was that was passing through his mind. He seemed to be considering something, but nevertheless gave no apparent hint of embarrassment or agitation. Then his answer came, but it was not quite in the form that Peter had anticipated.

"I'm afraid I can't help you, Mr. Bathurst. I certainly remember the screen, as I said just now. It was of some kind of beaten metal-work and about the size stated in the catalogue. When

I compiled the catalogue I had some notes of Mr. Stewart's to assist me in my classification—I remember I used his own description wherever possible, when it came to making up my own list. There were some objects in the collection that I was forced to raise certain questions about through lack of information in the notes, but this screen wasn't one of those. Mr. Stewart himself, I may add, approved the description in the catalogue in every instance."

Anthony had followed him very carefully as he furnished this explanation. "Did Mr. Stewart mention the matter of this screen to you in connection with his projected purchase of the other one?"

Llewellyn shook his head vigorously. "Never!" was his emphatic reply. "I knew that he was adding to his collection, but he never referred in any way to this screen that he already had in his possession. I'm absolutely sure on the point."

"Forgive me, Mr. Llewellyn, if I appear insistent, but I've understood since I've been here that you were a very zealous assistant to Mr. Stewart in this particular branch of his work. Is that true?"

Here Goodall intervened abruptly. "Yes, Mr. Llewellyn, how was it, if you were so intimate with Mr. Stewart in all his collecting work, that he didn't mention the fact of these two screens to you?" But Llewellyn was not to be so easily shaken.

"Without appearing to be disrespectful, I would suggest that Mr. Stewart would have been in a better position to answer that than I, Inspector," he replied smoothly.

Goodall flushed, but Llewellyn went on. "All I can say is that he *didn't* mention them."

Then Anthony countered with another question. "Had Mr. Stewart confided in you at any time—before—had he discussed similar purchases on previous occasions?"

"Many times," responded Llewellyn with absolute candour.

"Can you then account for a seeming lack of confidence on his part in this instance?"

"Frankly, Mr. Bathurst, I can't! But Mr. Stewart, if his son will pardon my outspokenness at such a time as this, was a man of quick impulses. He was very impetuous and utterly impatient—caught by this whim and influenced by that wave of feeling—therefore not exactly a man that you could call a model of consistency. Not that I have any reason or desire to find fault with him as an employer. He was always just and always generous—I cannot complain of his treatment of me." He looked up and caught Inspector Goodall's eye and he was quick enough to sense its disapproval. For Goodall's brain was considering several elements of doubt. "Why," said the Inspector to himself, "why does this young man talk like this when Miss Marjorie Lennox accuses him of harbouring revengeful feelings against the man of whom he speaks?" He decided that the solution to this little problem might possibly be more speedily forthcoming if he showed a little craft. So he affected an air of ingenuousness.

"The sentiments do you credit," he declared. "It's the fashion of the world nowadays to run down your employers as much as you can. Well, Mr. Bathurst, what about this screen of yours? I'm afraid there's nobody here that can help you with those details you asked for. You'll have to remain content with the description in the catalogue—'an antique metal-work screen.' I expect the only person that could have supplied more information was Mr. Stewart himself."

"That's not quite true!" A musical voice from the doorway tinkled across to the group of men. They all turned instantaneously as Marjorie Lennox picked her dainty way towards them. "No! That's not true," she reaffirmed. "Because I can! Charles—introduce me to these gentlemen." She spoke imperiously.

Peter Daventry realized when he bowed to this charming interruption that life had discovered for him an additional interest. He murmured a few words to a magical smile and thanked God for another blessing. Anthony expressed his intense satisfaction that Miss Lennox was able to help them so materially, in which statement he was gallantly seconded by Detective-Inspector Goodall, whose thoughts at the same time reverted to Sergeant Clegg and a lady's handkerchief!

"I overheard what was being said," exclaimed Miss Lennox demurely, "and I realized at once that I could help you. The night before he died, poor Uncle Laurence brought me in here specially to look at that screen. He was very excited about it and he explained to me that Lord Clavering's death and the sale of his property had given him the chance to get the two screens that had belonged to Mary, Queen of Scots, before the débâcle at Carbery Hill and her subsequent imprisonment. We looked at it together—I can describe it very fully."

"Just what I want, Miss Lennox," exclaimed Anthony. "As fully as you can, please—you will help me a lot."

Marjorie puckered her brow. Peter instantly formed the opinion that it made her distinctly more lovely than ever. "It stood about so high," she declared with an appropriate gesture, "and was made as far as I could judge of some kind of metal—copper I should imagine from the colour. Of course, being over 300 years old it was much darker and blacker than the beaten copper work that we see now." Here came more brow-puckering, to Peter's secret delight—Mr. Daventry, it must be remembered, had a keen eye and the soundest of discriminating tastes. "The next part is harder to remember," continued the charming chronicler, "but I think I'm right." She thought for a moment and then went on. "In the top left-hand corner there was Mary's Lion and in the right-hand corner the 'fleur-de-lis.' At the bottom of the screen—on the right—"

"Forgive me, Miss Lennox," said Peter under the influence of a sudden impulse, "it's awfully rude of me, I know, but let me see if I can finish the description for you—just a fancy of mine—that's all."

Miss Lennox looked very surprised and a little disdainful, but, "Go on then," was all she permitted herself to say. Thus encouraged, Peter did so.

"At the bottom," he declared oracularly, "were the Leopards and Lilies of England."

A pair of wonderful blue eyes seemed suddenly to become more wonderful. With the wonder of amazement.

"You're right—absolutely right," she said. "Where and when did you see Uncle's screen?"

But Peter proceeded with the assurance of the conqueror. "In the centre," he said, "were the words, 'Jesus Christ, God and Saviour.'" He paused and with his eyes invited her corroboration. But this time Marjorie corrected him—*very* disdainfully.

"Oh no," she remarked—"in the centre were two words in Latin. They had been scratched, or inscribed perhaps is the happier word, with a sharp-pointed instrument—at least that's what it looked like. The two words were *'Timeo Danaos.'* Here she stopped as all good story-tellers should when they have scored a good point.

"Translate, Mr. Bathurst," said Goodall with the suggestion of a grin, "my classics are rusty."

"*'Timeo Danaos,'*" repeated Anthony, "*'et dona ferentes'*— which being interpreted means, 'I fear the Greeks especially when they bring gifts.'"

"What the deuce are Greeks doing on this screen?" grumbled Goodall.

Anthony shook his head. "Can't see for the moment, I admit. Anything else, Miss Lennox?"

Marjorie nodded her little head in the affirmative. "Yes," she said, "right underneath the two words—almost exactly in the centre of the screen—was a big fish."

"A fish?" queried Anthony, wrinkling his forehead, "what sort of a fish?"

Marjorie shook her head. "Just an ordinary fish—that's all I could say about it. All the animals—the Lion, and the Leopards and the Fish—and the flowers too, were done in a kind of repoussé work—you know what I mean—they stood out as it were away from the surface of the screen itself."

Anthony nodded that he understood what she meant.

"You've been of tremendous assistance to me, Miss Lennox," he declared. "The case becomes more complicated than ever, but all the same I feel it in my bones that we shall solve it. Inspector Goodall here will confirm my opinion."

The Inspector smiled grimly, but whatever remark he may have been about to make was stifled by the reappearance of

Sergeant Clegg at the door of the Museum Room. Clegg saluted smartly.

"A word with you, Inspector, if you please."

Goodall turned to Charles Stewart. "Mr. Stewart," he said, "I should be obliged if you would take Miss Lennox and Mr. Llewellyn into the library—I will join you in a few moments—I want to have a little chat with them—thank you."

Peter Daventry had been half hoping that the Inspector would dismiss him too, but his luck failed. He was more reconciled, however, when he listened to Clegg's report.

"A trunk-call was put through on the night of the murder, Inspector, to Blanchard's Hotel, Clifford Street, W. I worked on the lines this gentleman suggested—although as it happened he was a good bit out in his reckoning as regards the time." This last remark left his lips triumphantly.

Anthony looked up—puzzled. "How much, Sergeant?" he inquired promptly.

"Eleven minutes," Clegg announced judicially.

"Good Lord, Sergeant," said Anthony, "I was afraid you meant hours"—he broke off and shrugged his shoulders.

The Sergeant looked aggrieved. "Eleven minutes is a long time, if I may say so," he urged—defending his position—"you try and catch a train when you're eleven minutes late."

"Come, Clegg," exclaimed Goodall impatiently, "what do they say at Blanchard's Hotel?"

Clegg resumed his narrative with an air of injury. "I 'phoned the Hotel and I've been able to trace that it was to a gentleman who was staying there with his wife. When the 'phone call had been answered they asked for the manager—immediately. They informed him that owing to the sudden serious illness of a near relative they were obliged to leave the hotel at once. They paid their bill, collected their luggage and departed."

"On foot?" cut in Goodall peremptorily.

"I didn't inquire," murmured Clegg, "I was too—er—taken aback with what I heard next. This gentleman and his wife had registered at the hotel in the names of Mr. and Mrs. Laurence Charles Stewart!"

Goodall whistled in amazement.

"From where?" flashed Anthony.

"From New York," replied the Sergeant.

Chapter XIII

COLONEL LEACH-FLETCHER IS AT HOME TO VISITORS

"Stewart!" echoed Goodall. "Great Scott! Where on earth are we getting to? Did you get a description of these people, Clegg?"

"I did, sir. According to my information the man was between thirty and forty—his wife about the same. They had been at Blanchard's Hotel about a week—I didn't wait for any more details—I was anxious to get back to you with the information I had got!"

Goodall gave him a quick nod of praise, then turned to Anthony. "Do you know what I'm thinking, Mr. Bathurst?" he said. "I'm thinking that this lady and gentleman who left this hotel so suddenly are the identical pair that lunched with Mr. Daventry. What do you think, yourself?"

Anthony considered for a brief moment. "Yes, Inspector, I'm inclined to agree with you—I *was* thinking the same, myself. And when you get them you'll clap your hands on the murderer of poor Mason, the night-watchman—you can bet your bottom dollar on that."

Goodall's jaw set tight. "Well, I *shall* clap my hands on them—if it means chasing them over two continents. At the same time—I've got precious little to go upon—two people from New York that put up at an hotel for a week and then walk out of it suddenly. It's a needle in a haystack job, very probably," he concluded pessimistically.

"You have two other facts besides that, Inspector," added Anthony. "They possess a tapestry fire-screen, stolen from Day, Forshaw and Palmers', and the lady sneezes."

Goodall snapped his fingers impatiently.

"All the same, Mr. Bathurst—that won't help me overmuch. But with regard to what you just said about the screen—have they one screen or two?"

"That's difficult to say, Inspector. I don't know what to think—upon reflection, perhaps two."

"That's what I think," agreed Goodall, "and when I've had my little interview with Miss Lennox and Llewellyn—I'll decide upon a plan of action." Half an hour later he joined Anthony and Peter. "I'm running up to Blanchard's Hotel," he announced. "It's imperative that I should have a look round there—there may be a most valuable clue left behind—you never know. What will you do, Mr. Bathurst?"

"I'm calling on a gentleman whose name has been mentioned more than once in connection with this case, Inspector—a gentleman who lives very near—Colonel Leach-Fletcher."

Goodall's face brightened. "Exactly my own idea," he exclaimed, "it was just on the cards that I called on him myself before getting my train up to town." He stopped and thought—then swung round quickly on the two men. "And I will, Mr. Bathurst," he declared, "I'll come with you—if anybody can tell us anything it's this Colonel chap."

"Right-o, there's no time like the present. What about getting away now?"

"Delighted—I'll just run back and tell Clegg." Goodall dashed back and within a couple of minutes had made a start. "The address is 'Neuve Chapelle'—it's a charming bungalow, I'm given to understand, on the road to Rockinge—a matter of about four miles. The gallant Colonel, I presume, judging from the name he has given his bungalow, saw service in the European War—I expect Stewart found him an interesting and delightful neighbour."

"No doubt," agreed the Inspector, "I hear from Clegg that they were pretty close cronies."

"Neuve Chapelle" was reached in an hour, and the smart maid-servant who answered their ring showed some signs of surprise at the number of the visitors. The Colonel evidently didn't have many friends who called upon him of mornings. Goodall took upon himself the post of spokesman.

"My compliments to Colonel Leach-Fletcher," he said, "and will you please tell him that Detective-Inspector Goodall, of Scotland Yard, would like to see him for a moment or two?"

The maid-servant looked scared and her rosy cheeks whitened a trifle. "Will you please step inside, I'll tell my master."

An interval of a few moments saw them ushered into what was evidently the lounge. It was altogether a charming room, furnished in irreproachable taste. A man in the early sixties was standing in the centre of the room—facing them as they entered. Colonel Leach-Fletcher was a man of fine physique—round about five feet ten and weighing as far as Anthony could judge from a quick glance, somewhere in the region of fourteen stone. His manner was very decisive—some people might have described it as curt.

"Good morning, gentlemen," he said rather abruptly. "I understand you wish to see me—about poor Stewart I presume?"

Goodall bowed. "These gentlemen are Mr. Anthony Bathurst and Mr. Peter Daventry—they represent Mr. Charles Stewart's interests."

Colonel Leach-Fletcher acknowledged the introduction with a quick inclination of the head—and a rather cavalier one, at that. "I am ready to tell you anything you think necessary—but really, I'm afraid you will find it of small consequence—sit down, gentlemen!" The Colonel took up his position in front of the mantelpiece as his self-invited guests accepted his invitation.

"In the first place, Colonel," said Goodall, opening the interview, "I am informed that you dined with the murdered man on the evening of the murder, and left Assynton Lodge somewhere about ten o'clock." Goodall looked up for the Colonel's corroboration. It came immediately.

"Quite correct!" Goodall waited to see if the Colonel purposed adding anything to his reply, but the Colonel didn't—he waited for Goodall.

"Was Mr. Stewart in normally good spirits during the evening, Colonel?"

Colonel Leach-Fletcher twirled his white moustache. Then he thrust his two hands deep into his trouser-pockets and stood still. "Look here, Inspector—what name did you say—Goodall?—look here, Inspector Goodall—I'm utterly opposed to beating about the bush, so I'll tell you straight to your face without any embroidery that I hate your infernal trade and all its tricks and practices. But I'm a man that realizes the exigencies of duty—so I'll waive my personal inclinations that prompt me to send you to the Devil—and I'll answer your question—even though I feel within me that I'm betraying a dead man's confidence. Mr. Stewart was *not* exactly in his ordinary cheerful frame of mind on the evening in question."

"H'm," said Goodall, "perhaps you will explain more fully."

Anthony's eyes never left the Colonel now—he realized that he might be on the point of hearing something that touched the crime very closely. The Colonel's steely-blue eyes were full of resolution and determination. He had made a decision, and though he found its carrying-out irksome and unpleasant, he was determined to see it through.

"You must understand that Stewart and I had become very friendly and were on very intimate terms. We had a number of common interests and we were almost neighbours, four miles isn't a great distance in the country. I am not sure that, when he invited me to dine with him that evening, he hadn't a special reason for so doing. If I may be permitted to say so—he valued my opinion on most things and regarded himself as privileged to consider me a friend. During the evening—after dinner—he took me into the library and told me of two matters that were causing him a good deal of uneasiness. The first was rather a surprising one. He told me that there was underhand work going on at Assynton Lodge."

Anthony, with a quick glance at Goodall, cut in. "Did he actually use the word 'underhand,' Colonel?"

The latter pursed his lips. "Upon reflection, I believe he used the word 'treacherous,' but I'm not absolutely certain on the point. Is it very important?"

Anthony shook his head. "Tell us more, Colonel—this is most illuminating." The Colonel appeared gratified at this testimony to his narrative powers. He proceeded.

"Mr. Stewart went on to tell me that more than once he had found that his private papers and documents had been interfered with. This fact was worrying him considerably and causing him great concern. It wasn't so much the espionage that troubled him, but the idea that there was somebody near to him that was acting treacherously. I gathered from his conversation with me that evening that he was determined to take the bull by the horns and endeavour to put a stop to it, if at all possible."

"Did he suspect anybody?" questioned Goodall.

"I think not," replied the Colonel, "at any rate, if he did, he refrained from taking me into his confidence to that extent."

"One point that strikes me as important, Colonel," interposed Anthony, "did Mr. Stewart give you any idea as to how long this had been going on?"

"Only for a matter of months at the most—that at all events is certain—it commenced, he told me, some time after he came to England."

"Had he mentioned it to you before?" Anthony watched the Colonel very keenly as he put this question to him.

"Not in actual terms," came the reply, "he had hinted once or twice very recently that he was disturbed about something, but he never gave me any actual details till that last night of his life."

The Colonel leaned his elbow on the mantelpiece and put his head in his hand.

"What was the second matter that Mr. Stewart spoke about?" queried Goodall.

The Colonel deliberated for a moment or two before he answered.

"There, gentlemen, you approach me on much more delicate ground. And in some ways, I regret having made the admission to you and the promise to tell you all I know. The dead man, if he still possesses a spiritual consciousness in some other sphere, will, I hope, understand. I can only hope also that the living man will understand too. Gentlemen, Mr. Stewart was extremely upset about the conduct of his son—Charles Stewart."

Goodall's body became all attention. It seemed to him that he was beginning to emerge into the light at last.

"What had Charles Stewart done to offend his father?" he demanded. The Colonel extended his hands towards them—palms upwards. It was a gesture of deprecation and at the same time seemed to contain a tinge of disappointment. "That is a question I cannot answer! Mr. Stewart did not enlighten me. He told me that he was grievously disappointed over something Charles had done. He said that it would make a difference to his whole life."

"*Whose* life?" Anthony shot the question at him. "His own life or his son's?"

"I understood him to mean his *own* life," rejoined the Colonel very quietly.

"And he gave you no inkling as to what this conduct was?"

"None at all!" The Colonel shook his head slowly, "and I didn't press him for any more information on the point. It would have been a breach of courtesy on my part to have appeared unwarrantably inquisitive. I let Mr. Stewart tell me as much as it pleased him—and I sympathized with him. He was deeply attached to Charles and felt the misunderstanding or whatever it was very keenly. There is just one more piece of information that I am in a position to give. Mr. Stewart intended having an interview with his son after I left that evening. Of course, I can't say that the interview ever took place." The Colonel caressed his moustache again.

Goodall sprang to his feet. "Good heavens, Colonel! Do you realize the gravity of this last statement? Do you know at what time Mr. Stewart's murder has been put at—pretty well *fixed*?"

"I do not, Inspector," responded the Colonel. "I have only heard the bare facts." He looked at Goodall with an invitation for information. The Inspector gave it to him.

"As far as we are able to judge—we who have been looking into the case—the late Mr. Stewart met his death somewhere about eleven o'clock—just about an hour after Butterworth saw you out."

The Colonel shrugged his square shoulders. "An hour is a long time, gentlemen, I would remind you! And Charles Stewart may not have been with his father after all. Events may have conspired to prevent it—there's no knowing. You are working more or less in the dark."

Anthony ranged himself with the Colonel. "I quite agree with you, sir. Half-a-dozen people might have been in the library with Mr. Stewart between ten and eleven o'clock that night—there is no evidence to the contrary—that's certain. But this interview that you mention, Colonel! Are you convinced that it was to be on the subject that had caused Mr. Stewart such displeasure? That seems to me to matter a great deal."

"I can't be certain with regard to that," was the Colonel's reply. "Mr. Stewart didn't tell me so exactly—but I think that I should be perfectly justified in assuming so—coming as it did after what he had just previously told me."

Goodall took a hand again. "Coming back to the details of your own visit, Colonel—I'm sure you won't mind answering a few more questions. How did you travel over to Assynton Lodge on that particular evening?"

The Colonel's reply came quickly with a touch of annoyance in his voice. "By car, of course, my own car. What's your point in asking a question like that?"

Goodall affected not to hear the question—he made no immediate answer. "So that I presume," he continued, "that you were home here by ten-fifteen easily?"

"I should imagine that would be about the time," said Colonel Leach-Fletcher testily, "though what the blazes all this has to do with the affair—"

Goodall intervened again. "In that quarter of an hour's journey—did you pass anybody or notice anybody on the road?"

"I did not," snapped the Colonel. "It was a perfectly glorious night, and if I had passed anybody, I probably shouldn't have seen them—my attention is always too much taken up in driving my car."

Anthony flashed him a cordial smile. "Fond of motoring, Colonel?"

"I am that. It's one of my hobbies—the roads are pretty good down this way, and I go for some fast spins."

Anthony rubbed his hands. "You're another like myself," he chuckled. "What's your car?"

"A Bentley—latest model," said the Colonel—"real beauty—I can knock an easy seventy-five out of her."

"I don't think I've seen the latest model," said Anthony reflectively, "I don't fancy—"

The Colonel broke in on his musings enthusiastically. "Come out to the garage then and have a look at mine. It won't take a moment."

They followed the Colonel, who explained the car's fine points with the eagerness of a schoolboy. Goodall looked at his watch.

"Good-bye, Colonel," he said, "I must be going! Many thanks for your kindness. You know where I'm off to, Mr. Bathurst—don't quite know when I shall be back—if you want me, 'phone the Yard."

The Colonel's eyes followed his retreating figure for some distance. "We must be going too, Colonel," exclaimed Anthony, "but there's one little point before I go. That last evening you spent with Mr. Stewart—did he refer to any book while you were there—was he reading any book at any time during the evening? Try to remember if you possibly can!"

The Colonel knitted his brows. "There was a book open on his desk, now you come to mention it—I remember seeing it there—what was it called now?" he searched his mind in the effort of remembrance—"I know—it was Renan's *Vie de Jésus*."

CHAPTER XIV

MR. BATHURST TAKES A BOOK FROM THE BOOKCASE

THE COLONEL made this announcement with an air! "By Gad!" it seemed to say—"I'll show these police fellers and detective Johnnies that they aren't the only people that can use their eyes or their memories!" Then Mr. Bathurst jerked him back from his ecstatic contemplation to stern reality.

"Now Colonel," he said, "think very carefully—when did you see this book lying on Mr. Stewart's desk—when you entered the library after dinner—or when you left him at ten o'clock?"

The Colonel frowned. "Damn it all, sir," he muttered, "you expect a man to remember a devil of a lot—had I known there was going to be a murder, I might have taken more particular notice," he glared at his questioner with growing impatience.

Anthony smiled. "As a matter of fact, sir—I wouldn't have troubled to ask that question of ninety-nine persons out of a hundred—because I know I should get no satisfaction. The ordinary person is very unobservant. But I have been so impressed with the various points that you have remembered."

The Colonel grunted his satisfaction—he was a soldier and therefore not unmoved by flattery. "Thank you—thank you," he muttered. "Now let me see if I *can* help you in this particular instance."

He closed his eyes for a few seconds seeking either concentration or inspiration—perhaps both. "The book was lying open on poor Stewart's desk when he took me into the library—I'm certain of that now I cast my mind back—and I'm almost equally certain that it was in exactly the same position when I said 'Good-bye'—I can't remember him closing it or putting it away—he was talking pretty seriously to me virtually the entire evening. Yes"—he reflected, giving himself a species of mental check—"I'm confident that's right." Anthony held out his hand.

"That's excellent, Colonel."

Colonel Leach-Fletcher took it in his. "Must you be going?"

"Afraid so, Colonel—we've a heap of things to see to, Mr. Daventry and I—and we haven't too much time at our disposal—coming over to see you has helped us no end—no doubt I shall see you again before the affair is finally settled."

"When is the inquest fixed for?" queried the Colonel.

"Haven't been told yet," answered Anthony, "but in all probability it will only be formal at the first inquiry. The Police will probably take evidence of identification and then ask the Coroner for an adjournment. I'll make arrangements for you to know as soon as we get the news at Assynton Lodge—still you'll be wanted yourself—I was forgetting that."

"I suppose you're right—it's a bad business and a nuisance—still it can't be helped now—what's done can't be undone. Good-bye, gentlemen." The Colonel waved his hand in dismissal. For a few minutes Anthony remained silent, and Peter Daventry was beginning to know him sufficiently well to realize that it was a thoroughly sound investment to let him alone during those moments. After a time his mood passed and Daventry saw his face break into a smile.

"Cigarette, Daventry?" he exclaimed, "and I'll join you in smoking the health of a very pretty little problem indeed. I am deeply in your debt, Daventry, for my introduction to it. I wouldn't have missed it for the world."

Peter took the cigarette and they lit up. "Glad to hear you say that, Bathurst," he rejoined, "but the question is will you be able to let daylight into it?"

Anthony rubbed his chin with his fingers. "As to that, Daventry," he said, "I am extremely confident—although I always try to school myself to remember that 'Pride goeth before a fall.'" He grinned.

"Look here, Bathurst," remarked Daventry, "I know in cases of this kind the Doctor Watson of the business is always a thick-headed sort of arrangement, and I don't suppose I'm any more brilliant than the majority." He stopped for a second—shame-faced and apologetic.

But he found Anthony the reverse of inaccessible. "Unload, Daventry," he said sympathetically, "what precisely is troubling you?"

"Well, it's like this," responded Peter, "everything points as far as I can see to this Assynton Lodge murder being an inside job—and yet everybody there seems unaffected—I'm afraid I'm not making myself too clear—everybody seems normal— nobody's bolted with the screen, for instance!" Anthony shook his head. "I know what you mean, but what you put forward is very easily explained, isn't it? The screen may have been handed to a confederate, or again, it may be more profitable for the criminal to hold up his activities for a while."

" H'm," said Peter, as he thought over what his companion said. "I see your point—but I'm not altogether satisfied."

"I don't suppose you are for a moment," was the rejoinder, "the case, as a whole, bristles with extremely puzzling details— and you don't know them all, Daventry, take it from me."

Peter looked at him incredulously. "Why—what do you mean?"

"I got one or two pieces of evidence from Sergeant Clegg that he collected before we arrived at the scene—I haven't told you of all of them yet."

"Tell me now," said Peter anxiously, "don't leave me in the dark."

"Let's take the case as a whole then, without stopping to attempt to think of what you know and what you don't know. Stewart is murdered, I'm confident I'm right here, about eleven P. M. Colonel Leach-Fletcher left at ten o'clock, Butterworth can give unimpeachable confirmation of *that*. The Colonel tells us that Stewart intended interviewing his son about some matter that was causing friction between them. We'll call it friction—although it may have been of more serious consequence. It is a significant fact that Charles Stewart, although calling you and me into the case, has maintained an eloquent silence concerning it, whatever it was. Now we arrive at a further complication. Butterworth tells Sergeant Clegg that he heard Stewart—*Laurence* Stewart—in conversation with somebody else in the library at *ten minutes past ten!*" He paused and watched Peter intently.

"You don't say so," exclaimed the latter. "Can he tell who it was?"

"Oh yes," murmured Anthony negligently, "he recognized the person's voice."

"Then who was it?" demanded Peter eagerly.

"Marjorie Lennox!" Anthony dropped the name daintily and delicately—he must have been thinking of the little lady herself.

"It's a lie," cried Peter. "The butler's lying—I refuse to believe it—it's not feasible—it's—"

"My dear Peter," cooed Anthony, "I am sorely afraid that I diagnosed your complaint a few hours ago—when Miss Lennox made her dramatic entrance into the Museum Room. I feel doubly sure now that I was right."

Peter looked somewhat sheepish.

"Unfortunately the excellent Butterworth's story has strong support."

"From whom?" asked Peter sullenly.

"Support of a peculiar and convincing nature," continued Mr. Bathurst nonchalantly. "When the Sergeant first examined the library—*the actual scene of the crime*, Daventry—he found a lady's handkerchief caught in the curtains that hang at the French doors." He took another cigarette with evident enjoyment.

"Doesn't necessarily belong to Miss Lennox," countered Peter.

"N—no," replied Anthony, calculatingly, "no, I admit that. But it has initials on it, in the corner, I believe—and those initials are 'M. L.'—perhaps it belongs to Mr. Morgan Llewellyn!"

Peter gasped.

"Is that a fact, Bathurst?"

"Absolutely, my boy—everything exactly as I've told you!"

"Well, all I can say," replied Peter, exercising his full powers of recovery, "I don't believe Miss Lennox has *anything* to do with the dreadful business and that she can give a perfectly reasonable account of how her handkerchief got there." He seemed very dogged as he made this last remark. But Anthony had not finished with him yet awhile.

"But she *won't*," he proceeded airily. "She was approached about having been in the library. And she *lied* about it, Daventry. It's no use disguising the fact, she *lied* about it—*and then made an attempt to get into the library*—presumably to look for her handkerchief."

"Do they suspect her—do *you* suspect her, Bathurst?" demanded Peter, "it seems impossible—that girl—mixed up in a monstrous affair of this sort"—he stopped at a loss for words to express his indignation adequately.

"I can't answer your first question—I can't answer for them," said Anthony, "but I certainly suspect her of knowing more than she has told us. For instance—why has she deliberately accused Morgan Llewellyn?"

"What?" muttered Peter again. "When?"

"To Sergeant Clegg when he first spoke to her—what do you make of that, Daventry?" Peter was non-committal. "Again," continued Bathurst relentlessly, "why were her initials in front of the dead man—scrawled by the dead man in his last conscious moments?"

"They mightn't have been intended for hers—you can't be certain," defended Peter.

"Of course not!" Anthony slapped him on the back. *"As a matter of fact they weren't!"*

Peter could hardly believe his ears at this sudden revelation. "How can you know that?" he demanded.

"Well, I don't know, Daventry," came the prompt reply, "but all the same, I'm pretty sure."

They were nearing their destination, and the edges of the grounds of Assynton Lodge were already coming into sight. Anthony became grave again.

"But there's one thing I don't know," he muttered. "What is the secret of these Stuart screens? What do they hold to make men murder for their possession? Why does one bear the first two words of a line from Virgil? 'I fear the Greeks'—why the Greeks?—there were no Greeks round Mary surely"—he turned to his companion. "Tell me again—what was the inscription on the tapestry screen at the Hanover Galleries?"

"It was done in coloured beads—the beads spelled the words, 'Jesus Christ, God and Saviour.'"

"Made by a monk, I suppose," murmured Anthony, "their work was usually dedicated in that way—still—"

Peter cut in. "I know! There's one thing I wanted to ask you—it slipped my mind just now. What made you suspect Colonel Leach-Fletcher?

Anthony showed signs of amusement. "Who says I suspect him?"

"I could see you did," replied Peter, "dash it all, I'm not so blind as all that."

"You're forgetting something, Daventry," said Anthony. "Leach-Fletcher's stay was from seven to ten, you know—three hours he spent with the murdered man!"

Peter looked blank. "Don't get you," he exclaimed. "If you want to suspect anybody—suspect that lying Butterworth. He must have some ulterior motive for hatching up that yarn about Miss Lennox."

Anthony shook his head in denial. "Butterworth told the truth, Daventry. What he said about Miss Lennox is entirely accurate."

They entered the gate and walked round to the back of the house, Peter growing moodier and more despondent. His championship of Miss Lennox, together with his denunciation of the butler, had proved profitless—his words had fallen on barren soil. Whereat he was distinctly crestfallen! He refused to harbour the idea for a mere moment that Miss Lennox could be implicated in the crime that he was helping to investigate. It was ridiculous! When he considered that only a couple of days ago he was craving for something exciting to turn up and now that "something exciting" *had* turned up—he found the whole thing extremely difficult to believe.

"When do you expect Goodall back?" he questioned as they entered the house.

"Can't say definitely," said Anthony, "it depends on how he gets on up in Clifford Street. London's a big place—he may have a ticklish job to trace 'Mr. and Mrs. Laurence Charles Stewart.' You can't tell."

Peter assented. "That's just what I'm thinking," he declared, "rather neat that, don't you think, to register in those names?"

Anthony turned to him—a serious look on his face. "You feel certain then—that they are assumed names, Daventry, and not their own?"

"Well," replied Peter, with a certain amount of hesitation, "I'm afraid I took that for granted—I hadn't been considering them as possible members of Stewart's family—do you really think they are?"

"I don't know quite what to think about it—I've nothing sound to work upon—I reserve my opinion till I know more—it's a habit of mine."

Charles Stewart came forward to greet them. "So Goodall's gone to town—eh? What about some lunch—you must be ready for some by now?"

"Yes, to both questions," laughed Anthony. "The Inspector thinks he can do better up in town for the time being than down here."

Stewart seemed disinclined for conversation at lunch, and with Llewellyn relapsing into taciturnity, Anthony was left to contemplate the *entente cordiale* that had so speedily arisen between Peter Daventry and Marjorie Lennox. It possessed several features of attraction for him. At the same time he realized that it might conceivably place Daventry in an awkward position as Charles Stewart's solicitor and indirectly affect himself. When they rose from the table he slipped his arm into Peter's.

"I want you for a moment, Daventry—I want to get into the library while the coast is reasonably clear, and I want you to help me."

Peter was pleased to hear this—action stimulated him just as much as passivity galled him. He cast one more adoring glance in the direction of the exquisite Marjorie and fell in at Anthony's side.

"It's just possible that I'm too late," remarked the latter, "that the bird has flown—or rather 'has been flown with'—still, we'll see."

Peter nodded in agreement, although of course he didn't see.

"Come in and close the door quietly," said Anthony, "and now you're in, sit down and make yourself comfortable—you're going to stay in here some little time." Peter found himself wondering what was coming. "I'm going to speak very quietly, Daventry, because something sinister is going on in this house— and as events have already shown—the persons concerned stick at nothing. I am particularly anxious not to be overheard or even overlooked. So we'll pretend, as far as we are able, to be indulging in just an ordinary conversation. Remember how careful I was first thing after breakfast this morning."

"Bank on me," came Peter's reply. This sort of thing rather appealed to him, it served to put him on his mettle.

"You will remember also," commenced Anthony, "that my rest was disturbed last night, or to be precise, this morning, by a gentleman who was indulging in a little walking exercise past my bedroom door and down the corridor to his own! You and I know that gentleman, my dear Daventry, as a Mr. Morgan Llewellyn. I formed the opinion that it must be a fairly strong motive that lures a man from his bed to promenade the house at night—what do you think, Daventry?"

"Absolutely," said Peter decisively, "I know it would have to be for me."

"We'll proceed then"—Anthony lit a cigarette and tossed his case to Peter. "From other symptoms that very quickly manifested themselves, I concluded that the gentleman in question was seeking something that he had dropped—or left by mistake, possibly—in this room—he was annoyed, you will remember, that he found his entrance barred by Clegg's arrangements. And he was so annoyed that he was indiscreet enough to *express* his annoyance. Of course I ought to mention that there's just one other possibility"—here Anthony glanced slyly at the attentive Daventry—"Mr. Llewellyn *may* have been worried about something that somebody else had left in here." He blew a cloud of smoke from his nostrils. "A lady's handkerchief, for example. What do you say to that—impossible?"

"I suppose it's possible," conceded Peter grudgingly, "I'll grant you that much."

"That's very sporting of you," declared Anthony. "But somehow I don't think that's the true explanation—Miss Lennox, Clegg tells me, was working on her own to recover the lost handkerchief—so I don't think she employed Mr. Llewellyn. Now—listen. I watched our gentleman very carefully when we were all in here this morning—when Stewart sent for him and also afterwards—and I'm pretty confident that he's uneasy about something in this library. From the way in which he used his eyes on this desk—I deduce a document or paper of some kind. I may be wrong, of course. This is where I come to the remark I made when we came in just now. During our absence at Colonel Leach-Fletcher's—Goodall came as well, remember— he may have made hay while the sun shone. But I think not, my dear Daventry, I think not." He crossed to Stewart's bookcase. "You may have noticed more than once in your experience that a man will very often put an important paper handed to him unexpectedly into a receptacle that he has handy at the moment. As I see the facts of the case after Colonel Leach-Fletcher said his 'good-bye' to Laurence Stewart, Stewart returned to the book that he had been reading. The Colonel was good enough to remember its title. It was Renan's *Vie de Jésus*." Anthony stopped and pondered for a minute or two. Peter wondered what was troubling him. Whatever it was, it soon passed. He lifted up the glass front of the bookcase and sought the book he had just mentioned. "A singularly beautiful piece of work, this, Daventry," he declared. "But I expect you've read it." He brought it over to Peter—then held it by the two sides of the cover and fluttered its leaves together quickly. A paper fell on the carpet. Peter's hand, disengaged and therefore at an advantage, beat Anthony's in its descent, by the merest fraction. He ran his eye over it with eager excitement.

"It's a letter," he cried—"from Morgan Llewellyn."

"Really," said Anthony—"and to whom?"

Peter's eyes searched for the information. "To Miss Lennox," he gasped.

"*Voilà!*" murmured Mr. Bathurst.

Chapter XV
MR. DAVENTRY GETS HIS FEET WET

"Read it to me, Daventry," said Anthony. "Upon what precisely does Mr. Llewellyn find time to write to Miss Lennox? For the sake of her '*beaux yeux*'?"

Peter tossed it to him—rather ungraciously let it be said. "Read it yourself, though it seems to me to concern Miss Lennox herself and Miss Lennox only." He pushed his hands into his pockets and strode to the bookcase—where he stood, moodily, with his back to his companion.

"'Dear Incomparable Marjorie'"—read Mr. Bathurst—"'At the risk of punishing myself far too severely to contemplate, by driving the smile from your two wonderful eyes'—Mr. Llewellyn wields a pretty pen, Daventry—you'd better listen to this—'I once again write to you to ask you to reconsider the answer you gave me a little while ago to a very important question. A question that affects me—body and soul. For, dear, peerless Marjorie, monotonous though it may sound to you—I love you! To say that I worship the ground that you walk upon is by no means an exaggeration—judge then how much more I worship *you*! When you are away from me life is most unutterably empty—the sun ceases to shine—the flower to bloom—the bird to sing—everything is bitter emptiness and desperate waste. Marjorie—marry me! I refuse to accept your previous answers as final! And if your guardian endeavours to interfere between us, as you threaten will happen—his blood be upon his own head! I am a desperate man—desperate with love for you, Marjorie—and desperate men have a habit of using desperate remedies. Let me know your answer after dinner to-night, and may that answer bring mad joy to the heart of—Morgan Llewellyn.'" Anthony whistled,

"Dear me, Daventry, do you know I hardly suspected anything quite so ardent as this!" He looked up, and although his tone still contained a hint of raillery, there was at the same time a strong hint of gravity also. But Peter was in no mood for banter and in none too good a temper for serious discussion.

"After all, say what you like," he muttered, "that letter was written to Miss Marjorie Lennox, and it hardly seems decent to me for us to have read it—that's the worst of this investigation business."

"You feel this particular instance rather too acutely, I fear, Daventry," said Anthony gaily, "it touches you on a tender spot." Peter's sole reply was inarticulate—a grunt. Anthony tried a different tack. "I had hoped," he chided gently, "that a rather effective piece of work on my part might have received some measure of congratulation."

Peter swung round—instant with shamefaced apology. "I say, I'm frightfully sorry, Bathurst. It was too bad of me altogether. Really I do congratulate you on a topping shot—forgive my discourtesy—it was inexcusable on my part."

Anthony grinned—pleased nevertheless at the unmistakable sincerity of the compliment. "Thank you—it wasn't too bad a shot—although I candidly admit the actual result has surprised me." He tapped the letter with his forefinger. "At the same time we must realize that this is most important. It explains a good deal that was previously somewhat puzzling. We know now for certain why Miss Lennox was in here with her guardian after the Colonel's departure."

Peter raised his eyebrows. "Why—exactly?"

"To show him this letter! Don't be alarmed—the lady does not eye Llewellyn's suit with any favour. She has threatened him doubtless that if he continued to pester her with his attentions, she would report the whole affair to Stewart. Somewhere about five minutes past ten on the fatal night—she did so."

"What happened after that?" queried Peter, breathlessly.

"That, of course, I can't answer," replied Anthony. "I can only enter and subsequently explore the realm of conjecture. I assume that Stewart found this to be yet another trouble to add to his worries. He was probably incensed at what he would naturally term his secretary's effrontery. I think his interview with his ward was short—he would deal with Mr. Llewellyn in the morning. I imagine also that Miss Lennox left by the French doors and made her way into the garden."

"Why?" demanded Peter quickly.

"That was when I suggest she dropped her handkerchief."

"Of course—I should have remembered."

"We know now," continued Anthony, "the reason underlying her accusation of Llewellyn. Which you observe was a merely *general-indefinite* sort of accusation. She wouldn't give a definite reason for it—she kept silent about his attitude towards her—even to denying that she had been in this room."

"But why did she do that?" questioned Peter again.

Anthony shrugged his shoulders. "Most women are different about their love affairs in matters of this kind—after all Llewellyn found her attractive—she would probably forgive him that much more quickly than indifference—for instance. All women like to be liked—you know!"

"I don't think Miss Lennox is a girl of that type," asserted Peter vigorously. "I think she has proved that by—"

"Of course you don't," chaffed Anthony. "But whether you do or you don't is of no consequence—take it from me."

Peter relapsed into a chair. It was gradually being driven home to him that he was not showing himself to the best advantage this afternoon. "What are you going to do now?" he asked. Anthony carefully put the letter into his breast pocket.

"This certainly places Llewellyn in an unfavourable light," he remarked. "He threatens the dead man—he's Welsh, too—and has struck me throughout as a man who might make a dangerous enemy—still"—he pointed to the desk at the side of which Peter had seated himself. "Give me that bowl of ink," he commanded. Peter obeyed—wondering again. Anthony held it up to the light. "Remember what Goodall said when he looked at this?"

"Yes," said Peter. "Something about understanding what you meant."

"Quite right—though I'm not absolutely sure that friend Goodall really did." He glanced quickly round the room as though in search of something—"hand me that glass, will you, Daventry?" Holding the glass in his left hand, he carefully poured the ink from the bowl into it—very slowly—almost as though measuring it drop by drop. At last the bowl appeared empty—of ink. He handed it back to Peter. *"The other tiny stone* I mentioned a little time ago—see it at the bottom there—I knew it was there—I could hear it the first time I shook up the ink!"

Peter gazed into the ink-bowl with a feeling that he had gone back to school once more and was being confronted again with mathematical mysteries that he had never been too successful in solving. "A similar stone, Daventry, to those we found in the coal-scuttle."

The use of the plural pronoun stimulated Peter immensely. "Yes—yes, of course," he contributed.

Anthony continued with the expression of his theory. "The murderer cleared the table to the best of his ability—but he—(or she)—forgot the ink. And as it happened he had dropped some dirt *into the bowl where the ink was."*

Peter's wonderment increased. "Really, I don't altogether follow you," he declared. "What did he do to make the table dirty—I don't know?"

Anthony poured the ink back into the bowl—after carefully removing the tell-tale stone. "I'll retrace my steps then a trifle," he remarked. "First of all, I am fairly confident that this murder was not a premeditated one. It was deliberate and brutal, but as I read the case, something unexpected happened that forced the murderer into what he considered was an impossible situation and one that called for the murder of Stewart—*quickly.*"

"You mean that Stewart fired at him and he killed Stewart in a sort of self-defence?"

Anthony thought over that for a moment—then shook his head. "No—not that exactly—Stewart was murdered treacherously—as he sat there," he pointed to the seat by the desk—"killed from behind—but I think you're right in your assumption that Stewart fired at him—we'll look into that question in a moment."

"How do you mean, then, that the murderer was *forced* into killing Stewart?"

"Dead men tell no tales," replied Anthony gravely.

Peter nodded. "I see what you mean. But I'll tell you something that I can't quite get the hang of!"

"I'm listening," said Anthony. "Fire away."

"Well, it's like this—all the way through the case—the tendency has been for all of you to take the view that somebody in the house was implicated—everything seems to me to point in that direction! Well"—he stopped for a moment at a loss for words. Anthony said nothing, but waited interestedly for him to continue. Bathurst's attention, and silent attention at that, gave Peter encouragement. "Well—if that's so—what made Stewart fire his revolver—as you suggest he did?—it seems to me he would hardly fire a shot at somebody whom he *knew*—somebody with whom he was familiar!"

Anthony considered his statement very carefully. "Supposing he suddenly found that particular somebody acting dishonestly or treacherously towards him—mightn't he fire then—what do you think?"

"I don't think he would even then," contended Peter, "unless they attacked him, of course!"

"H'm," muttered Anthony, "I'm inclined to appreciate your point, Daventry—you've given me something to think over."

He paced up and down the room turning over this new aspect of the case that had just been presented to him. Suddenly he turned quickly. "We'll look into that point a bit later on, Daventry—in the meantime, I want you to accompany me—I'm going to look for something else—come along." He opened the French doors and stepped out—Peter immediately following him. A moment's walk brought them to the rockery garden. The fountain, continually throwing up its sparkling cascade, to fall in widening ripples into the water of the pool that surrounded it, brought a delicious touch of coolness to the warmth of the June afternoon. The rock garden had been built all around it—the pieces of crazy paving, with the green blades of grass peeping inquisitively between them—lying around it on all sides and in all shapes and sizes. Bathurst's eyes took it all in quickly and alertly. The larger pieces formed the floor of the rockery, the smaller pieces having doubtless been selected for building and banking up the sides. Anthony scrambled to the top and stood there for a second or two—astraddle almost—one foot poised on the top—the other on a pointed stone a trifle lower down. He called to Peter Daventry. "Come up here a minute, Daventry—will you?" Peter scrambled up behind him. Anthony pointed to the spaces between the pieces of stone and rock. "Look in there," he said. Peter looked! "See those little brown stones? Seen anything like them before?"

"Of course—from Stewart's table—in the coal-scuttle."

They stepped down. "That's right, Daventry—that's where you saw them—and I've one in my pocket as well—that I took from the ink-bowl." He started to walk round the rockery—his eyes searching everywhere—keenly alert but apparently anxious as well. "I can do with half a dozen of these pieces of paving," he called over his shoulder to Peter. "Half a dozen of the smaller pieces—the size that I could pick up pretty comfortably—get them for me, will you—you'll probably find the kind I want round the top of the garden." Peter made his second undignified scramble to the summit of the rockery. He quickly collected a few and tossed them one by one down to Anthony below. He watched the latter pick them up and in turn examine them with the greatest care. Peter noticed that he paid particular attention to the underneath part of each piece that he looked at. Then he shook his head doubtfully as though dissatisfied with the turn that events were taking. Picking the rocky pieces up again, he subjected them to a further examination. "You command the back of the house from where you're standing, Daventry—or at any rate part of it—is there anybody about?"

Peter looked across—and then back over the stretch of grass that ran to the doors of the library, and saw no one. "Not a soul," he called with cheerful assurance.

"Good man," said Anthony, "I'm rather keen that we shouldn't be observed at this particular moment." Then an idea seemed to strike him suddenly. With his eyes on the path of the rock garden he began to walk around—keeping the fountain in the centre. He had almost completed the entire circle when he came to an abrupt stop. "Quick, Daventry—come down here." Peter picked his way down. "Look at the side of this path—the side nearest the pool—does anything suggest itself to you?"

Peter adjusted his thinking-cap. He gazed carefully at the side that Anthony indicated—there was a slight declivity where the path made its natural shelving towards the pool. The meaning of what he saw was instantaneously obvious to the most elementary powers of observation. There was the impression of a stone—but there was no stone near anything like the shape delineated in the soft soil. Anthony rubbed his hands. Peter knew the gesture to signify pleasure and success.

"I see what you mean," said the latter, "there's a piece of paving missing!"

Anthony looked all round. Then came to a decision. "Daventry," he said, "I'm going to ask you to do me a favour. Somewhere in that pool lies the missing stone—you know its shape." He bent down and inspected the impression at the side of the path. "It's roughly the shape of a magnum of champagne—about fourteen inches in length and at its widest part—the part corresponding to the bottom of the bottle—about half that size."

"What do you want me to do?" inquired Peter.

Anthony grinned. "I want you to go paddling."

Peter looked into the water. "Not deep," he remarked. He pulled off his shoes and socks, hitched up his trousers, and waded in.

"Don't move round too quickly," called Anthony. "It won't be healthy for bare toes when you do find it."

Peter trudged round treading the mud at the bottom with the utmost respect. Step by step he circled the water-pool—then suddenly Bathurst saw him bend down. When he straightened himself he held a longish piece of stone just as had been described to him. One end resembled the neck of a bottle and it broadened out towards its other end to a width of about seven inches. This end had sharp jagged edges. Anthony took it from Peter's outstretched hand.

"As I thought, Daventry," he declared, as Peter made the path again, "a short time ago this piece of stone formed part of the path that we are now standing upon—you know what it is of course?"

Peter replied very promptly. "I've a very shrewd idea," he declared. "I'm just beginning to see daylight—your theory is that that piece of jagged stone—"

"Was used to kill Laurence Stewart," said Anthony, "and then thrown into that pool—and it's more than a theory—it's a fact."

Chapter XVI
MR. BATHURST AGAIN SAMPLES THE BOOKCASE

PETER WHISTLED. "You seem pretty sure of it. But all the same—"

Anthony interrupted him a trifle impatiently. "Those little mud pellets and small stones told me an unmistakable story. It seemed to me a most important factor in the case—remember no weapon was found near the body. It was obvious that Stewart had been struck from behind—I immediately deduced a sharp and heavy piece of stone. But if it hadn't been for the proximity of the ink-bowl to the dead man's head, the true significance would probably have escaped me. For the wound on the head was clean—I inquired of the doctor through Goodall. The murderer held the piece of stone by the neck-end—soil side uppermost—and struck Stewart with the comparatively clean part, and the force of the blows caused the small stones underneath (as they lay originally) to be dislodged." He held out the weapon to Daventry. "Of course the water in the pool has cleaned it, but I daresay a thorough and scientific examination may yield us some little evidences to support my theory. Time will tell—we'll take it back to the library and hand it over to Goodall upon his return from London, as a souvenir." He turned to Peter. "But not a word till I say when."

Back in the library, Anthony got to work again very quickly. "Stay here a moment, Daventry," he said, "while I have a word with young Stewart—I won't keep you waiting long—put this in a safe place"—he handed over the recent discovery. A matter of ten minutes saw him back, and then Peter was destined to receive yet another surprise. "Get that revolver of yours, will you, Daventry—I told you to bring one down here with you, didn't I?"

"It's upstairs in my bedroom—I shall have to go to get it."

"Do—and load it—in all six chambers—I suppose you haven't brought any 'blanks'?"

Peter shook his head. "Sorry—I haven't!"

"H'm," muttered Anthony, "never mind. We shall have to take care—that's all!"

It was the work of a few moments that brought Peter back to the library with his revolver.

"Now listen," directed Anthony, "I want you to fire two separate shots—you'll have to fire of course out into the garden—fire in the direction of the fountain, for instance—that will do—make sure there's nobody about—stand in the centre of the room when you fire."

He walked to the library door.

"Where are you going?" questioned Peter. "Aren't you going to stop to enjoy the performance?"

"I'm going to shut this door, which I want you to *keep* shut—then I'm going upstairs to my own bedroom—look at your watch—in five minutes' time fire one shot—then wait till you hear from me—clear on everything?"

"Right-o," murmured Peter. "I understand perfectly."

Anthony closed the door. Peter watched the hand of his watch travel the five appointed minutes. Then he walked to the French doors and opened them. The coast was clear—the walk to the rockery entirely deserted. He returned to the centre of the room as he had been directed and pulled the trigger. Then he grinned to himself. "Expect the inhabitants of Assynton Lodge that hear that will be scared stiff unless old Bathurst tipped them the bright idea just now." The door opened behind him.

"Well?" said Bathurst.

"Well?" said Peter.

"I lay on my bed just as I should if I were there in the ordinary way, and although I was *listening*, old son, *I never heard a sound.*" His face showed obvious signs of pleasure.

"What makes you so pleased about that?" queried Peter.

"What makes me pleased?" echoed Anthony. "Why, it fits in with my theory beautifully—that's what pleases me. Now I'm going again—wait another five minutes and then fire a second shot exactly similar to the previous one."

He slipped out again noiselessly. Peter waited patiently for the second spell of five minutes to pass. Taking care again that all was in order in the garden, he walked back to the centre of the library as before and for the second time discharged his revolver. "Where did that one go to?" he murmured reminiscently—then sat on the table till the arrival of Bathurst.

"Just the same as before," announced the latter. "I took the liberty of using Charles Stewart's bedroom for that little experiment—it's on the floor below ours, you know—I asked him if I might just now—and once again, Daventry, *I heard nothing at all.*" He thrust his hands into his pockets and walked to the bookcase. "That experiment that we have just conducted," he continued, "proves to me conclusively that the shot that we know had *at some time* been fired from Stewart's revolver *had been fired by him on the night of the murder*, but why—why?" He paced backwards and forwards three or four times.

"Perhaps the shot was fired by the murderer after Stewart was dead," volunteered Peter.

"Why?" demanded Anthony immediately. "Why should the murderer fire a shot that for all he knew might awaken the whole house?"

"Well—as a blind," supplemented Peter somewhat feebly.

"Don't think so—it doesn't fit," said Anthony, in summary dismissal of the theory. "The shot is fired," reflected Anthony, "by Stewart, who has—according to his dress at the moment—come down to the library from his bedroom in a hurry—why does he fire—he doesn't seem to have been attacked *then*, but afterwards—as you said earlier, the treachery and the attack appear to come from inside his own ménage and yet he *fires*—why?" His eyes wandered round the room—intent and purposeful. "Also, my dear Daventry, if he fires, as I'm out to assert that he *did*—where's the bullet—eh—tell me that?" He stood with his left hand caressing his chin. "Supposing he didn't know—supposing he wasn't sure—that's certainly an idea—that would account for the pocketing of his revolver *subsequently*—a feeling of safety—of security that came to him—false as it eventually turned out to be—but yet conveyed to him temporarily by the conditions." He came across to Peter full of this latest piece of theorizing. "Look here, Daventry—let's remember what Colonel Leach-Fletcher told us. He was Stewart's friend—his evidence should be reliable. He was insistent that Stewart was worried about something that was going on in his house. The word that Stewart used, according to the Colonel, imputed *treachery* on the part of somebody here! Now do you remember what the Colonel went on to say? He stated that in his opinion Stewart had come to a decision 'to take the bull by the horns' in an attempt to put a stop to whatever was happening. Remember that?"

Peter agreed. "Yes."

"Well now," continued Anthony, "let's assume that Stewart was thoroughly on the *qui vive* that night, and succeeded in identifying this disturber of his peace. He comes hurriedly downstairs—armed—ready to defend himself if necessary—prepared to see the thing through to the bitter end—as he comes down"—he swung round on to Peter in violent enthusiasm—"I deserve to be kicked, Daventry, I've been painfully slow to appreciate what actually happened—but I think I'm clear now. Go and stand at the door, will you—just where you would be if you had just opened it and entered." Peter stared wonderingly but obeyed him. Anthony went to the side of the bookcase and faced the opening door.

"This is where the murderer stood," he declared gravely, "when Stewart opened the door. He came here from that chair." He indicated the chair by the desk—the chair in which the dead man had been discovered.

"How do you know that?" demanded Peter. "Never mind for the time being—but if you look carefully at where I'm standing—you'll be able to see for yourself." Peter looked—but saw nothing to solve his own difficulty. He shook his head, as though to give point to his failure to grasp Anthony's idea. The next words the latter spoke rather startled him. "Stewart stood where you are standing and fired in the direction of where I am standing—then something happened that caused him to put his revolver back in the pocket of his dressing-gown—the left-hand pocket, remember—and to take a rather changed view of the situation in which he found himself."

"What was that?" demanded Peter.

"He recognized the interloper—the interloper who afterwards murdered him."

"Why then," countered Peter instantly, "didn't he recognize him at first—before he fired the shot? You either know or don't know a person—it isn't as though Stewart fired from a distance—you say yourself that he fired from the doorway only a few feet away—when he entered the room—the fact that he *did* fire in that way seems to me to show conclusively that he *didn't* know the person—that he fired at a stranger. You don't blaze away with a revolver at anybody you happen to see—regardless of consequences." He lit a cigarette with the air of a man that defies contradiction.

"An excellent piece of reasoning on your part," smiled Anthony, "but there's one little possibility that I fear you may have been tempted to overlook."

"What's that?" retorted Peter.

"I'm not blaming you, my dear chap. I overlooked it myself in the first place; *supposing the conditions changed.*"

Peter wrinkled his brow. "Conditions," he said, in a puzzled kind of way, "what conditions do you mean?"

"The conditions of the room!" Anthony watched Peter's mystified expression. "As I said just now, Daventry, I was slow myself to pick up the crucial point. When Stewart fired his shot—he fired *in the dark*. When the intruder disclosed his identity, Stewart put his revolver away—he felt safe. So safe that he put it away in his left-hand pocket—a right-handed man doesn't do that if he wants to use it again. And unhappily, events proved that his faith in the situation brought about his death—that was why I told you to look where I was standing."

He pointed to the wall to the right of the bookcase directly facing the doorway. Peter's eyes followed the direction of his finger.

"The electric light switch?" he queried.

"That's what I think," exclaimed Anthony. "It seems to me that whoever was in here heard Stewart coming down from his bedroom and just had time to get over there and switch off the light. Stewart probably challenged from the doorway, and either at some movement on the part of the intruder or out of intense anxiety—he had been worrying, you know—he fired. Then I suggest that the burglar disclosed his identity deliberately to safeguard his own skin or that something happened that caused Stewart to discover it. That's the reason, Daventry, why I say that we ought to find a bullet somewhere in here."

Peter grunted. "Might be in the burglar's body for all you know!"

"A thousand to one against that," returned Anthony, as he came to the middle of the room. "It should be somewhere in the vicinity of that electric light switch," he asserted. "The intruder would be standing there when Stewart fired."

But the wall was untouched—not a vestige of a scratch upon it anywhere. His eyes travelled to the bookcase. "What about the bookcase, Daventry?"

"It's sectional," replied Peter, "and every section is protected by a glass shutter—no bullet can possibly have touched any of them—look for yourself—they're all sound." He motioned towards them with his hand.

"Quite true," said Anthony. "Then where the devil"—he paused for a second; "supposing one of the glass fronts was up—eh—what then?"

"Then the bullet would hit the back of one of the books, of course."

"Supposing there were blank spaces—where books were missing from their places on the shelves?"

Peter scratched his chin. "Then the bullet would go through the back of the bookcase—but it's tremendous odds on a shot fired like this one was finding such a space as you describe—it would border on the miraculous."

Anthony nodded in acquiescence. "I agree." Then he broke out again. "Damn it all, Daventry, I'm certain I'm right in my conclusion—that bullet must be somewhere about. Take down the books on the top shelves—that's the nearest height, I should say, to where Stewart would have fired—and start with the top shelf nearest to the switch."

Peter somewhat reluctantly moved about three dozen volumes, tossing each one on to the floor as he did so. The woodwork at the back of the shelf was clean and unimpaired— no bullet had torn its destructive way through there. "Nothing here," he declared over his shoulder to Anthony. But the latter was studying the books that Peter had just moved. One in particular seemed to be affording him particular interest. It was the thickest and bulkiest of them all.

"Come here, Daventry, will you?" said Anthony. Peter strolled across. Anthony pointed to a hole neatly drilled in the back of the cover. He opened the book at a page near the beginning. "There's our bullet—embedded in this book. The thickness of the paper and the size of the book—848 pages to be exact— were sufficient to arrest its further progress—it was the only possible solution that remained to us."

Peter Daventry gasped! "By Jove," he muttered, "who'd have thought it?"

"Also, my dear Daventry," remarked Mr. Bathurst, "let me call your attention to the title—'The Memoirs of René de St. Maure—one-time Page to Mary Stuart.' Altogether a most fascinating work, I should imagine."

CHAPTER XVII

THE MEMOIRS OF RÉNÉ DE ST. MAURE

ANTHONY TOOK out his pocket-knife and carefully extracted the bullet from its paper bed. "I think that Goodall will have little difficulty in fitting this to Stewart's own revolver," he declared. He turned to Peter. "It's easier to piece the affair together now. When the burglar—the murderer if you prefer to call him so—cut across the room to put out the light he was holding this book in his hand—*so.*" He placed the fingers of his left hand on the switch and held the book in his right—with the back of the cover facing the door." Peter nodded—the scene was now becoming plainer to him, and its visualization most intriguing. "Stewart entered in the dark as I told you—and challenged the person he knew was facing him. At first he got no reply, but the intruder *attempted to replace the book on its shelf in the book-case at his side*—he was familiar with its location because he had replaced it *on many occasions before.* Stewart detected the movement and instantly fired *in the direction of the sound.* Then the gentleman concerned so closely with historical research considered his safest plan was to disclose his identity—it might save his life for one thing. You know the result!"

"Wonderful—Bathurst!" said Peter. "I can see the whole thing as you depict it—there isn't a weak link in your chain."

Anthony flushed with pleasure. "A closer study of M. Réné will, I think, more than repay us for any little trouble we have taken"—he tapped the cover of the book playfully.

"I've been thinking, Bathurst," said Peter, "if this book is so important, if, for example, it holds the key to the entire mystery, why on earth did the murderer leave it behind—especially as it held the tell-tale evidence of the bullet?"

"There may be several answers to that question. The right one may be difficult to name. When the revolver was fired the book was sent spinning from the murderer's hand! Possibly Stewart himself replaced it on the shelf in the bookcase. Also—after the murder, the paramount question was to get away, remember!" He opened the book and examined it with some care. "There's one thing, Daventry, if this book has been in constant use recently, and I'm convinced it has—there shouldn't be too much difficulty in discovering the particular page or pages that have been pored over so many times so very assiduously. Remarkable how the Stuart connection keeps cropping up, isn't it?"

"I'd like to know what we're on the track of," interjected Peter. "It's a positive strain to keep on wondering like we do—or like *I* do—to be properly precise."

Anthony smiled at him. "Include me, Daventry—for the time being at least." He walked to the chair by the desk and sat down. "The question of 'how long' depends on what success I have with the estimable de St. Maure—let's have a preliminary look."

Peter went to his side and sprawled on the table—his elbows supporting his head. It was a ponderous and bulky book, and the ravages made by the passage of the bullet only served to make its examination more awkward.

"M. René was blessed with an unusually prodigal fund of reminiscence," remarked Mr. Bathurst—"what has he handed down in the pages of this dainty little treatise that has turned men's minds to murder—I wonder?" He turned to Peter. "I'm going to try a little experiment—yet another one."

Peter still watched him with interest. He inserted the forefinger of each hand at the back of the book—between the binding and the massed pages—the left finger holding the top and the right the bottom. The book, of course, hung down loosely—the pages swinging a trifle and presenting openings in three or four places. "Put a thin slip of paper where you see the pages separating," said Anthony, "a book invariably opens at the places where it has been well used. See that they hold, Daventry." When the book was turned over, the first two marked places yielded nothing that seemed to have the slightest bearing on their quest. At the third, Anthony let go a whoop of triumph. Peter bent over him and read the printed matter with avidity. The passage that was pointed out to him read as follows: "Now in these days the knowledge came to my Queen-Mistress that her Cause had been betrayed, and that nothing short of a miracle from High Heaven could succour it. Whereupon there was much secret to-do and conniving amongst her chief adherents. I happened more times than once to find the Queen in her Seton's arms or whispering to Mary Fleming. At four o'clock of the tenth day of the six month the Queen-Mistress sent for Thibaut Girardier—he that had been her Chief Armourer since she left my beloved country—and it was bruited abroad in the household both that night and during the days that followed that much wealth had been very secretly disposed of in many secret places of Wild Scotland. Messengers that carried her full faith and trust were employed and despatched to many of these secret spots. But Girardier was summoned so it was whispered by them that should have known, in the matter of the Cardinal's great gift—'the Black Twenty-Two.' I know not, for it was never my practice to seek out or spy, what handiwork it was that he did. Sufficient be it to say that he made the Queen-Mistress two screens—one of Tapestrie and one of some specimen of beaten metal—and they twain shall tell the generations that are to come all that is deemed necessary of the 'Black Twenty-Two.' But the riddle of this message cannot be read from one of the twain alone. Thibaut had special audience of the Queen for many of these days."

"Well?" inquired Anthony—"and what do you make of all that?"

"Dashed if I know," replied Peter. "Who is this St. Maure Johnny anyway, and what is it that he's gassing about?"

Anthony pointed to the title page again. "'One-time Page to Mary Stuart,'" he quoted; "I presume he escaped from the wreck of that lady's fortunes and lived to a ripe old age to inflict these memories on us."

"What the hell does he mean by the 'Black Twenty-Two'?" questioned Peter irreverently.

Anthony shook his head. "I can't answer that, Daventry—my history's too rusty altogether. I shall have to undertake a little research on my own before I can properly tell you that—but at any rate, I promise you, it sha'n't be long." He rubbed his hands. "Make a copy of that for me, will you—and then we'll put the message back on the bookshelf. It won't be the first time that that particular piece has been copied."

Peter set to work on his task.

"When Goodall comes back," continued Anthony, "we shall have several little things to show him. Daventry, I owe you an eternal debt of gratitude. I wouldn't have missed this case for worlds—this time next week I shall be bored stiff—I shall have nothing exciting to occupy my mind."

Peter stared. "What exactly do you mean—what about this affair—aren't you going to stick to it and see it out?"

"Of course," responded Anthony, "but it will be all over by then—because in about three days at the most, I shall have much pleasure in the performance of three duties. Firstly, I shall introduce the police to the murderer of Mason the night-watchman—secondly, I shall introduce the police and you yourself to the murderer of Laurence P. Stewart, and thirdly, I have high hopes of reading to a distinguished audience *the secret of the screens*."

Peter handed him the copy for which he had asked. Words failed him. But he permitted himself one exclamation—unhappily it was not altogether free from profanity. A little failing of Mr. Daventry!

CHAPTER XVIII
THE ROOM AT BLANCHARD'S HOTEL

OUTSIDE the library Anthony ran into Charles Stewart. "With your permission, Mr. Stewart," he said, "I should like to run up to town this evening on an urgent matter. I've just telephoned Goodall and made arrangements to see him this side of nine o'clock to-night." Stewart lifted his eyebrows.

"Any startling discoveries, Mr. Bathurst?"

"Not exactly startling—but I want to look into one or two things that have suggested themselves to me, at the London end of the tangle—I'm sure you understand."

Stewart bowed. "I presume you are accompanying Mr. Bathurst, Mr. Daventry—I had hoped that we could have—"

Before Peter could frame an affirmative reply, Anthony had spoken for him. "Mr. Daventry will be remaining here until I return," he intervened.

Stewart's face showed a certain amount of surprise, but he accepted Anthony's statement without demur.

"I'll get Llewellyn to look up a train for you, Bathurst, and get one of the cars ordered for you."

Anthony thanked him and turned away. "I'm afraid he's a trifle disappointed in your choice of me as an investigator," he murmured to Peter, "but perhaps in a few days I shall be able to rehabilitate myself in his good graces—or perhaps not—you never know, do you, Daventry?"

"I'm rather hipped at having to stay behind," responded the latter.

Anthony caught his arm lightly and spoke in a low-toned voice. "You're staying behind on special service. You're on guard—and you must watch everybody without them having the ghost of an idea that you *are* watching them. Particularly you must see that *nobody leaves this house on a journey to London without you follow him or her*. If that does occur, let me know at once—understand?"

"Where shall I find you?"

"Telephone Goodall at the 'Yard'—he'll put you in touch with me."

Peter nodded with understanding. Then an idea came to him. "You say 'a journey to London.' Why London? Supposing I find somebody leaving for Stow-on-the-Wold? Or Husband's Bosworth?" He grinned in appreciation of his poser.

Anthony stood still a moment and thought. "Everybody here must be watched by *you*," he declared. "If anyone tries to leave here you must follow him and get the news through to me at once. You'll find the destination will be London, though, should the contingency occur. It's what the racing fraternity describe as a 'stone-ginger.'"

Peter indulged in a burlesque salute. "Very good, Sergeant. I'm your man!"

Anthony shook him by the hand. "I know I can rely on you implicitly, Daventry—that's why I feel safe in leaving you here—if you weren't here I couldn't undertake this journey to town, I don't mind telling you that. I want to see Goodall, I want to put in a quiet hour or two at the British Museum, and I also desire to have a look at the hotel in Clifford Street. When you see me again I have high hopes that my case will be complete—good-bye, old chap."

"Shall I come down to the station with you?" asked Peter.

"Better not, I think, in the circumstances—I shall feel easier in my mind to think that you will be here on the spot all the time. What I'm relying on you to prevent is the one thing that might cause my plans to miscarry. I'll tell you one more thing that will make you realize how important your job is." He bent forward and whispered in Peter's ear. "The key to the secret is still in Assynton Lodge—I want it to stay there—get me?"

Peter's expression grew serious, although he felt more reconciled to staying behind now that he had a job of work to do. He whistled—the situation was a little clearer to him and more attractive of acceptance. He watched Anthony's car purr down the drive, turn the corner and go over the crest of the hill. And he wondered when he would welcome him back.

Arrived at Paddington, Anthony entered a public telephone box and was connected with Goodall.

"Wasn't sure that I should catch you, Inspector," he opened. "I'm speaking from Paddington—I've come up myself you see—close on your heels too! What's that? No—not exactly—what I wanted to know was this. Have you had time to go over to Blanchard's Hotel yet? To-night? Good man—I'll come with you—if you don't mind—I'll meet you in Clifford Street at nine o'clock. Right-o—I'll have a little light refreshment and come round." Punctually to the time arranged he turned the corner of Clifford Street from New Bond Street, to walk into the arms almost of Detective-Inspector Goodall and a plain clothes officer. The Inspector greeted him cordially.

"Good evening, Mr. Bathurst—I've been engaged on following up a clue in connection with these two Stewarts from America—that's why I've left this job round here till now."

"Any luck, Inspector?"

"Not up to the moment, Mr. Bathurst. They seem to have walked out of this hotel and been swallowed up—but I'll get 'em—you can rest assured on that. When I got back to the 'Yard' this afternoon, I was sent hot-foot to a house in Wimbledon where they were supposed to be—not a doubt about it, I was informed! That's the worst of our game, Mr. Bathurst—we have to listen to all sorts of information that can't be tested till *we* test it. And it often means the waste of valuable time." He clicked his tongue in emphasis of his dissatisfaction. "But I'll comb 'em out—if it takes me six months—the teeth of my comb will pick 'em up somewhere—Scotland Yard may be slow but it's sure—and remarkably patient. Here we are, Mr. Bathurst—they're expecting me here."

The reception clerk telephoned news of their arrival.

"Mr. Blanchard says will you please go up to his private room. Atkins! Show these gentlemen up to the governor's room, will you?"

Atkins, a uniformed attendant, quickly piloted them to the proper quarters.

"Come in, Inspector! Good evening, gentlemen. I've been expecting you ever since your telephone inquiry of this morning."

Blanchard was a fair, stout man, somewhere, at a glance, in the early fifties. His eyelashes and eyebrows were so fair as to be almost invisible—giving his eyes a strange protruding tendency. He had a nervous habit of throwing his eyes down to the floor, immediately after he addressed a remark to anybody, which gave him a bird-like appearance.

"Sit down, gentlemen." He waved a pudgy hand—much be-ringed—towards an arm-chair and a comfortable looking settee. Anthony selected the former.

"This gentleman is Mr. Bathurst—he is acting for Mr. Charles Stewart, of Assynton Lodge, Berkshire. Doubtless you have heard of the tragedy that has taken place down there?" The Inspector made the introduction.

"I read of it in this evening's paper, Inspector," replied Blanchard. He looked at Anthony. "Good evening, sir. I'm sorry that we haven't met under more pleasant circumstances. Now, Inspector, what is it you want of me?"

Inspector Goodall leaned forward in his chair and fixed his eyes intently on Blanchard. The latter fluttered his lids and became more ornithological than ever.

"You will remember, I think," commenced Goodall, "that my inquiries this morning elicited the fact that a lady and gentleman stopping here, under the names of Mr. and Mrs. Laurence Charles Stewart, received a telephone call late on Wednesday evening. The call was answered in all probability by the man." Blanchard intervened. "Quite correct, Inspector! I was downstairs at the time when the 'phone rang. Mr. Stewart went into the smoke-room to answer it."

"Good," rapped Goodall. "What happened after that?"

"Directly afterwards, Mr. Stewart came to me and asked for his bill. He said that he had just received bad news concerning a near relation. Serious illness of some kind—they would have to leave at once. They paid the bill and went off at once."

"H'm," said Goodall. "Now a few questions, Mr. Blanchard. I may as well tell you that this pair that we've been discussing are strongly suspected in connection with the Hanover Galleries murder, so I'll trouble you to be as careful and explicit in answering as possible."

Blanchard's fat face paled. Such things were not good advertisements for his hotel!

"Count on me, Inspector," he fluttered. "Ask me your questions!"

"How long had they been stopping here?" Blanchard picked up the receiver and pressed a button. "That you, Miss Fortescue? Bring me up the reception register, at once, please. Ask Atkins to stand by till you get back!" Blanchard opened the register; ran his finger down two or three pages—then looked up. "Here you are, Inspector—came in on the 28th May—the last Saturday of the month." He pushed the book across to Goodall.

"From New York, I see," said the Inspector. "Did they strike you as being American?"

Blanchard nodded. "Yes, I should have put them down as American anywhere had I been asked—not knowing!"

"How did he pay you when he left that night?"

"Let me think—the bill was a little over fourteen pounds, I remember—he gave me the exact money in Treasury notes and silver!"

"A man between thirty and forty, you say—and wife about the same—anything distinctive about either of them?"

Blanchard hesitated. "Possibly some of my chaps here could answer that more satisfactorily than I can. I can't say that I noticed anything."

"How many rooms did they have?"

"Only one—their bedroom—they took all the meals that they had here in the hotel dining-room."

"Can you remember any letters coming here for them?"

"I couldn't answer that either—my clerk downstairs might be able to remember."

Blanchard's fat fingers stroked his cheek as he answered. Then he continued quickly. "There's one thing I am in a position to tell you—they were out of the hotel a good deal during the day—I do know that."

The Inspector nodded. "Sight-seeing, I suppose—eh?"

"That's what I thought myself," responded Blanchard.

"Pardon me," interposed Anthony, "when Mr. and Mrs. Stewart, to grant them temporarily the name they gave themselves, left here in a hurry—do you happen to remember if they went by taxi?"

"Atkins might know—would you care to ask him?"

"Thank you," replied Anthony.

Blanchard repeated his previous business with the telephone and in ready response the porter arrived.

"You remember Mr. and Mrs. Stewart, Atkins, the lady and gentleman that left in such an almighty hurry on Wednesday night?"

"Yes, sir—very well, sir—I was on duty down below, sir, when they went out."

"Very well, then—you'll be able to answer what this gentleman wishes to know—did you call a taxi for them?"

Atkins shook his head. "No, sir! They went on foot—each of 'em carrying a suitcase."

"Another piece of bad luck," muttered Goodall to Anthony. "We always seem to run up against a brick wall!"

Anthony plied the porter with another question. "Any special points about either of them, Atkins, during their stay here?"

The porter's shrewd face wrinkled in thought. "Well, sir," he said, after a few seconds' consideration, "you mightn't call it a *special* point—and there again, you *might*, but I did spot something you might call peculiar on the part of the lady—Mrs. Stewart as we called her."

"Let's hear it," exclaimed Anthony—"little things count in cases of this description. Try to remember carefully."

Atkins rubbed his fingers across his nose. "Well, sir—it was like this 'ere. I happened to be on duty in the 'foyer' when Mr. and Mrs. Stewart first arrived. And I noticed that Mrs. Stewart was able to tell the time from the clock that hangs right at the other end of the vestibule. I remember 'er saying to 'im—'Look—we're late—it's nearly half-past six.' Now, you can take it from me, sir, a woman's got to 'ave blinkin' good sight to see the time that distance—you 'ave a look yourself, sir, when you go out."

"I will," said Anthony encouragingly. "Go on, Atkins."

"Well, sir, two days after that little incident and almost what you might call regular ever since—Mrs. Stewart went about wearing black glasses—in fact, she was wearing 'em when 'er husband was in the smoke-room answering that telephone call that caused 'em to skip out so quick."

"How do you know that?" rapped Goodall. Atkins turned to him and answered him—unperturbed and unabashed. "I was in there, sir, when Mr. Stewart came in and his wife followed on be'ind. They 'ad the call put through from downstairs. A gent sent for me to 'ave a word with me about getting his luggage orf—that's 'ow I came to be in there."

"This gets better and better," declared Anthony. "Did you happen by any chance to overhear any of the Stewarts' conversation?"

Atkins rubbed his nose again—possibly as an incentive to remembrance. "Nothing to speak of, sir—but I heard the lady say something about her father."

Anthony interrupted him promptly. "What do you mean, Atkins—did she say 'my father' or 'her father'—you appreciate the difference, don't you?" Atkins regarded him with an air of pained surprise. "The words she used, sir, were 'my father'! I took it as 'ow she was alludin' to 'er own male parent."

"Thank you, Atkins." He discovered the exact position of the palm of the porter's right hand. "You've been a great help to me."

"Thank you, sir. It's been a real pleasure." Inspector Goodall chewed the end of his cigarette. "Some relation of the murdered man, Mr. Bathurst, without a doubt. Fits in with my own theory, too—born the wrong side of the blanket perhaps over in the States somewhere—used the black glasses as a disguise. Worked the two jobs I shouldn't wonder, in a way that we can't quite fathom at the moment—there's a missing link somewhere. Also—where does Mr. *Charles* Stewart come in?"—he leaned right across in Anthony's direction—"supposing it affects his inheritance—eh?"

Anthony waved his hand and harked back to the proprietor of Blanchard's hotel. "Mr. Blanchard—would you be good enough to turn up Mr. and Mrs. Stewart's account—the one they settled when they went?"

"I'll go down and get it for you," said Blanchard. "A matter of a few moments only."

"After he's brought you that," interjected the Inspector, "we'll go and have a look at the room they occupied."

Blanchard was as good as his word. "I have what you asked for, sir! What was it in particular you wanted?"

"Refer to the last day of their stay here, will you, Mr. Blanchard—did they lunch here?"

Blanchard's eyes travelled down the columns of the account. Then he shook his head. "No, sir, apparently they did not—it must have been one of the days when they were out—one of the days I mentioned!"

Anthony looked across at Goodall. The latter smiled. "Testing Mr. Daventry's theory, aren't you—and it holds good—eh?"

"What about that bedroom, Goodall?"

"Just what I was thinking," said the latter, rising from his seat. "Mr. Blanchard, we should like to have a look at the bedroom that Mr. and Mrs. Stewart occupied while they were staying here—I hope no newcomer is in it."

Blanchard was all attention. "Nobody at all, Inspector. The room is as they left it—except that the chambermaid may have tidied it up."

"That's what I was afraid of," groaned Goodall. "That gentle little operation known as 'tidying up'—however, we'll hope for the best."

Blanchard referred to a book. "Number fifty-four," he announced. "I'll take you up."

Goodall turned to his assistant. "Stay here, Waring—I don't expect to be very long"—then followed the other two upstairs. It was a large room, furnished with wardrobe, dressing-table, wash-hand stand, double bed—half a dozen chairs, one wicker arm-chair and a box-divan. Every piece of furniture was subjected by Goodall to a thorough investigation. But they yielded nothing. He then went to the various ornaments of the china trinket-set that stood on the dressing-table. They were all empty—as was the grate. Anthony went to the wardrobe.

"Nothing here, either, Inspector," he declared. The Inspector came and tried the lower drawers. They also were all empty.

"Drawn a proper blank—as I thought," muttered Goodall. "Everything that might have whispered the words of the chorus to us has been 'tidied up.' What have you got there, Mr. Bathurst?"

Anthony was standing by the fireplace examining something on the mantelpiece. "What do you make of that, Inspector?" he asked. Holding his right hand to the edge of the mantel, he very carefully swept something into it with his left.

Goodall looked at it curiously. "Looks like a few grains of dust of some kind," he said. "Sort of dried grass—what do you think?"

Anthony put his nose to it and smelled it. "Pungent," he exclaimed. "Not exactly aromatic." He blew it away from the palm of his hand, Goodall patching him.

"Would you care to have a chat with the chambermaid that attends to this room?" inquired Blanchard.

"That's an idea, certainly," said Goodall. "Have her up, by all means."

Blanchard went out and called down the speaking-tube.

"I don't think we shall find anything more, Inspector," said Anthony. "I expect—"

"*More!*" exclaimed Goodall with evident disgust. "I like the '*more,*' Mr. Bathurst. It seems to me we've run across precious little—I don't know what you think about it." Anthony grinned, as they both turned to welcome Rabjohns, the chambermaid.

"I'm a Police Inspector," announced Goodall terrifyingly, "so be careful what you say! When you 'tidied up' this room after Mr. and Mrs. Stewart left it—did you destroy any papers or letters that you found here?"

Rabjohns slowly wiped her hands on her apron. "No, sir—that I didn't. There was nothing left in here, Mr. Inspector, not even a 'bob' on the dressing-table."

Blanchard frowned at her—after all, he thought, it was not seemly that she should obtrude her trivial personal "grouses" at a critical time such as this.

"You're sure of that," barked the Inspector. "Certain you found and destroyed nothing?"

"Positive, sir. You can rely on what I'm tellin' yer, sir—you can put your shirt—sorry, sir!" She caught Blanchard's eye and amended her ways.

"One question I'd like to ask you before you go," intervened Anthony. She turned and faced him. "Yes, sir?"

"When you have entered this room, first thing in the morning—during Mr. and Mrs. Stewart's stay here I mean—have you ever detected a peculiar odour in the room?"

Rabjohns dropped her hands in astonishment. "That I have, sir! Not one morning, but *every* morning—I even mentioned it down in the kitchen. Smelt like something burning, it did, sir—but however did you know about it, sir?"

Anthony turned to Goodall. "We all have our little secrets, haven't we, Inspector? As I've reminded people before."

The Inspector coughed. What exactly did Mr. Bathurst mean?

Chapter XIX
INSPECTOR GOODALL IS ENTERTAINED

When they left Blanchard's, Anthony decided to have a few additional words with Goodall. "What do you say to a little supper with me, Inspector?"

Goodall caught eagerly at the idea. "Waring," he said to his subordinate—"you can get along now. Report to me at the 'Yard' in the morning—I'm going along with Mr. Bathurst here."

Waring saluted and quickly made himself scarce.

"I know a nice quiet little place in Soho," said Anthony, "where I can give you Omelette Espagnol, Homard Americaine, a delicious piece of Stilton and a really excellent Burgundy—you will be my guest, of course, Inspector!"

"I shall be delighted, Mr. Bathurst—may I ask what else you intend to give me?" His eyes twinkled shrewdly.

"Patience, Inspector—there are one or two things I want to tell you, but Ricardo's will be a better setting for them than the street we are in now."

Ricardo's was all that Anthony had claimed for it. Inspector Goodall warmed under its cheering influence, and with his fourth glass of the really excellent Burgundy toasted Mr.

Bathurst almost hilariously, and Mr. Bathurst was pleased to reciprocate.

Eventually the latter pushed his chair back and recalled Goodall to the business of life.

"Before you tell me what you thought of tonight's jaunt, Inspector, I'll tell you briefly what I did at Assynton after you left us at Colonel Leach-Fletcher's—try one of these cigars, Goodall—they'll suit your palate."

Goodall lit up, leaned back and prepared to listen.

"I conducted a series of little experiments," continued Anthony. Goodall nodded complacently. The cigar really *was* intended for a man of discernment. "First of all," proceeded Anthony, "I was able to trace a letter that had been lying in the library since the fatal evening." He took the letter from his breast pocket. "Read that, Goodall, will you?"

The effect was electrical—Goodall's complacency became a thing of the past. "Morgan Llewellyn," he muttered grimly. "I had a pretty shrewd idea that he was interested in that little baggage that treated old Clegg so contemptuously." He tapped the letter with his forefinger. "I don't know that I'm altogether too pleased to get hold of this."

Anthony appeared to disregard the last remark and went on. "Then I set to work on another point. You remember the condition of the ink in front of where the dead man was found?" Goodall frowned an affirmative. "I had a strong impression, Inspector, that I should find some weapon—near at hand—in the garden in all probability, from which that débris had come. *I was right in that impression.*"

Goodall sat up straight in his chair. "You don't mean to say—"

Anthony knocked the ash from the end of his cigar. "I'm confident that I have found the weapon with which Mr. Stewart was killed. It's a sharp jagged piece of stone that once formed part of the path leading from the Assynton Lodge rockery. At the present moment, I believe, it resides somewhere in the library where Daventry has concealed it."

"That's risky, Mr. Bathurst, supposing!"

"It's quite safe there, Inspector. Daventry fished it up from the pool where the murderer had slung it. Acting upon my instructions, of course—I showed him where to look for it."

Goodall's eyes widened with amazement and incredulity. "But where's all this leading to—I'm getting bewildered!"

"Sit still, Inspector," went on Anthony, "I haven't quite finished yet. The curtain isn't up for the third act yet—then there's still the fourth to come." He pushed his fingers into the left-hand pocket of his waistcoat. "The bullet that Stewart fired at his murderer, Inspector—take a good look at it!" He tossed it across, nonchalantly.

Goodall's eyes almost started from his head as he handled the little messenger of Death. "And how the hell did you find this, Mr. Bathurst, and where?"

Anthony smiled at the Inspector's astonishment. "I was convinced that Stewart *had* fired his revolver on the fatal night, so it was fairly conclusive to me that the bullet should be in the library somewhere. I tried to reconstruct the whole scene as I had imagined it! The result of this little attempt at reconstruction brought me round about the bookcase. Eventually, Daventry and I found a book—embedded in this particular book was the bullet you are now holding."

Goodall sank back in his chair with the appearance of a man who, after repeated and ineffectual struggling and striving, at last reluctantly bows to Fate and accepts the inevitable. "You'll tell me you've arrested the murderer next, Mr. Bathurst! When are you starting on the Hanover Galleries case?" His mouth might have been described as cynical.

Anthony leaned across the table. "Not yet, Inspector! I told you the fourth act was still to come! I must ask you to give me another forty-eight hours say—then I hope to put the entire threads of the case in your hands. You will then proceed to make your arrests." His grey eyes danced, and even his hard-bitten companion caught something of the domination of his personality. "The following day we shall read with our early morning cup of tea—'Dramatic Double Arrest—Police Swoop in Hanover Galleries' and Assynton Lodge Murders—Triumph of Detective-Inspector Goodall.'" His mouth twisted into a smile. "Does the prospect please you, Inspector?"

"That's a hard question to answer," grunted Goodall. "I feel that I'd rather see my way than have somebody hold my hand—with all due respect, Mr. Bathurst."

"Of course, Inspector—any man would! I promise you, you shall see every step of the way, before I ask you to take the *final* steps—there's my hand on it."

The Inspector grasped his hand warmly. "You've made me feel easier," he conceded. "I've only known you a couple of days, and yet I seem to have known you all my life."

"One point I want to mention now, Inspector—before I forget it. I've left Mr. Daventry in charge down at Assynton. I've told him, if he wants me in a hurry—and it's just possible, in the circumstances, that he may—to ring you up at 'the Yard.' I sha'n't be wanted to-night—I'm certain of that. If he should ring you to-morrow or Sunday—that address will find me"—he scribbled an address on his visiting card and pushed it across to the Inspector. Goodall transferred it to his pocket-book.

"All Sir Garnet, Mr. Bathurst. That shall be attended to, if required!"

Anthony called their waiter and settled the bill. "Perhaps you'll be good enough to return to Assynton with me when I go back—will you, Inspector? Don't worry about this end of the tangle—it will solve itself with the other, take it from me. I've another difficulty, unfortunately, at the moment—I have to solve a third mystery." He rose to go and Goodall followed his example.

"I don't quite understand, Mr. Bathurst."

Anthony's eyes glinted. "I have to solve 'the riddle of the screens,' or in the picturesque language of M. Réné de St. Maure—the problem of the 'Black Twenty-Two'—but that, Inspector, is another story." He took the Inspector by the arm. "The British Museum is going to be my H.Q. for to-morrow, Inspector—if that interests you at all—don't forget—if you should want me at the address I just gave you."

They passed out into the street. "There's one thing I forgot to tell you," remarked Anthony. "There's a woman in the case,

as I expect you know. But here's something you may not know—
she suffers a good deal from hay fever—and although I can't tell
you her name—I could tell you what it was before she married—
good-night, Goodall."

Goodall turned quickly at the surprising intelligence, but all
he could see was Mr. Bathurst's retreating figure. Which, as may
be guessed, afforded him no enlightenment.

CHAPTER XX
MR. BATHURST BRUSHES UP HIS HISTORY

AN OBSERVER of discernment would have formed the opinion that Mr. Bathurst had fallen a victim to the fascination of
the history of the Stuarts. At least half a dozen volumes were
ranged round him; and the same discerning observer, had
he been sufficiently discourteous to peer over Mr. Bathurst's
shoulder as he read, would have discovered that the life of
Mary, Queen of Scots, appeared to present special features of
absorbing interest. "Before we begin looking for anything"—
murmured Mr. Bathurst to himself—"it will probably be as well
if we attempt to satisfy ourselves as to what exactly we are looking for." He took from his pocket-book a copy of the paragraph
from "The Memoirs of M. Réné de St. Maure" that Peter Daventry had made, and read it through carefully more than once.
"If these memoirs are in any way reliable and authentic," he
reasoned, "two screens were used in some special way towards
the temporary disposal, at least, of part of Mary's possessions.
My task then, is to discover (a) what particular part this was?
(b) are the two screens mentioned by M. de St. Maure the two
that have figured so prominently in the Hanover Galleries and
Assynton Lodge murders? and (c) if so, what is the secret the
screens contain that affects the hiding-place of whatever was
hidden?" He turned again, to the paragraph. At any rate, there
was a distinct reference within it that bore unmistakably on the

query he had designated as (a)—"The Cardinal's great gift"! So far so good—but which Cardinal? Mr. Bathurst had a shrewd suspicion that more than one gentleman entitled to the description of "His Eminence" had figured in the life of the tragic Mary. That was certainly one point upon which it would be necessary for him to reassure himself. "If I had the wretched screens in front of me, it wouldn't be so bad," he mused—"as it is I'm working with a couple of second-hand descriptions of them." He tapped his front teeth with the butt of his fountain-pen; Peter Daventry in the one instance and Miss Lennox in the other, might have missed vital points in their descriptions. He looked through two of the histories that seemed to deal more closely with the minute details of Mary's career than any of the others and was successful after a time in finding three references to the Chief Armourer—Thibaut Girardier. But no mention could be discovered concerning Girardier's special work in connection with the two screens. "Many secret places of Wild Scotland," he quoted—"would give us a pretty extensive field to cover—'O Caledonia, stern and wild!'" Then his thoughts reverted again to the one bizarre description that he did possess of "The Cardinal's great gift"—"The Black Twenty-Two!" What was meant exactly by that? "Might be a couple of football elevens," he muttered with a shade of sarcastic bitterness. "Only one thing for it," he concluded after seven abortive attempts to extract any pertinent information from a number of dead and gone historians—"only one thing for it, and that is to work systematically and methodically right through the incidents of Mary's life as I find them recorded here." He arranged all the volumes he had requisitioned, side by side, and started to go through them, as far as possible, simultaneously. An hour and a half's arduous exertion yielded him nothing, and even his own inexhaustible supply of patience combined with intellectual optimism began to feel the strain. But it is the darkest hour before the dawn—suddenly a sentence from the fourth of his arranged books seemed to leap from the page upon which it was printed! Anthony's eyes glistened—he read on with feverish excitement—he felt certain in his mind that at last he had run to earth his first clue to the identification of "The Cardinal's great gift." At least, here was a definite start and a start of the right kind! Fortified with this piece of knowledge, he ransacked every book for additional data. Fruitlessly! Here all success ended—not a single page told him anything more. He worked on for another hour; then he began to tell himself that he was ploughing the sands. "After all," he soliloquized, "what more can I really reasonably expect to find? If Réné de St. Maure knew what he did know and yet remained ignorant of the real secret of Girardier's work—how can I expect to find any trace of this knowledge in other historians who were probably nothing like so well placed for knowledge as de St. Maure himself? This part of the problem I shall have to solve by my own ingenuity." He pushed his chair back from the table— and thought the whole question over very carefully, omitting nothing and giving every possible point the fullest examination and consideration. Suddenly he came to a decision. He returned the books he had requisitioned to the appropriate attendant, at the same time requesting access to recent files of "The Times" and "The Daily Telegraph."

"Those two will do for a start," he said to himself—"it's only an idea on my part and it may lead nowhere, but I should like to test my theory before relinquishing it." Starting with "The Times," he ran his eye down the "Personal" column on the front page—day by day—six copies to each week—till he had worked back as far as the 1st January. Nothing caught his eye as being likely to be what he wanted. He paused at several—considering them with the utmost discrimination—but eventually, occasionally perhaps with a certain amount of reluctance, decided to discard them as inappropriate. He then commenced on the file of the "Daily Telegraph." The first few days were quickly disposed of. But at the second item of the "Personal" column of the copy for Monday, May 30th, he paused. The message ran as follows:—"M. S. Ring Regent 9999 till further notice. Both well!" His eyes narrowed as he reread this—weighing every syllable. "'M. S.' might very well be 'Mary Stewart,' which in itself might very well be a 'code word' used to convey messages relative to this particular little conspiracy;" his thoughts raced on—"then we get a telephone number which is of course the pith of the message that is required to be communicated and an intimation that two people are in good health." He thought for a moment and then the truth leaped to his brain. "By Jove—nothing of the kind—idiot that I was—'both well' is simply 'Bothwell'—the other code word—just a word I might have looked for in relation to the 'Mary Stuart'!" He searched the remaining papers through rapidly, in case there were other previous communications of a similar nature. To no effect! This was the only one! Anthony surrendered the files, conscious of an excellent morning's work—he had started badly, but had finished well. At the first opportunity he walked into a public telephone call-box. He lifted the dog's-eared Directory that swung at the side of the receiver, true to the tradition of such Directories, and opened it at the "B's." His finger traced the names down till he came to the particular one he desired. "Blanchard's Hotel—Regent 9999." Mr. Bathurst replaced the Directory and allowed himself the satisfaction of a smile. "But Regent 9999 doesn't harbour Mr. and Mrs. Bothwell now—if it did once, when they preferred to call themselves Mr. and Mrs. Laurence C. Stewart." He walked to his flat. "Any message come for me while I've been out, Emily?" he inquired of a girl who met him as he entered—a maid on the housekeeper's staff.

"Yes, Mr. Bathurst! A telephone message came through for you about eleven o'clock this morning—I said you were out and that I didn't know when you would be back—it's a gentleman that rang up—he's promised to ring up again in the afternoon—he told me to tell you not to worry about not getting the message in the first place."

Anthony heaved a sigh of relief. Emily's statement meant that Peter Daventry had telephoned Scotland Yard as he had arranged with him and through the offices of Inspector Goodall had been put through to the flat. He had realized that failure to deliver his message might conceivably be a source of anxiety to Anthony and had very sensibly endeavoured to allay possible fears by the injunction not to worry. It was simply a question now of waiting for the promised ring and hearing what Peter had to tell him. Meanwhile he would seek the seclusion of an easy chair, fill his pipe, and concentrate on the secret of the screens. "The riddle cannot be read from one of the twain—alone." As far as he could see only the screen stolen from Stewart's museum room contained anything in the nature of a message. *"Timeo Danaos,"* he reflected. "'I fear the Greeks'—once again, why the Greeks?" His mind went back to his Uppingham days and groped for the Virgil context. He was delighted to find that his memory didn't fail him. *"Quid quid id est, timeo Danaos et dona ferentes, sic fatus validis ingentem viribus hastam"* . . . what the blazes came next—anyhow it didn't matter much that was evident—none of it seemed to have any intelligent bearing on Thibaut Girardier . . . yet he had put *"Timeo Danaos"* on the one screen . . . what was it Daventry had said was on the other . . . the two would have to be taken together if any sense was to be knocked out of them . . . those animals . . . he could understand the Lion, and the Leopards . . . and the fleur-de-lis . . . why the devil was the Fish there . . . he had read enough that morning to authenticate most of it . . . but that Fish . . . "I fear the Greeks" . . . what was that he had read . . . The telephone bell rang peremptorily. He lifted the receiver. "Speaking, Daventry! What is it?"

CHAPTER XXI
MR. FERGUSON OF NEW YORK

ANTHONY LISTENED. "Yes—that's all right, old man. I got your message and of course I knew from that that everything was O.K. down at Assynton . . . What . . . When? . . . Monday? You say Stewart would like me to come down . . . well I should rather like it myself . . . it will suit me all right, too . . . I had intended returning on Monday in any case . . . Goodall will be coming too . . . Ferguson, you said . . . he's been pretty quick over it, hasn't he? . . . don't quite see how it's been possible . . . right-o then . . . be very careful over the week-end, won't you? . . . keep your eyes skinned on every man Jack of 'em . . . Good-bye." He sank back in his chair.

Ferguson of Crake and Ferguson, New York! Laurence Stewart's solicitors! But how Mr. Ferguson could have arrived in England so quickly after the murder wasn't clear to him—"he must have flown over," he remarked to himself somewhat jocularly. His train of thought, however, didn't last for long. His mind was soon back to the problem of the screens. Where was he when that confounded telephone rang? He closed his eyes in an attempt to recapture his concentration and the exact point to which he had arrived. He had been wondering about two things—he remarked. The Latin tag and the Fish in the center of the screen. It was becoming increasingly plain to him that he would have to get into touch with the Hanover Galleries screen! Without that, he was merely beating the air. He decided to speak to Goodall at once. He was instantly put through. Goodall seemed anxious for news. "We are no nearer a solution this end, Mr. Bathurst," he announced rather gloomily, "every clue seems to lead nowhere—the pretty pair I'm after seem to have been spirited off the face of the earth."

"I wanted to speak to you about them, Goodall, among other things," replied Anthony. "Get into touch with the New York police as quickly as you possibly can—I have a strong presentiment that the gentleman we're after has a considerable reputation as a 'crook' over the other side. Who is he? Haven't the least idea, Goodall—ask them if any particularly promising specimen of the unsavoury sort has slipped out of the States recently—from little old New York, in all probability. You can give them a rough description of the man you want."

"Very well," answered Goodall, "although I think you're drawing a bow at a venture—still I'll try it! What else did you want to say?"

"I've two more pieces of news for you, Inspector—the first will make you sit up a bit."

"I've been doing quite a lot of that lately, Mr. Bathurst—what's the latest development?"

"Have a glance at the Personal Column of the 'Telegraph' for the 30th of last month—see what you make of it!"

"All right," assented the Inspector. "What else?"

"I want you to come down to Assynton with me on Monday morning. There's a train at a quarter to eleven. I've just heard from Mr. Daventry that Mr. Stewart's solicitor from New York is expected down there and I'm required to be there as well. It isn't putting me out at all, because it was my intention to return then—I dare not delay action much longer. I'll meet you then at Paddington."

"I hope to be in a position to report some progress this end by that time," declared Goodall, in a tone of voice not exactly distinguished by hopefulness.

"I hope so too, Goodall," added Anthony, "but never mind if you aren't. I forgot to tell you something! When you come down on Monday—bring a couple of pairs of handcuffs, will you?" He chuckled, and put the receiver back with the fervent wish that he could have witnessed the expression on the Inspector's face. It was during the week-end that followed that an idea began to take very definite shape in Mr. Bathurst's brain. In fact, so definite did it become that he was sorely tempted more than once to put a telephone call through to Assynton. But he desisted— there would be plenty of time on the morrow—and there was more important work to be done than the solving of the problem of the "Black Twenty-Two"! Goodall was straining at the leash, eager and impatient to land his man—to land his *men* in both affairs. Goodall should be satisfied!

When he met him in the morning at Paddington, Anthony could see that the Inspector was looking very finely-drawn. Anthony touched him on the arm. "Don't worry, Inspector," he exclaimed with a note of gaiety in his voice, "the curtain is just going up for those third and fourth acts I mentioned, and you and I are not going to miss any of it. Also, Inspector," he grinned broadly, "the bouquets will be for you when it goes down—so possess your soul in patience and wait for that 'soothsome' moment—that 'fragrant minute.'"

Goodall's eyes twinkled—not necessarily in anticipation of the coming event as depicted by Mr. Bathurst. "Bouquets aren't much in my line! Still, I've brought what you asked me." He patted his left-hand pocket with the palm of his hand. "Optimist—aren't I?"

"Good man," said Anthony, "for you'll certainly want them. By the way—any news from New York yet?"

"I've got on to them, but there's no news as yet!"

The journey down was comparatively uneventful.

"It's been an interesting little problem, Goodall," said Anthony as they ran into the drab station at Assynton, "and not the least interesting part is yet to come. I hope you are thoroughly prepared for a rather dramatic *dénouement*?"

"I shall be there," retorted Goodall with grim determination, "whatever the *dénouement* is! Whenever! And *wherever*!" He stepped into the car that was waiting for them.

Peter Daventry met them in the hall immediately upon their arrival. Anthony put his finger to his lips.

"All serene, Daventry?" he whispered.

Peter nodded briskly and elevated his two thumbs. "The entire household is as you left it—the people indoors and the outside staff as well—you need have no qualms."

Anthony patted him on the shoulder. "Excellent, Daventry—I felt I could rely upon you."

Charles Stewart came from the library with out-stretched hand. "I'm glad you're back, Bathurst. I suppose it's too much to ask you if there have been any developments?" He rattled on without giving Anthony a chance to reply. "Good morning, Inspector! You look a trifle tired! Mr. Ferguson hasn't arrived yet, but I'm expecting him any minute now. I'm pleased you're both back with us—I feel that you should be here to hear what Ferguson has to say—come into the library!" The three men followed him in. "The inquest is this afternoon," continued Stewart, "and we are burying my father early to-morrow morning—it will be very quiet—we have very few friends in this country—we haven't been here long enough to make many. Colonel Leach-Fletcher will be present—it is very considerate of him."

He went across to the French doors and looked out on to the garden. It was an easy matter to see that the tragic events of the last week had left their mark upon him. He was over-young to bear alone the burden of the blow that had befallen his house. It seemed unfair that it should rest entirely upon his own shoulders. Anthony walked over to him.

"Mr. Stewart," he said very quietly, "immediately the inquest is over this afternoon I should like to have a talk with you. There are one or two little matters that I should like to settle as soon as possible. Will it be convenient?" Charles Stewart paled a little.

"Only too pleased, Bathurst," came his reply. "Let me know when you want me—will in here do?"

"Excellently!"

As Anthony spoke the word, the noise of a car was heard humming up the gravel approach to Assynton Lodge. The door opened to admit a stout, clean-shaven man—dressed in a fashionable lounge-suit of light-grey—double-breasted. Holding his grey Homburg to his chest he bowed to Charles Stewart, at the same time making his own introduction.

"My dear Mr. Stewart," he said in a pleasantly modulated voice, with just a touch of American accent, "I am Andrew Ferguson, of Crake and Ferguson, of New York. I am grieved beyond measure that our first meeting should be taking place under such heart-breaking circumstances. My very sincerest sympathy—Mr. Stewart." He clasped the young man's hand warmly in his own. "These gentlemen"—he inquired, raising his eyebrows.

"Mr. Peter Daventry, representing a London firm, similar to your own—Mr. Anthony Bathurst, whom I've called in to watch my interests, and Detective-Inspector Goodall, of Scotland Yard." Stewart motioned towards the three in turn. Ferguson bowed again. "Come to the library, Mr. Ferguson, will you?" said Stewart, "and no doubt, you will stay for lunch."

"As a matter of fact," said the lawyer, "my presence here to-day is rather remarkable. When you cabled last Thursday to our New York offices—I had already sailed for London. We have some very important business to transact over here in connection with one of our most esteemed clients, and Mr. Crake and I decided that I had better run over myself. So I sailed on the *Mauretania*. I was, naturally, most distressed and shocked to get a wireless message from my partner, Crake, late last Friday, informing me of the sad news of Mr. Laurence Stewart's death—and asking me if I would call down here to see you immediately upon my landing. My dear Mr. Stewart—I have lost no time!" He beamed on the assembled company. "By the way, Inspector, has the inquest been held yet?" He turned towards Goodall.

"Not yet—it is to be held this afternoon."

"H'm—pardon any—er—possible—er—laceration of your feelings, Mr. Stewart—I am sure—in the circumstances you will understand thoroughly my motive in asking—but I presume that there is no possible doubt that my unfortunate client was murdered?" He removed his glasses and wiped them nervously.

Charles Stewart looked across at the Inspector. The latter took it as his cue to reply to Andrew Ferguson's question. "Unfortunately—no—Mr. Ferguson—as far as I can see at the moment—there is not the vestige of a doubt." Ferguson replaced his glasses on his nose and blinked at Goodall. "Have the police any—"

Goodall cut him short, breaking in abruptly. "As far as the inquest this afternoon is concerned—the police will content themselves with offering merely formal evidence of identification and then asking for an adjournment."

"Quite so—I see," responded the lawyer. He paused for a moment. "Well, what I was about to say was this. Mr. Crake in his message—sent me in our own private professional code, of course—the major provisions of your father's will. Have I your permission to make them public here and now, Mr. Stewart?"

Charles Stewart waved his hand in assent. "Certainly—I shall be rather glad if you will. I had intended to ask you."

Ferguson took a document from his pocket. "As you know, your father was a very rich man. His investments, which were many and varied, have almost, without exception, turned out to be excessively lucrative. He had with him very much more than a mere touch of financial genius." He looked up. "You will understand that I have only, at this juncture, received from my partner what I termed the *major* provisions. Legacies are left to all members of the late Mr. Stewart's household who had been in his service for any length of time—I can safely say that nobody with any claim at all has been forgotten. Mr. Stewart was always most generous. For example," he broke off and referred to his paper—"Mr. Morgan Llewellyn receives an annuity of £300— John Butterworth £500 per annum, 'in recognition of many years' faithful and devoted service'—several other servants have been remembered very kindly. The rest of the will is rather surprising." He wiped his glasses and blinked at the company again. "£250,000 is devised and bequeathed to Miss Marjorie Lennox—Mr. Stewart's ward—and the whole of the residue of the estate to Mr. Charles Stewart—in respect of both real and personal property. But there are important conditions attached to each of these two bequests. In Miss Lennox's case, the capital sum is to be held in trust until she reaches the age of forty, and in Mr. Stewart's case similar conditions apply till the age of forty-five, unless they marry each other, when the capital sums pass into their respective possessions immediately upon such marriage. Should, however, either Miss Lennox or Mr. Stewart marry a third party—when marriage to the other principal legatee is possible and legal—the contractor of such marriage forfeits his or her bequest under this will and the said bequest passes to various charitable institutions." He waved his hands with a gesture of semi-apology. "It was pointed out to Mr. Stewart when he first outlined these provisions that there might be several flaws in the disposition, but"—he shrugged his ample shoulders—"he was absolutely determined upon the matter."

Charles Stewart was very white and kept biting at his underlip in nervous excitement. "You will be a very rich man, Mr. Stewart," said Mr. Ferguson of New York—"provided, of course—but there." He smiled somewhat fatuously—"I know how perfectly charming the lady is—I have no doubt—"

"Come in and have some lunch, Mr. Ferguson, will you?" responded Mr. Charles Stewart. It will be noticed that Mr.

Ferguson's remark provoked in him no particular enthusiasm. Certainly Mr. Bathurst noticed the fact!

Chapter XXII

MR. BATHURST BAITS THE HOOK

The inquest that afternoon took its course as Inspector Goodall had foreshadowed. Formal identification of the body was taken by the Coroner, and almost immediately afterwards, Sergeant Clegg asked for an adjournment. The Coroner granted the Sergeant's request without demur. Goodall attended—he told Anthony that he always made a special point of attending inquests—he had more than once during his career picked up an hitherto elusive trail from some unexpected turn an inquest had taken, and he also liked to have a good look at all the people who made it their business to be present—but Peter stayed in the house with Anthony. The latter's first remark after lunch was surprising. "What daily papers come to Assynton Lodge, Daventry, any idea?"

"You bet I have," replied Peter. "I was only too glad of them during my enforced term of Sentinel-in-Chief—'The Times,' 'The Telegraph,' and 'The Morning Post'—also a financial paper of some kind—I didn't look at it."

"Good," said Anthony—it flashed through his mind that Goodall had never informed him whether the "Telegraph" for the 30th ultimo had afforded him any special information. He would have to ask him that when he came in.

"Tell me," said Peter, "I haven't had a chance of speaking to you quietly—how did you get on—what are the latest developments—what's been doing?"

"Matters have gone very well," rejoined Anthony. "There is still one little point upon which I am not yet quite clear, but I hope to clear that up before many hours have passed. I also wish to amend with all apologies a statement that I made—rather carelessly perhaps—to you!" He swung one leg over the other and clasped the knee with his two hands. "I told you, Daventry, that I would introduce the police to the murderer of Mason the night-watchman—and you yourself to the murderer of Laurence P. Stewart! I was wrong!" He paused, and Peter looked up! What had gone wrong to cause Anthony Bathurst to retract a statement like that? Disillusionment on that score came quickly. "I was wrong," repeated Anthony, "inasmuch as I shall have the pleasure, my dear Daventry, of introducing you to *both murderers.*"

"I'm sure I shall be charmed," murmured Peter, responsively. "But before that happens I should like to be enlightened a bit. What do you make of that wretched will?"

"You shall see, Daventry," responded Anthony, ignoring the last question, "my final plans are not quite complete—they will be to-night—when they are—you shall know more. I shall have to take Goodall into my confidence, too—I've promised him as much." His words coincided with the sound of the latter's voice outside the door. Anthony went to the door and beckoned to him. The Inspector came, scratching his head thoughtfully.

"That will—Mr. Bathurst! You must have noticed how young Stewart kept away from it all the time during lunch—yet I'll swear it was the only thing that he was really thinking about. I can't help feeling that that will contains the key to the whole business!" He made the statement emphatically, and watched Anthony's face carefully to see the effect of his words.

But Mr. Bathurst's face remained impassive. "What do you think, yourself?" persisted Goodall—definitely putting the opinion to the test.

"I think it certainly had something to do with the *second* murder," conceded Anthony. "But possibly not altogether in the way you think." He turned the subject. "What about that Personal message in the 'Telegraph,' Goodall? You never told me what you made of it."

The Inspector fished out a newspaper cutting. "I certainly must congratulate you again over that, Mr. Bathurst," he declared. "The telephone number mentioned is assuredly that of Blanchard's Hotel—though I don't altogether see how you got on to it—the 'M. S.' *could* also be linked up with the affair to read 'Mary Stuart,' but even there—"

Anthony cut in. "I was actually looking for something of the sort," he confessed. "I had thought previously that the 'Agony Column' might very probably prove to be one of their most likely means of communication! The combination of 'M. S.' and 'Bothwell' was too strong a coincidence to be passed over without investigation." He paused to see how the Inspector would take this last remark.

Goodall's eyes opened! "Well, I'm blessed," he exclaimed. "I see now what you mean—I'm afraid I missed the second point—that was real smart now."

Peter held out his hand for the paragraph, which he read with interest. Interest which was all the more intense on account of the explanation that had preceded it. Anthony's next words brought both him and the Inspector to a keener alertness. "Make sure your revolver's in working order, Daventry, and you, Inspector, keep those handcuffs close to you. I sha'n't ask you to wait very much longer now. I want to have a chat with Stewart this evening before the funeral to-morrow morning—then all we shall have to do will be to await events. Somehow I don't think we shall be kept in suspense very long. Our birds are a bit impatient *now* I fancy." The door opened suddenly to admit Morgan Llewellyn.

"You're wanted on the telephone, Inspector Goodall," he announced. "In the hall." Goodall disappeared quickly.

Anthony motioned to Peter to await his return. Five minutes saw the Inspector back. "From the 'Yard,' gentlemen! In answer to the inquiry I put through at your instigation, Mr. Bathurst. New York has sent a message through that I fancy identifies our 'Mr. Laurence C. Stewart the second' of Blanchard's Hotel and the Hanover Galleries. In the opinion of the New York Police, he's no less a person than 'Snoop' Mortimer—otherwise known as 'Flash Alf'—they've been after him for months in connection with some very cute jobs over the other side—he slipped out of the country about a month ago—they're pretty certain that he's our man."

Goodall's manner was becoming more jaunty—he felt he was "getting hold" at last. Anthony weighed the information over in his mind. It tallied with what he had been expecting. She had met him in New York—no doubt—when Stewart had moved there from Washington. That would account for the entry of Mr. Mortimer into the cast. "Is Mr. Charles Stewart back yet, Inspector?"

"He should be by now, Mr. Bathurst. I left him talking to Mr. Llewellyn—but no doubt he came up by car. Very likely he passed me on the road—I walked up."

Anthony nodded in an understanding manner. "I'm going to see him—you stay and talk to the Inspector—Daventry!"

The two latter looked at each other in some amusement as Anthony slipped from the room. "He's actually arranging my amusements now," commented Goodall ruefully. "I shall be thundering glad when we clear the decks for action."

Anthony found Charles Stewart in Llewellyn's room—the secretary was busy writing. He glanced at Stewart, who rose to greet him. "I hadn't forgotten I promised to have a word with you, Mr. Bathurst. I'll come along now." He pushed some papers into his pocket and accompanied Anthony down the corridor. "In the library?" he suggested.

Anthony declined. "Daventry and Inspector Goodall are in there—come in the Museum Room—is it unlocked?"

Stewart pushed open the door of the room in question and waved Anthony to a seat. He chose a Chippendale chair—his host followed his example. Anthony cut no time to waste and speedily got to grips with what he wanted to do.

"Mr. Stewart," he said, leaning across with a mixture of interest and sympathy, "I am going to ask you one or two more questions that possibly may border upon the personal. You will, I am sure, pardon any seeming directness—but I am *nearing the end of my case*, and I wish to handle all the facts firmly and confidently."

Stewart's cheeks flushed quickly. "I don't quite under-stand—"

Anthony extended a protesting hand. "I think you will. Who is the lady you wish to marry?"

Stewart half rose in his chair. Then he sank back, as though resigned to anything that might come next.

"I think I am able, Mr. Stewart," continued Anthony, "to put my finger on the subject of the interview that you had with your father, not long before he was killed—it concerned a lady—the lady you are desirous of marrying—who is she?"

Stewart's emotion got the better of him for a brief period. Then he made a big effort and succeeded in pulling himself together. "That's been one of the hardest things I've had to bear, Mr. Bathurst," he stated. "The thought that my last words with my father had been bitter ones. Ever since that awful morning when I realized that I should never speak to him again—that I should never again hear his voice speaking to me, that thought haunted me—every moment almost. And another thought has accompanied it. This! If by any miracle I could bring my father back to life and have that interview over again, I don't see that I could conscientiously end it or even carry it on, in any other way." He looked pathetically at Anthony.

"You have my very profound sympathy, Mr. Stewart. But you mustn't upset yourself needlessly. Tell me all about it." He put his arm on the young man's shoulder. Stewart drew his hand across his forehead and tossed his hair back from his brow.

"Well, of course, Mr. Bathurst, you have been able to see, from what Ferguson has told us to-day—exactly how the land lay. My father was fond of me as a man is of his only son, but he was also passionately attached to Marjorie—Miss Lennox! I think, perhaps, he was the type of man that prefers girls to boys, and although she was his ward—he always regarded her as a daughter. *More than as a daughter." He brought his fist down in the palm of his other hand. "*More*—because he cherished the idea that one day she and I would marry. But I don't think either of us care for the other in that way. We've always been tremendous pals and all that—but there it ended! Somehow we didn't want to marry. I'm speaking more for myself than I possibly can for Marjorie—naturally—but I don't think she has ever wanted to marry me any more than I have ever wanted to marry her. How the idea obsessed my father's mind you can judge after hearing what Ferguson told us with regard to his will. My father couldn't bear to be thwarted in anything." He stopped, and once again the colour flaunted its red banner in his cheeks. "Soon after we came to Assynton, I met a lady to whom I was instantly attracted, and now I am very happy to say there is a complete understanding between us. She is a Miss Rosemary Armitage, of 'The Towers'—seven miles from here. I had been playing tennis there the night Colonel Leach-Fletcher dined with my father. I don't know if anything was said during the evening, but when the Colonel went, my father sent for me and in his own words—'had it out with me.' He had heard of my admiration for Miss Armitage and it had upset him."

"What time was that?" interjected Anthony.

"At a quarter-past ten—I looked at my wrist-watch as I entered the library! I wondered what it was my father wanted to see me about so late—he sent for me—you see."

Anthony thought for a second. "That leaves a quarter of an hour between the Colonel's departure and his sending for you. Whom did he send for you?"

"Marjorie," replied Stewart listlessly.

"Miss Lennox has made no mention, as far as my knowledge and memory go, of having been in here after Colonel Leach-Fletcher went. Yet I am certain she came in, and I am equally certain of the reason that brought her. When she left your father, he sent her to fetch you." Anthony made this statement very confidently and went straight on to invest it with more significance. "It was *because* of what Miss Lennox told your father that he *immediately* sent for you—she went to him to complain of the lover-like attentions of his secretary."

"Of course," burst out Stewart, "you can't be sure of that—you're speculating somewhat, aren't you?"

"On the contrary, Mr. Stewart," came Anthony's reply, "I have been able to obtain conclusive proof of what I have just said!"

"What sort of proof?" demanded Stewart.

"Proof about which there isn't a shadow of a doubt—*proof in Morgan Llewellyn's own handwriting.*"

Stewart let a look of complete astonishment pass over his face. "Honestly, I hadn't the least idea."

"I don't suppose you had! Now I want to talk about another matter. And I want you to give me your absolute confidence again, and eventually, your entire obedience. I want this house to be shut up after to-morrow morning's ceremony!"

"What?" muttered Stewart.

Anthony leaned over to him and spoke in very quiet tones.

"I want you to announce this evening to all your staff that Assynton Lodge is to be left empty from say to-morrow midday. Tell Llewellyn to take a month's leave—tell all the servants the same thing. Send Miss Lennox to friends or to an hotel in town, and tell her you will join her in a few days. I shall want you with me. Let Colonel Leach-Fletcher know—let the whole world know—make it as public as you possibly can—and leave the place as soon as is convenient to you, to-morrow afternoon."

Stewart looked dumbfounded. "But I must leave somebody here. How about all the valuables—I shouldn't care to lose them all."

Anthony considered the point that he raised. "I see your point. Very well, then—leave Butterworth and his wife here— he's the best to stay behind—*but nobody else!*"

Stewart still looked at him in amazement. "Where am I to go myself?" he questioned.

"I'll tell you to-morrow midday," answered Anthony. "Meanwhile will you do as I suggest?"

Stewart's answer came a trifle wearily. "I've placed myself in your hands, Mr. Bathurst—I must be content to leave the matter entirely to you." Then he seemed to think of something. "What about Mr. Daventry and Inspector Goodall?"

"Leave them to me—and answer me one more question. When your father had that interview with you—did he by any chance mention to you the peculiar provisions of his will?"

Stewart hesitated for just the fraction of a second before his answer came. "Certainly not, Mr. Bathurst—when Ferguson told me the provisions of the will this morning nobody was more surprised than I. My father was angry at my not falling in with this supreme desire of his—furiously angry I may say! He so far forgot himself to say things about Miss Armitage which were as absurd as they were untrue, to anybody that knew her—he even threatened me in a way—a vague sort of way. But—"

"How do you mean?" interrupted Anthony abruptly. "How did he threaten you?"

Stewart gnawed at his lower lip. "As I said—vaguely! That it would be the worse for me if I persisted in acting in opposition to his wishes—just that—nothing more. Why do you ask?"

"The point occurred to me—that's all—go on!"

"Well—that's all," concluded Stewart. "The word 'will' was never mentioned—I left my father hoping that he would cool down and see things eventually from my point of view—and Marjorie's."

"When Miss Lennox came to tell you your father wanted you, did she seem upset or distressed at all?"

Stewart reflected for a second or two. "No," he declared. "But I'll tell you what I did notice about her—her cheeks were very flushed—as though she were labouring under great excitement—I certainly did notice that."

Anthony rose and walked across to one of the tables. He picked up a dainty piece of glass—almost gossamer-like in its texture and quality.

"You understand, don't you? I want that announcement about closing the house up to be made *to-night*. Inform all the servants—arrange with Llewellyn and Miss Lennox on the lines that I suggested see Butterworth about taking charge during the time you will be away—'phone Colonel Leach-Fletcher in short make all the necessary arrangements as soon as possible. If it could be managed—don't come back to the house after the funeral. What a lovely piece of glass this is!" He rang his finger-nail against its edge.

"Very well," said Stewart. "I will do exactly as you wish."

"I'm obliged," returned Anthony. He walked to the door—then stopped and looked back at Stewart.

"By the way," he exclaimed, "would you kindly arrange for me to have a word with young O'Connor before he goes for his unexpected month's holiday?"

Chapter XXIII
WHEN THE CAT'S AWAY

"Goodall," murmured Anthony, "I shall never be able to forget entirely the look on your face this afternoon when I asked you to fall m with my arrangements. It was an education on its own—really in some ways I regard it as sufficient reward in itself for the trouble I have taken over the matter. Have another slice of this cold lamb, you two."

The two people addressed pushed their plates towards him, the Inspector grinning somewhat feebly.

"It might even have been a better education for you had you felt disposed to tell me a bit more—even now you haven't put me wise to all that's going on—thanks, Mr. Bathurst."

"Well, Inspector, you do know more than I do," grumbled Peter. "If anybody's got a real legitimate 'grouse' it's little Peter—that's enough—thanks—I haven't got an appetite like the Inspector here."

Anthony drained the contents of his tankard and surveyed his two companions with an almost fatherly air of condescension and regard.

"You must allow me to stage-manage the show in the way I think best. Really—I could charge you both with downright ingratitude! I procure a topping car for you—if you prefer the word procure to borrow—I drive you out into some most charming country—and I carefully select an inn that provides you with delicious cold lamb, admirable new potatoes, delightful green peas, singularly delectable mint-sauce, excellent Cheddar—all washed down with cooling draughts of the wine of the country. In exchange for all this—you censure me for what you both appear to consider excessive reticence."

Goodall looked intently at him. "'Borrow,' did you say? Now I thought I'd seen that car before now I know where it was—that's Colonel Leach-Fletcher's 'Bentley' we've been joy-riding in!" He slapped his hand on his thigh.

"Quite, Inspector," exclaimed Anthony. "I thought you would spot its identity when I invited you to get in and be seated!"

"Wasn't thinking of it then—I was wondering where you were taking us to and what was the big idea!"

"'Journeys end in lovers meeting,'" quoth Mr. Bathurst "I didn't want to meet people—two in particular." He looked at his watch. "It's half-past eight, Goodall," he announced; "I asked Stewart to be here at nine."

"Stewart?" questioned the Inspector.

"Yes. he's coming back, according to my intentions, with the three of us to Assynton Lodge—and we're going via 'Neuve Chapelle'—Colonel Leach-Fletcher's house is the Rockinge side of Assynton—that's why we're going round that way. It will be safer!" Goodall nodded an assent. "Of course," continued Anthony—"it's just on the cards that we shall draw a complete blank—but as I said before, I don't think so. Impatience is a tyrannical taskmaster—ask any woman! Come into the smoke-room!" They made themselves comfortable. "I calculate that it will be dark about a quarter-past ten—we have three-quarters of an hour's journey from here by car—let alone the walk from the Colonel's. We should leave here, to be on the safe side, directly Stewart comes."

"You think it's certain that nothing will happen before dark?" asked Goodall.

"I don't think any attempt will be made," answered Anthony, "*before midnight*! They will wait until it's really dark—still we mustn't give any chances away. Now, Daventry—I want to talk to you. That screen you saw at the Hanover Galleries! If my memory isn't faulty, it was covered with the words, 'Jesus Christ, God and Saviour,' in beads. Am I right?" Peter nodded.

"That's right," he admitted cheerfully, "I can see it now. Brightly-coloured beads they were under a kind of glass covering."

"Was the word 'and' shown in full—with its full complement of letters—that is?"

"What do you mean?"

"Just this! In the present day, and is often expressed by a kind of hieroglyphic—you know what I mean—I don't quite know how old the practice is—but counting 'and' as one—if it had been shown-like that—there would have been just twenty-two letters in the inscription—see what I'm getting at?"

Peter shook his head. "That theory goes 'phut,' old man," he declared, "'and' was depicted in full—the three letters, a-n-d."

"Thank you," replied Anthony somewhat surprisingly cheerfully. "I'm rather glad, as a matter of fact, to hear you say that—it rather strengthens my belief in my other theory." Goodall looked up at the clock anxiously.

"Mr. Stewart should be here, Mr. Bathurst—I don't want to stay in here too long, you know. I shall be getting uneasy."

"Neither do I. Let's go and have a look outside!"

They scanned the white stretch of road that wound its serpentine-like way through the green of e countryside. For the moment their eyes saw nothing—then Anthony spoke to his companions. "Our man I fancy!" He pointed in the reverse direction to that in which they had been looking.

"Travelling pretty fast, too," muttered Goodall.

"He's a trifle late—that's why," replied Anthony. In a few moments the big car spun into the inn-yard with Charles Stewart at the wheel. His face seemed set and anxious.

"Sorry if I'm a bit behind time, Bathurst," he apologized, "I miscalculated the distance this place was away—I hope it hasn't inconvenienced you."

Anthony got into the car and sat next to him. "We were getting a bit worried about you—that was all. I'll travel back with you! Daventry—you drive the Inspector in the Colonel's car. Make straight for 'Neuve Chapelle'!"

The two cars swung out on to the road Peter in the "Bentley" leading.

"I should like to get back to the Colonel's by ten to ten at the latest," exclaimed Anthony. "Can we do it?"

"Easy," said Stewart. "I'll let her out when we get on to the Rockinge road—it's bound to be pretty clear there—it always is."

"What about O'Connor, Bathurst?" he continued. "Did you see him all right as you desired?"

"Yes—thanks! I've arranged all that I wanted." He paused and looked at his companion. "I'm rather afraid that events have crowded upon us very quickly, Mr. Stewart, and that coming so soon after this morning they may have proved a severe strain upon you—but there is this much to be said, I hope to clear up the whole business within the next few hours."

Stewart nodded. "It will be a great relief—perhaps in time I may school myself to forget it all . . . except that wretched will, though . . . that's likely to be a permanent obstacle."

"Nine-fifty-two," he announced eventually as they drew up outside Colonel Leach-Fletcher's. "Not bad going that."

The Colonel was not in, the maid-servant informed them. He had gone out after ten on foot and had not yet returned. Mr. Bathurst thanked her, and in the circumstances would put the "Bentley" into the garage if she would see that it was unlocked for him! Peter ran it in as smoothly and in as business-like a manner as possible.

"Yours too, Mr. Stewart," instructed Anthony. "You're leaving it here to-night—you know—and completing the rest of the journey with us on foot!"

Stewart looked a little bewildered, but by this time had become quite prepared to obey Mr. Bathurst's orders without asking too many questions.

"If we walk smartly," declared Goodall, "we ought to be there by a quarter to eleven, and that's quite late enough in my opinion. . . . Step it out gentlemen, until I give the word to stop you."

The four were quickly into their stride—Peter Daventry wondering where it was all going to end. He put his hand in the pocket of his coat and felt the butt of his revolver. He was prepared, at any rate, should it turn out to be a "rough house." Old Bathurst evidently thought it might by his references to the revolver. He jerked at Anthony's sleeve. "That's the second milestone since we started—another quarter of an hour or so ought to bring us pretty close to the Lodge."

Anthony nodded, and for the next ten minutes or thereabouts the little party walked in silence. Suddenly Goodall, who was leading, stopped, and turning in his tracks, approached the others. "We're just on there," he whispered, "and we must all keep very quiet. Is there anything more you want seen to, Mr. Bathurst?"

"How many men have you posted round the house, Goodall?" asked Anthony.

"Half a dozen. Every point is well watched—I've seen to that!"

"Better make sure they're there before we do anything," suggested Anthony.

"Wait, then," snapped Goodall. He was soon back. "All O.K.," he declared very quietly.

"What I propose, then, is this—we four will keep well away from the entrance that leads to the front of the house on the Assynton side. We'll climb the garden wall at the back—we shall come to it first, approaching from this direction, and once inside the grounds we'll take cover—somewhere near the rock garden say. We oughtn't to stand much chance of being spotted round there." He looked up at the sky. "The moon's in our favour!" Goodall appeared to be considering the plan very carefully. "Yes," he said, after a pause, "I don't think we can do very much better than that. I'll go and have another word with Sergeant Clegg and wait for you under the shadow of the wall." He was as good as his word, and shortly afterwards the four figures dropped silently from the wall and stealthily made their way nearer to the house. Not a glimmer of light showed, and the dim foreboding that the night was destined to produce nothing sensational smote Anthony for a brief moment. Then his reason re-asserted itself and he shook off the idea of failure.

"Deuced peculiar way of entering my own garden," muttered Charles Stewart.

Goodall put his fingers to his lips. "Silence everybody—please—not a syllable—gentlemen."

Suddenly a figure flitted out from behind a bush. Peter quivered with excitement. Anthony caught it softly by the arm. "That you, Patrick?" he whispered.

Goodall turned round again angrily, but Anthony held up his finger with a gesture that betokened silence.

"Ay, sir, it's Patrick O'Connor. I fixed that little job for you and father's up near the window—as you told him, sir. Nothing's happened yet, sir—I've watched since the time you mentioned." Anthony expressed approval. "Fall in with us, Patrick—and as quietly as you know how."

Two or three minutes later came another order from the Inspector. "Now sort yourselves out—and keep within half a dozen yards of one another—and nobody's to move forward after taking up position unless ordered by me or Mr. Bathurst here." As he spoke a light suddenly flashed and lit up one of the rooms. Peter started as he saw it. "Which room's that?" he queried of Anthony in a whisper.

"Not sure—watch the house carefully—get away to my right—three yards will be ample."

For a long time nothing happened—till just as suddenly as previously a second room flashed into light. Anthony tiptoed over to Daventry. "One of the bedrooms now—on the second floor—I really think things are moving. I'm going forward a bit to have a word with Goodall."

The Inspector listened sagely and was on the point of making his reply when Anthony gripped his arm.

"Listen, Goodall, listen. Hear that? A car! It's driven up to the house—it's going up the drive now—can't you hear it?"

Goodall cocked his head in the darkness—then turned swiftly and silently.

"Get the men to their places, Mr. Bathurst—we haven't long to wait now, I'll lay any odds."

Goodall's instructions were instantly obeyed, and Peter Daventry was perfectly certain in his own mind that everybody could hear plainly the sound of his heart beating. But nobody appeared to—nobody turned on him angrily with an order to stop the noise his heart was making—so he concluded after a time that the noise wasn't anything like as bad as he imagined and that his fears were exaggerated.

Anthony flitted noiselessly across to the Inspector. "Stay here—all of you—I'm going forward a bit—don't do anything till I come back and give you the word." He slipped away in the darkness. Keeping well in the shadow, he silently approached the library. A figure suddenly materialized, peering at him for a brief moment of palpitating suspense. Suddenly Anthony felt his hand gripped in a grasp that would have made many a man wince.

"All right, O'Connor," he whispered, "be careful not to make the slightest sound—*they're somewhere in the house.*" The giant flashed back a smile, white teeth gleaming in the darkness. Simultaneously the library flooded into light! Anthony in the stress of his excitement dug his fingers into the foundryman's shoulder. "I'm going right up to the French doors," he whispered again, "in a very few minutes from now—get well back for a moment or two in case they open them and come out." They crouched together in the darkest patch they could find. The few minutes seemed an eternity. O'Connor's breath came in short sharp gasps—inactivity fretted him and he found this period of waiting and suspense well-nigh intolerable. Then his heart went to his mouth as he saw Anthony go forward, very slowly and silently—on the grass as much as possible—step by step—and reach the doors of the lighted library. He saw Bathurst's body worm to one side, seeking a favourable chink of vantage—he saw it stiffen to rigid attention as this chink was apparently gained . . . the rest he had to leave to the flights of his imagination. Then as he looked he saw Bathurst drop down from his full height and begin to tiptoe again on his return journey. Anthony answered his companion's unspoken question. "Couldn't be better—stay here while I go back to get Goodall and the others." O'Connor could just see that the speaker's face was shining with a mixture of excitement and elation. Goodall heard Anthony's news with quiet satisfaction.

"Good," was all he permitted himself. He collected Peter and Charles Stewart, sent young O'Connor down to Sergeant Clegg and issued his final instructions. "Your revolver, Mr. Daventry?

Right! You're perfectly certain about the doors, Mr. Bathurst, aren't you?"

"They've been attended to, Inspector—be easy on that point." The four men crept forward and joined the elder O'Connor. And at last they reached the point they wanted. Anthony listened for a single tense moment—then beckoned to Goodall, who stole silently to his side. "Look through there," he whispered. Goodall peered into the room. Two men were standing with their backs to the French doors, but the form of one of them was vaguely familiar to him. A woman was kneeling on the floor in front of two objects the exact shape of which her body hid from the watchers' sight. Anthony caught at Goodall's arm and pulled him away— then he whispered a few words into the Inspector's ear.

"Good God!" muttered Goodall. Then he made a sign to Peter and the others, and with a sudden sharp movement of his hands pulled open the doors. The woman sprang to her feet with a scream that rang in Peter's ears as he levelled his revolver. Goodall was at his side, and Peter could see a second automatic gleaming in the Inspector's hand. The two men in the library pivoted round in amazement, and the smaller man's hand dropped like lightning to his hip pocket.

"Put your hands up," roared Goodall, "or, by God, I'll let daylight through you."

Four hands went sullenly up, while the woman sank quivering to the floor. Goodall walked to the man that was armed and quietly took the revolver from his hip pocket. "'Snoop' Mortimer and Alice Mortimer," he said deliberately, "I arrest you on the charge of murdering James Mason at the Hanover Galleries on the morning of June 9th last."

Sergeant Clegg came out of the circle of light by the doors and clicked the handcuffs on the man's wrists. The woman lay prostrate on the floor. Goodall administered the usual caution. He then walked to the elder man who stood grey and ashen by the library table, completely paralyzed at the dramatic interruption. "I also arrest you, John Butterworth," he said, "for the murder of your master, Laurence P. Stewart, on the night of June 8th!" Butterworth reeled and swayed like a tree shaken in the wind—

then held out his hands mechanically for the handcuffs—the bracelets from which, for murderers, there is no escape.

CHAPTER XXIV
THE SECRET OF THE SCREENS

THE LIBRARY door closed upon the three prisoners. Goodall's mouth was set in lines that were grim and hard—the man-hunting game is no occupation for the squeamish. "Clegg and his men will have them in the cells in no time," he declared. "And the papers will sell well to-morrow morning."

But his remark evoked no response from the others—all eyes had gone to Charles Stewart. He had sunk into a chair—the very chair, as it happened, where his father had been sitting when he had met his death—thoroughly overcome by the events of the evening. "Butterworth," he muttered incredulously in a broken voice—"Butterworth! A man that my father would have trusted with anything"—he put his head into his hands and his shoulders shook in his emotion.

"Come—come," said Anthony, "you mustn't break down like this—personally I was somewhat relieved to find that it was Butterworth whom we were trailing and not anybody else."

Stewart lifted up his face and looked at Anthony searchingly. "You were *relieved*?" he queried. "Didn't you know then till to-night?"

"Some time before to-night, Mr. Stewart," replied Bathurst with a sympathetic movement of the head. "You see I had some occasion to suspect him from the very first."

Stewart looked at him again blankly and a trifle doubtfully. "To me," he continued, "it has come as a very great shock. I don't think I shall ever be able to forget it."

Anthony patted him on the shoulder and went across to the others in the room. Goodall picked up the two screens—the two objects that had been engaging the attention of Alice Mortimer as she knelt upon the floor just prior to the arrest. He placed them on the table—in its centre—Anthony removing everything else to obtain clear room-space. Then he looked carefully at the screens. There they stood the one that had come back to the house from which it had been removed—the other just as Peter Daventry had seen it in the Hanover Galleries before the murders. The first had been the property of Laurence P. Stewart, who had been murdered. The second had been the property of Lord Clavering, who had died in his bed. The screens were as they had been for over three hundred years—they had defied Time, and up to now had defied also the challenging and predatory lusts of men. Stewart's screen was of the dark bronze-like metal work that Marjorie Lennox had described. It stood about four feet high, with the Queen's Lion in the top left-hand corner and the "fleur-de-lis" in the corresponding position on the right. In the middle could be read the two words from Virgil—"Timeo Danaos"—they had been scratched on with infinite care and patience. Below them swam the fish just as Miss Lennox had pictured it. At the bottom, in the two corners, were the Leopards and Lilies of England—the Leopards directly beneath the Lion and the Lilies below the "fleur-de-lis." Lord Clavering's screen, that had traveled to Day, Forshaw and Palmers' and thence to Mr. and Mrs. "Snoop" Mortimer, stood perhaps an inch or two higher—upon a carved wood pedestal. The glass-shielded tapestry was just as Peter Daventry remembered it. It was the counterpart of the other as regards decoration and ornament, save for its centerpiece. The coloured beads took the place of the Latin words—they were all that there was there—"JESUS CHRIST, GOD AND SAVIOUR." Peter pointed to the fourth word, "It is written in full," he exclaimed, "just as I told you." Anthony nodded.

"Yes—that's all right. I've abandoned that particular theory." He turned to the others, who were beginning to be infected with his strange combination of eagerness, enthusiasm and excitement. "Judging from the faces of the little gathering that we were discourteous enough just recently to interrupt," he declared, "I don't fancy that the lady had successfully interpreted the riddle that her father had put in front of her."

"Her father," interjected Goodall, "you mean her husband, Mr. Bathurst!"

"I don't," smiled Anthony, "I mean her father, as I said—you will find that Alice Mortimer was *née* Butterworth—she met her esteemed husband in the States."

Charles Stewart gasped and Peter Daventry raised his eyes in astonishment.

"Assuming therefore," continued Anthony, "that the secret of the screens still remains unsolved, I purpose putting a little idea of mine to the test—I think you will find it interesting, gentlemen." He walked to the French doors. "O'Connor," he called. The black-bearded giant stepped smartly into the room.

"At your service, Mr. Bathurst—what is it that you're wantin' of me?"

Anthony pointed to the smaller of the two screens. "You know a good deal about metal work, O'Connor," he exclaimed, "have a look over here, will you?" Michael O'Connor strode across to the table. "What would be the effect, O'Connor, of heavy blows upon this metal work?"

O'Connor ran his fingers over the embossed surface of the screen. Then he ran them through his hair. "Would it be with a hammer that you mean?" he questioned doubtfully.

"Yes—something of that kind."

"Well"—he scratched his head still more doubtfully—"you could beat it and beat it and kept on beatin' it. You could knock it into all shapes and that 'ud be about all you could do—you couldn't knock holes into it. It's old and hard that metal work is—and it 'ud stand all the banging you could give it. That's my opinion, sir." He paused and looked round at them, as though inviting either a criticism or a confirmation of what he had stated.

From Anthony there came the latter. "Just my own opinion, O'Connor," he declared, "it would stand as much hammering as you chose to give it." He walked up to the table and inspected the two screens intently. Goodall and Peter Daventry joined him, while Charles Stewart came round to the other side of them. Suddenly Bathurst put his finger on the point of the metal work that comprised the eye of the swimming fish. But to no purpose—and his circle of spectators saw something like a gleam of disappointment cross his face. Then he tried a second time—the forefinger of his left hand pushing on the fish's eye and the forefinger of his right pressing on its tail! There was a sudden clicking sound and a sharp exclamation of amazement from Charles Stewart. As though by magic the embossed body of the fish on the reverse side of the screen to which Bathurst had pressed, swung away—revealing a cavity in the metal work the size of a man's hand. Anthony plunged his hand into it and drew out what looked like a wad of discoloured cotton wool.

"Gentlemen," he cried, with dramatic triumph, "allow me to introduce you to the 'Twenty-Two Black Pearls of Lorraine.'"

Chapter XXV

THE RIDDLE OF THE BLACK TWENTY-TWO

HE LAID the dirty padded mass on the library table, and started to pull the soft fleecy substance to pieces. From the first corner he extracted a magnificent specimen of a black pearl. Then the others came to his assistance with exclamations of delight, wonder and incredulity. In a few moments the twenty-two black pearls lay on the table in front of them—none the worse to all appearances for their three hundred odd years' concealment. Every one was a truly magnificent specimen. Goodall, Peter and Charles Stewart handled them in a kind of amazed bewilderment, marvelling at their size and beauty. Michael O'Connor's two eyes were nearly falling from his head. This would make a story for many future generations of O'Connors to smack their lips over. After a time the reason of the other three reasserted itself, and they turned to Bathurst—their questions in their eyes.

"Hadn't you better tell us all about it, Mr. Bathurst," suggested the Inspector, "it's the nearest approach to the Arabian Nights that ever I've run up against."

Anthony selected a comfortable corner of the table and swung himself on to it. The others seated themselves round him. "I had better begin at the beginning," he said. "Although the case appeared very involved and complicated in its initial stages—one of the points that seemed to border upon the impossible and which seemed also to be perhaps the most difficult one to surmount—actually simplified matters enormously and gave me my starting-point. I refer to the fact that when you, Mr. Stewart, accompanied by Llewellyn and Butterworth, broke down the library door on the morning when you discovered the body of your father—the key was in the door on the inside and the bolts of the French doors were firmly shot in their sockets. All three of you were agreed on the matter. Inasmuch as these were the only two exits from the room by which the murderer *could possibly have escaped*—this evidence must have been false—faked if you like. One of the three people had been quick enough and clever enough on his entry to *impose* this piece of evidence upon the minds of the other two. Quite easily done, too, when their attention was so distracted. It was the only possible solution to the mystery, and when you find the only possible solution, gentlemen, you hang on to it. The question then arose which one of the three was it? I made up my mind to await events a bit before deciding prematurely and to preserve an open mind. The next important step in my investigations was the letter found on the murdered man's desk—the few words that had been scribbled by him just before he met his death. They were, you will remember—'Urgent—in the morning. M. L.' Now I suggest, gentlemen, that most of you—perhaps all of you—were inclined to associate either Mr. Morgan Llewellyn or Miss Marjorie Lennox with the initials there written—I considered those possibilities very carefully, but after a time I rejected them. If it were in the nature of an instruction—then it would almost certainly be intended for Llewellyn—and he would scarcely be reminded in that particular way of anything about *himself*. Also would Stewart put initials if he were referring to the lady whom he looked upon as a daughter? Surely she would be 'Marjorie' to him, without any surname? No, gentlemen! I came to the conclusion that 'M.

L.' stood for the abbreviated and incompleted form of 'Merry-weather, Linnell and Daventry.'"

He paused and looked across at Peter, who allowed an exclamation of "By Jove!" to escape his lips.

Goodall said laconically, "Go on!"

Anthony proceeded. "Assuming this to be a sound theory, then—what had happened in the library that night to cause Stewart to scrawl the words? That was what I had to find out. It seemed to me pretty conclusive that if Merryweather, Linnell and Daventry were coming into the picture, then what I had suspected for some time was true—*that the kernel of the matter lay in the screen that I discovered to be missing from the Museum Room and in the strange coincidence of the murder at the Hanover Galleries with yet another missing screen.* I was indebted to Colonel Leach-Fletcher for the next important piece of assistance. Stewart, he informed us—you remember, Goodall—was very troubled about what he described as some treachery happening in his house. Private papers and documents were being tampered with. Was this the same trouble that he was feeling over his son? I decided no! Mr. Charles Stewart here had no reason to acquire information from his father by stealth or underhand methods. He could have obtained it in the open—in many ways. I then began to centre my suspicions upon two people—Llewellyn and Butterworth. Also, I considered the evidence of Patrick O'Connor's bicycle. I was able to establish—with your help, Inspector, that communication had undoubtedly passed on the night of the crime between the murderer this end and Blanchard's Hotel. Something had happened suddenly down here that made the immediate acquisition of the tapestry screen imperative—it was to be obtained at any cost! Then I reconstructed the crime—finding the missing bullet and the weapon that the murderer had used. The location of the bullet was most interesting—but of that more later. Also I found the answer to my question as to what was making Llewellyn so uneasy. It was a love-interest—concerned at the moment with a love-letter! I began to think seriously then about Butterworth—John Butterworth, the trusted butler. 'Treachery,' you will agree, is a good interpretation of betrayed trust. This is what I think happened on the night of the murder." He stopped again to light a cigarette. "We know that Stewart had confided to the Colonel that he intended to take immediate steps to probe the treachery that he imagined was going on around him. In my opinion he had formed certain suspicions and intended to take action, that very night. But something happened directly after his guest left that he hadn't been expecting. Marjorie Lennox had been waiting for Colonel Leach-Fletcher to leave to get into the library and to put before her 'Uncle' documentary evidence of the unwelcome attentions to which she was being subjected by Llewellyn. We know that she had threatened to do so, by the terms of Llewellyn's letter. We can only conjecture what happened—but it is plain that the question of Marjorie's affections caused your father, Mr. Stewart, to send for you directly after she left him—in the hope of arranging matters more on the lines of what he desired."

Charles Stewart nodded his head in acquiescence. "That is so—Mr. Bathurst."

"After your talk with your father finished—your father went to bed—but only ostensibly. He was on the *qui vive* that night— he undressed—slipped a dressing-gown over his pyjamas—a revolver into the right-hand pocket—"

"Left," cut in Peter Daventry crisply. Anthony ignored the interruption.

"—And waited until something happened that brought him downstairs. To the library—for this was the room where he had previously discovered signs of interference with his private papers. Butterworth was in there—engaged on a book of French memoirs to which I shall refer again. Like 'John Shand,' he had always been a natural scholar—with an unusual aptitude for learning and culture—this aptitude unhappily has brought him, finally, to what I believe is sometimes described as 'the nine o'clock walk.' But I digress! Butterworth heard his master's footsteps—sprang to the light switch and snapped out the light. Stewart fired at the unknown intruder—we know where the bullet went. Butterworth then disclosed his identity—probably with an instinct for self-preservation. Shocked at the perfidy of the man he trusted implicitly, but at the same time realizing that he surely would not need the revolver again, Stewart then replaced it in his left-hand pocket. Do you agree, Daventry?" Peter nodded rather shamefacedly and could have kicked himself for his recent interruption. Anthony smiled. "Stewart wrested part of the truth from him, in all probability, and then heaped rebuke and scathing censure on his head. And I think—although perhaps it's largely guess-work—that he let Butterworth know that the provision that he had made for him in his will would be immediately negatived. Then the butler was dismissed and Stewart sat down to think things over. He didn't notice that Butterworth had *made his exit by the French doors into the garden and not by the door*. Stewart scrawled his few words—intended for Llewellyn—I suggest it would have read had it been completed—'urgent in the morning. M. L. and Co. to act re'—well—what shall we say—perhaps a new will—perhaps they were to receive more explicit instructions re the tapestry screen that had now been invested with an intrinsic value concerning which his curiosity had been considerably whetted. But Butterworth, with his half-share in the proceeds of the 'Twenty-Two Black Pearls of Lorraine' greatly imperilled, to say nothing of an immediate pension of five hundred pounds a year at stake, *came back* from the garden with murder in his heart. Fate had placed his weapon handy. He struck! As we know, he cleaned as much of the dirt from the table as he could see—he forgot the proximity of the bowl of ink. He then collected the Museum Room screen, locked the library door on the inside, went out by the French doors, borrowed O'Connor's bicycle and 'phoned his daughter at Blanchard's Hotel. Her precious husband—a real product of the Bowery—went on with her to the Hanover Galleries and completed the job. Meanwhile, Butterworth returned, disposed of the screen somewhere, and went to bed."

"Just a minute, Mr. Bathurst," interposed Goodall. "Why did Butterworth replace the book he was at work on—I can't understand that?"

"It's hard to say—I question very much if he knew that the bullet was embedded in it—he was probably obsessed with the idea of leaving the room quite normal. Alternatively, Stewart may have replaced it."

"I think it was a mistake," declared the Inspector.

"We all make 'em," continued Anthony. "That's why we're waiting for the perfect crime. Where was I? Oh, I remember. Well, I now began to consider what it was that lay behind it all. M. Réné, Daventry, please?" He pointed to the bookcase. Mr. Daventry took down once again "The Memoirs of Réné de St. Maure" and handed it to him. Anthony read the paragraph to them. Goodall's face was a study, and Michael O'Connor's black eyes gleamed with excitement.

"Pretty vague," commented Charles Stewart.

"Vague, certainly," said Anthony, "but it told me conclusively that they were after something valuable—the clue to which lay in some way in these two screens. Butterworth no doubt had got on the track of it through his delvings into your father's library, had realized that the late Lord Clavering's screen—advertised for sale—would give him the evidence that he had been wanting and had brought his choice specimen of a son-in-law over from the States to take a hand in the game. A morning's research gave me a hint as to what the query might very well be. Perhaps you would care to listen to a little history. Mary, Queen of Scots, besides being Queen of Scotland, was Dowager of France, the widow of the little King Francis. She was also the niece of His Eminence the Cardinal of Lorraine. He showered upon her a much greater measure of affection than was usual in those days, and when she eventually sailed for Scotland he made her a 'great gift' of twenty-two black pearls—you've handled some of them to-night, gentlemen. When Mary suffered her defeat years afterwards at Carbery Hill, which meant the complete overthrow of her fortunes, she took the steps about which you have just heard to preserve many of her treasures—the Cardinal's gift among them. First of all I anticipated that they were buried somewhere in Scotland and the clue to their hiding-place was contained somewhere on the screens. So I set to work to read the riddle."

He walked up to the two screens and beckoned up the others. They crowded round. "Look at them," he exclaimed. "What strikes you as strange about either of them?"

"A good many things," muttered Goodall. "But I don't know that I can pick out anything in particular!"

"Go on, Bathurst," prompted Peter. "Put us out of our misery."

"Well," said Anthony. "There is this. There is one thing—on the metal-work screen—that appeals to me as extraordinary. By extraordinary, I mean out of place—something you wouldn't expect to be there. The inscription to Our Lord—the fleur-de-lis, the Lilies—the Leopards—all these are historically sound—normal—but what about the Latin words '*Timeo Danaos*'—'fear the *Greeks*'? It struck me that the word 'Greek' might contain an important significance. I toyed with the idea for some time—trying this and that attempt at solution. Then I began to dwell on the other inscription—'JESUS CHRIST, GOD AND SAVIOUR.' I turned it into Greek form— thus 'Ἰησοῦς Χριστὸς Θεοῦ Σωτήρ.'

"I knew then that I had solved the puzzle! Take the initial letters of each word—I'll put them in English form to help you—I—CH—TH—S. You have there four of the five Greek letters that make up the Greek word for 'Fish'! ICHTHUS! In relation to that—the Early Christians in the agonizing days of their first bitter persecutions used to signify their secret allegiance to the Christ by drawing a fish upon the ground when they encountered a stranger of whose Faith they were doubtful. He was tested by that sign. When I thought of that fish on the other screen I knew I was home at last. It then remained for me to entice the murdering devils here—I thought the empty house would lure them—it was all so beautifully convenient with Butterworth left behind. Mortimer brought the tapestry screen down by car, and Butterworth, who induced him down, of course, had the other in safe hiding somewhere. They were desperately impatient to turn their knowledge to account and profit. The rest you know! When I saw the screens for the first

192 | BRIAN FLYNN

time to-night I guessed the fish had a secret cavity somewhere—luckily at the second attempt I found it."

Stewart and Goodall advanced to him with out-stretched hands. "A wonderful piece of work, Mr. Bathurst," said the former, "and worthy of the heartiest congratulations."

"Mine also," grunted the Inspector. "I'm very much in your debt—like Mr. Stewart here."

Anthony, flushed with triumph, waved their praise on one side.

"There's one thing I *can* take credit for," added Peter. "I told you he was a liar when he tried to implicate Miss Lennox—I was certain of it."

Goodall laughed at Daventry's plea for recognition—then turned to Anthony.

"One last point, Mr. Bathurst. What made you state to me that the woman we were looking for suffered from hay fever?"

"Come, Goodall," replied Mr. Bathurst. "Remember Druce's evidence—continuous sneezing—Atkins' evidence—the occasional use of dark spectacles by a woman possessed of excellent sight—a few fragments of 'Asthma Cure' on the mantelpiece of the room at Blanchard's Hotel—Rabjohns' story of the odour in the bedroom—the time of the year, June—it was a comparatively easy matter to deduce a hay-fever patient—any more questions?"

"No more," said the Inspector promptly and decisively. "I'm perfectly satisfied."

"There's still that awkward will," put in Charles Stewart. "That's got to be faced."

"Quite easy, Mr. Stewart," said Anthony. "Miss Lennox will marry a very rich man, so that forfeiting her share of your father's money will matter little to her. That will leave you free and unhampered to marry Miss Armitage—I think that's the lady's name, isn't it? And when we remember that the metal-work screen—*your* property, Mr. Stewart—was the one that contained the 'Cardinal's Great Gift'—what better wedding present could you give Miss Marjorie Lennox than the 'Black Twenty-Two'?" He pointed to the table. "Splendid compensation—you know."

Charles Stewart smiled a little sadly—then shook him by the hand again.

"I'm jolly glad," he exclaimed, "that old Thibaut Girardier picked the right screen in which to hide them."

"So am I," responded Mr. Bathurst.

THE END

CPSIA information can be obtained
at www.ICGtesting.com
Printed in the USA
LVHW111403230919
631940LV00002B/92/P

9 781913 054373